THE CONDUCTOR

THE BEATRIX PATTERSON MYSTERIES

The Seer

The Finder

The Pursuer

The Conductor

The Conductor

a Beatrix Patterson mystery

Eva Shaw

Torchflame Books

Vista, CA

ISBN: 978-1-61153-613-3 (paperback)

ISBN: 978-1-61153-614-0 (ebook)

ISBN: 978-1-61153-659-1 (large print)

Library of Congress Control Number: 2024922003

The Conductor is published by: Torchflame Books, an imprint of Top Reads Publishing, LLC, 1035 E. Vista Way, Suite 205, Vista, CA 92084, USA

Cover design and interior layout: Jori Hanna

To my grandparents, all immigrants, who willingly chose unimaginable hardships to have a better life and unknowingly offered that gift to me. I never knew them; I only heard snatches of stories, and they were brave, creative, savvy, and smart. They were entrepreneurs. If there is a heaven (which I am certain that there is), someday I'm going to finally be able to thank them with big hugs and happy tears.

Therefore, this book is dedicated to my maternal grandparents, Paulena Schwartz Miller and Joseph Miller, and paternal grandparents, Laura Schatz Rosenbaum Klein and Jacob Rosenbaum.

CHAPTER ONE
SANTA BARBARA, CALIFORNIA. MARCH 1948

"Fancy a snog?"

Thomas didn't wait for a reply as he kissed his wife once and then again before holding up their infant, Birdy, to place a soft peck on Beatrix's cheek. The little one waved with both chubby arms, and her almond-shaped eyes always made Beatrix blink in astonishment, feeling wonder and joy, fear and gratitude, all balled together. It was nothing she'd ever experienced.

"Can't you just say 'kiss' rather than snog, darling? It sounds scandalous," Beatrix protested.

"My point exactly." He kissed Beatrix again, then turned to the nearly year-old baby. "Amazing wave there, Birdy, and now, come on. You can do it. You can say 'Daddy.'" Thomas had been coaching her to wave and say Daddy, consumed with it for weeks.

"You know, Thomas, that Birdy might not actually speak until after her first birthday. And 'Ma' is the easiest sound for her. The wave, however, is quite genius," Beatrix said.

"Isn't she just? Don't wait up for us." He laughed again.

They'd just finished breakfast, so this made Beatrix chuckle, her brown hair with the auburn highlights stuck back in a loose

1

ponytail. She was dressed for the garden in green denim overalls and a blue, lightweight pullover. She was eager to get digging in the dirt. In another month, the flower beds would be exploding with a riot of reds, yellows, and orange nasturtiums, happy-faced Marguerite daisies, and yellow coreopsis with white cosmos accenting the design. Sweet alyssum in puffy clouds would round out the color scheme. She planned to jam the beds and pots with everything the local nursery offered.

As anxious as she was to plant the starters she'd bought at the nursery center the previous day, Beatrix never rushed their goodbyes. Not in the most secret places of her heart or her wildest dreams, in the darkest times of her life as an unwanted orphan, lost in a series of boarding schools as a teenager, and floundering to make a living during the horrors of the war, did she ever think her life would be filled with the love of a devoted husband and the cutest baby on the planet.

Standing on the sidewalk in front of their ever-so-slowly-being-renovated Victorian mansion in the sleepy, little California beach town of Santa Barbara, Beatrix moved closer to Thomas, slipped her arm around his trim middle, and moved in for a hug. In the cheerless days of World War II, all the gratitude she felt in that moment had been impossible even to dream about. She trailed her fingers down her cheek, where soft baby lips had just been, and sighed.

"Think we'll saunter over to Woolworths Five and Dime for an escapade, and certainly we'll be back before elevenses, which I prefer to call it over your Americanized 'snack time.' That chocolate chip scone in the pantry is to share with our tea, my dearest Bea. Not my best baking, but it had better be there when I return." He produced a frown, knowing she had a penchant for chocolate—the reason he'd baked them.

"Wave goodbye to Mummy, Birdy pet. We're off for a jaunt," he said, and Birdy did exactly as her daddy asked. Then the twosome was off for their quick spin in the neighborhood or

2

even farther to Sterns Wharf or north to the mission. Down the sidewalk they went, and Beatrix waved to their backs. She loved his smile and knew how broad it would be, even as she watched them moving toward the shops.

Thomas had procured, somehow, an honest-to-goodness British pram in the traditional navy blue fabric. She often thought he got more British by the day, although they'd lived in this community since the end of the war. He insisted that sweaters were jumpers and knackered meant that he or the baby was tired.

Just like Thomas, Birdy seemed to mostly have an "on" switch where she was happily and thoroughly engaged with toys, cooing, and making sounds that would eventually become words, and the rare "off" one, where she, as Thomas did, slept like a bag of rocks. While they had fostered and then adopted Birdy as an infant, it was remarkable to friends, family, and strangers how much the baby looked like Thomas and Beatrix. She had striking, intelligent eyes that constantly watched where her parents were, wild hair just like Thomas's, and smooth, creamy skin like Beatrix's. Most likely, they'd discussed, they'd never find her birth parents—who had left her, hours after her birth, at Cottage Hospital—or know her heritage.

Thomas had researched the possibility of using blood samples or even the cutting-edge science of gene testing to determine her ethnicity, but without any way to find Birdy's biological parents, it hardly mattered. They had just the previous evening talked about adopting more children and knew as soon as was appropriate that they'd explain to all the Patterson-Ling kids that they had been chosen, just like Mummy and Daddy had chosen each other.

They'd decided to name the little girl after all of their mothers and call her Jay. She would be Jennie, for Beatrix's adoptive mother; Adelina, for her biological mother; and Ya, for Thomas's mother, which in Chinese meant refined, elegant, and graceful. About a month after the baby came into their lives, there was a flock of squawking and comical California scrub jays frolicking the bird bath in the garden, and the little girl's nickname morphed into Birdy.

Thomas moved with grace and a quiet confidence, which Beatrix knew came from his years of martial arts training. Thomas was lithe and just an inch taller than his wife at five foot eight. He never thought there was anything unmanly about strolling around the city with the little girl and was totally in love with the child, as he'd told Beatrix that morning and every morning since the little one had joined their lives.

Thomas felt burdened with guilt as he headed into downtown Santa Barbara. He knew it was not cricket to conceal the letter he'd placed in his jacket's pocket when he picked up the morning mail. Yet, as with everything in his well-organized life, he dreamed it would be better to wait until evening to discuss what had been written. Was this an opportunity or madness? He liked to think he made wise decisions, calculated and smart. Yet the contents of the letter could change everything about their future and their family life in the tranquil beach city.

Was it a lie not to tell Beatrix at once? He thought not, except one could say it was a lie of omission. He mentally calculated what the effect caused by the letter would be on his family and sighed deeply. Beatrix had just established her practice as a psychologist focusing on returning veterans who suffered from mental damage as well as physical issues during and after the war. The effects of trauma on soldiers during the Great War was a field she'd studied at length, and now she was compiling data on the current mass of returning veterans, wounded inside and out from the Second World War.

Then there was the house. It still needed a multitude of improvements. Thomas thought, *What houses built in the late 1800s didn't?* However, it was livable, warm in the winter, and cool in summertime, thanks to the oversized windows letting in the playful ocean breezes.

Then there were the friends, closer than family, they'd made in the city. Sam and Jo Conrad lived just blocks away. The couples and their kids dined together once and sometimes twice a week. They were already planning summer picnics on Arroyo Burro Beach, also known as Hendry's Beach by locals, with its wide sandy shore and cliffs perfect for boys like the Conrads' eldest, Sammy, to scurry up. Thomas imagined Birdy following the Conrad twins and Sammy, running through the waves, unaware of how idyllic their childhoods would be away from the recent nightmares of war, with loving parents and a safe community in which to grow, learn, and follow their dreams.

After the war, when he could safely cross the Atlantic and travel from England to Santa Barbara to see his lover, he vowed never to forget how fortunate he was. This letter? The knowledge of it felt like a fire in his pocket, as its contents would change every aspect of their lives.

Can I do that? Am I dedicated enough? Why am I even considering it? It's utter madness, he thought.

Earlier that morning, he shook his head in dismay at the sheer contentment on his wife's face as she stroked Birdy's pitch-black hair. They'd been through so much together, individually and now as a family, after adopting Birdy. They were on a journey that made them both feel at peace. Once Beatrix read the letter and acknowledged its content, the future would flip, a dangerous somersault to their tranquil life. There would be no going back.

Whatever the result, we'll never be the same. That frightened Thomas, and he thought, *For now, I best wait. A few more hours of bliss before* . . . He couldn't even *think* the words—didn't want to face what would be the outcome when he did.

Beatrix continued to watch the pair and imagined Thomas chatting with the baby in Cantonese as they ambled down serene Anapamu Street in the heart of the city and onward to State Street, the main shopping street. Truth be told, she'd had doubts about becoming a mother to the fostered little one and then again when they applied to adopt the infant. At thirty, she didn't know if she'd have the patience of younger moms, but the moment Birdy arrived in their arms, Beatrix never looked back. Thomas, on the other hand, never doubted the decision. He jumped in, taking over the hourly feedings when Birdy was tiny, changing the nappies, walking the floor, sterilizing glass baby bottles, and suddenly becoming an expert on burping the baby. Because of Beatrix's incredible memory, she'd cataloged and compiled every event in their lives since the child had come to them. Often, when she was alone or taking a quiet walk on the beach, she'd think of how they'd come together and what their future could possibly hold.

At least once a day, Thomas would remark, "I was born to be a father." Thomas told this to anyone and everyone who would listen. He'd even taken a year's leave of absence from the University of California researching clean energy and teaching so he could be there for Beatrix and Birdy. "I do not want to forgo a second of our daughter's first year." The year was closing in, which made him blink back tears more often than not when he talked about returning to the university.

Beatrix thought of how, since the day Birdy was placed in his arms, Thomas sang the same Chinese lullabies his grandmother crooned to him. After all this time, Beatrix could finally join him, still fuzzy on the translated words. Thomas assured her one song was Birdy's favorite and performed it regularly at bedtime. "It's all about how the moon protects little ones," he'd told her. Then he winked and looked like a mischievous boy—a look she loved.

Beatrix remembered pointing out that the song sounded like a rude sea shanty that his grandmother also sang. She had learned that possibility from one of Thomas' sisters when the entire Ling clan had visited for December and January to get away from the chill of London. More so, to admire and love Birdy Patterson-Ling. And they did.

Beatrix knew that Thomas regularly held deep scientific conversations, talking to the infant as if she were a colleague. Other times, Beatrix had seen him get teary-eyed watching their exquisite little girl just sleeping. He'd whisper to Beatrix, "She's dreaming. Look at her fingers move. Look at that heart-shaped mouth. Bea, whatever do babies dream about?"

Truth be told, Beatrix did the same, humming French songs and reciting poems that her Parisian biological mother had taught her, also wondering what babies dreamed of.

Beatrix often found Thomas sitting near Birdy's bassinet, holding her plump little foot or stroking it while the baby napped. He balanced a book of advanced physics or some scientific theory Beatrix barely grasped and stayed close to the tot, sheer bliss etched on his face.

Birdy's arrival was unexpected and awe-inspiring. Thomas and Beatrix were the only couple on the county's foster parent list who asked for a child of mixed race, so the county of Santa Barbara quickly granted them the opportunity to adopt Birdy. Hence, the plans to visit London and Thomas's family were postponed, mandating immediately that the entire Ling clan came to Santa Barbara. Thomas and Beatrix put off visiting Paris to reunite with Beatrix's biological father, General Charles de Gaulle. After discovering Beatrix was de Gaulle's daughter, his family refused to speak with her, respond to her letters, or any attempts at reconciliation. Growing up, Beatrix had always thought that de Gaulle was an unofficial uncle, a kindly and generous man. Now, they were all, including her father, estranged from Beatrix.

Beatrix felt content, more than she'd ever experienced. That surprised and pleased her. She was just climbing the last of the front steps when the buzzing of the big, black Bakelite telephone in the front room of the Victorian home demanded her full attention. She swung open the screen door and dashed for the phone.

"Hello, Dr. Beatrix Patterson speaking," she said.

Beatrix felt fear shoot through her, and her forehead wrinkled when she heard the caller sob. "What is it? Who is this?"

It certainly could not be the person she'd expected to call. She glanced at her watch. No, it was too early.

That cry was completely out of character for her first counseling client of the day, as the woman always called to confirm before an appointment. Gloria Rayne had been in the South Pacific as a surgeon throughout the war, bobbing around on a naval hospital ship, often being harassed and bombed by the enemy as she performed surgeries with limited resources. Beatrix met her by chance during a previous investigation of a local religious leader who died under suspicious circumstances and the murder of a federal agent connected with the local Indigenous people, the Chumash Indians. Gloria had enough courage to do her job with the utmost confidence and then the wherewithal to seek counseling when she returned to the home front.

To the city's population, Santa Barbara's esteemed coroner, Dr. Rayne, seemed like the poster model for a competent, modern woman. "I can hide my pain well," she'd told Beatrix at their first counseling session, although the scars from Japanese bullets hitting her neck were visible still. Explaining the injury, she shook her head. "I was stupid, Beatrix. Went on deck. It had been a horrible night, filled with death, and unless I saw the sun that fateful morning, I knew I wouldn't be fit for the next surgery. I was sun-deprived and naïve. I walked to the edge of the ship and turned to see—truly, I could see the pilot's eyes on me—I saw the plane swoop down. He aimed at me, a woman." Her palm covered the scream that was in her throat. "I was the only one injured that day as our boys shot that killer out of the sky. I found myself in surgery, but not as the doctor."

While her external wartime wounds had left a mark, the psychological ones were deeper. Loud noises, barking dogs, and screaming children all sent her into a well-concealed panic. She'd come to Beatrix knowing that therapy could help with "combat fatigue." Over the past five months, they had been working to desensitize her crippling fears. Fortunately, Gloria could now enter a shop or restaurant where there was chaos and deafening noises without breaking out in a drenching sweat.

The caller was not the coroner. The sob Beatrix heard sent a chill to the hair on the back of her neck.

"Beatrix, it's Jo." Jo's voice quivered, and that never happened. "I'm sick with fear."

CHAPTER TWO

"WHAT'S WRONG?"

Beatrix always smiled when she thought of Josephine Conrad, who ran the local branch of the Women's Christian Temperance Union. She was a staunch supporter of women's rights, mother of four under the age of seven, and wife to Sam, a good man and railroad engineer. She was a brave crusader against human trafficking and violence against women and children, and Beatrix was honored to be her confident and best friend. Even with the trauma she carried, she always appeared calm and collected. That was why the sob panicked Beatrix.

"I'm scared. I can't stop shaking. Oh, Beatrix. They've arrested Sam. He called from jail, his one call. He sounded okay when he explained what happened and asked me to telephone you. I didn't realize the extent until one of the other guys who works on the railroad lines drove over and told me that thugs had beaten Sam. They knocked him down and kicked him, spitting and swearing at him."

"What? Why Sam? Is he all right?" Beatrix realized she was hammering out questions and not giving Jo time to even process them.

"It—is—the—strike," Jo said through choked sobs.

The strike? "What strike? Another with the Union Pacific Railroad? That was over two years ago," Beatrix said.

Beatrix remembered everything, word for word, from the reports in the morning's paper. There had been a mention of labor issues and lengthy discussions at the depot, in steel factories in the East, and the meat packers in Chicago, but nothing about violence.

Her incredible ability to recall the most minute fact was a condition called hypermnesia and helped her at once. Her hypermnesia, she believed, had been amplified by trauma when she and her parents, wealthy Jennie and William Randolph Patterson, had been in a car crash that took the lives of her adopted parents. They realized when she first started talking that their daughter had a keen memory. It was part of her, like her auburn hair. She was twelve, she'd escaped death, and yet her world had fallen apart, and that odd ability to remember everything had gone into overdrive.

As she'd read in the morning's newspaper, the journalists were predicting an even worse strike than what had happened in 1946. But the papers always went for sensationalism. But in 1946, there was massive outrage. It was like the American Civil War, but this time, it was the pro-union workers against big business, big greed.

There had been upheavals, uprisings, and far too much anger, brutality, lies, and chaos throughout America as the union and the business leaders fought against each other. The bloodshed, the hate, and the racist violence had begun after the war when the good, right, and honorable cause for better working conditions for those who kept America moving and functioning was being threatened for more profits going to stockholders. It had been painfully settled, with both sides still smarting from the disagreements. Resentments and fury still bubbled just under the surface for those who joined the unions and the corporations who fought against them.

"Not Sam, he's so gentle," Beatrix whispered more to herself than to her dear friend.

"He didn't do *anything*. He wanted to go to work, Bea. There was a demonstration. Sam said he didn't recognize any of the men in that crowd from around town. Apparently, two of the goons led the charge against Sam while the others stood back and cheered." Jo gulped, panic underlining every word she'd said.

"He's hurt badly? Did anyone get him medical care?" Beatrix pictured muscular Sam Conrad, military posture and a smile that lit up a room. Sam was one of those oversized humans who was a teddy bear at heart, who would do anything for his wife, his kids, his chosen *and* biological family, and his friends. Beatrix, Thomas, and year-old Birdy were fortunate to be counted as chosen family.

"He wouldn't say. He told me not to worry. How can I not? You have to help me. I can barely think of what to do. He told me you'd know." A moan escaped her throat, and Beatrix could hear one of Jo and Sam's twins crying in the background.

"Take a breath, honey. Whatever you need, I'm here for you," Beatrix said.

"Beatrix, I'm petrified. He's being held in the jail downtown, but one of his pals who came to the house said he'd heard talk of sending Sam to some makeshift federal prison out in the desert. A hell hole in Arizona. This kindly older man, Marcus, said he heard that the government was going to keep the supposed instigators there until it's sorted out. Sam is not some goon; I've never even seen him get angry. He would not pick a fight."

"This is horrible, Jo. We'll get to the bottom of it, I promise," she assured her friend but thought, *Without knowing everything, can I keep that promise?*

Beatrix felt her palm sweat as she held the heavy receiver and thought of the history of labor disputes in the country. She recalled every article she'd read during that time and thought of the details of the news she'd heard on the radio. After the slow-down of the post-WWII economy, the unions banded together. The Railroad Workers of America joined the CIO (Congress of Industrial Organizations), which was affiliated with the Marine and Shipbuilding Workers of America and the AFL (American Federation of Labor). They'd been vocal with their demands as the unions were becoming more powerful. Corporate America was even more so, and Sam had told Thomas and Beatrix how each group agitated the other, and yet, their fighting had been kept private for the most part. Recently, rumors surfaced of the union workers demanding more rights, and there were open clashes and public skirmishes with megacorporations insisting that the unions were still trying to cripple America's commerce.

"These are paid mobsters, Beatrix. I'm sure of it. They have been harassing the workers, even those like Sam, who are part of the railroad workers union. Sam thinks the corporations are behind this."

That moment was not the time to grill her friend or expound on a history lesson of organized labor in the US, which had been contemptuous since the start.

Beatrix smoothed her hands on the denim overalls, too large but so comfortable. Not appropriate at all for charging into the police station demanding answers.

"Listen, sweetie, Thomas just took Birdy out for their morning trot around town. He'll be back in ten minutes, as that's all it takes to settle her for a nap. The second he gets home, I'll pick you up, and we'll go to the police station. I am not a lawyer, but I doubt they can just take prisoners like that and transport them across state lines, especially since Sam hasn't done anything except his job."

"What if he fought back?" came a tiny voice, not recognizable but definitely from her frightened friend. "What if he hit someone?"

"Did he?" Beatrix asked.

"I don't know. I don't know anything anymore," Jo cried.

"Okay, Jo. Drink some water. Make a cup of tea. Can you call your mom to look after the little ones?" Beatrix asked.

"She's pulling into my driveway right now. Must have heard about the riots from the radio report or something. Hold on, Bea. Come in, Mama," Jo called to her mother.

"Tell your mom what we're going to do, and I'll call John Brockman. He's powerful and knows people. He'll know a good lawyer, and we'll get Sam back home to you and the kids. You need to be brave for him. Now hang up the phone in case anyone wants to call you," Beatrix instructed.

Beatrix heard Jo's mother's voice and knew the situation— any situation—would be competently taken care of. Lillian was a nurse who'd recently been let go because of a staff reduction at the hospital. Like Jo, Lillian was a force to be reckoned with, and she was also Birdy's chosen nana.

Beatrix sat for a moment staring at her hands, at the slim wedding ring and the five gold bracelets that she always wore—a symbol of Thomas's love and their desire to include four more children in their lives.

Her head still had trouble getting around whatever happened at the railroad yard. Sam, she remembered, had voted for the union, and he was a shop steward, who had volunteered to be part of the bargaining committee. A man of intense principles, he believed that everyone should be able to work and be paid adequately. He knew the union deal wasn't perfect and had said so to Thomas and Beatrix at dinner the evening before. Critical safety issues were being addressed, and there were fewer accidents ruining families, and that made joining the union, to Sam, the best choice.

Why, when he tried to get to work, did thugs stop him? Why hurt him? Did he fight back? Why did the police arrest him and potentially use brutality against him? Because he's Black? Because he's a powerful figure? Pandemonium brawled within her typically cool-in-a-crisis demeanor. She loved the Conrad family. This was wrong.

She slapped the table at the same instant the oversized Bakelite telephone rang once more, which made her flinch.

Before she could speak, John Brockman said, "Beatrix?"

"John. I was about to call you."

There was a silent second and then both said at the same time, "I need your help."

While living in New Orleans at the beginning of the war, John and Beatrix had businesses next to one another in the French Quarter. John's antiquarian bookstore was the front for an illegal gambling hall, which often drew in wealthy politicians from the city, and in turn, John always made generous contributions when those same public servants ran for reelection.

John considered Beatrix to be an astute judge of people's character, especially since she could read microfacial changes. He'd hired Beatrix to give her impression of a potential and expensive business partnership that was being presented to him by the Department of the Army. The business arrangement and loan of millions helped fund the famous Higgins boats used during the Normandy landings on D-Day. Beatrix had advised her friend to offer financial support with Mr. Higgins alone, leaving the US government out of the bargain. It was not because she had psychic powers; it was because she knew how to investigate and find the truth. They'd remained friends, and now he needed her help once again.

"John, you go first, please. What's happened?"

"You know me, Beatrix. I may not be as honest as the next crook, but I am not evil."

"What is it? Please. Who thinks you're evil?" Beatrix pressed.

"I'm being blackmailed," John said.

"Is there merit to the extortion?" Beatrix asked.

"No. Yes. The person is insisting that I'm un-American," John said.

"You? A Communist?" Beatrix asked in disbelief.

"Yeah, a Red," John said.

The new slang was familiar to most, including Beatrix and others who were socially aware of slurs. This term was gaining momentum as Communists were referred to as "Reds" and Communism as the "Red Peril" or the "Red Scare." It had been derived from the frequent use of red as the dominant color in flags of communist countries. Some Americans who sided with the work ethic of Communism were scorned, bullied, blackballed, and threatened. Beatrix knew the Red Scare was hysteria over the perceived threat posed by Communists in the US, which was being called the "Cold War" between the Soviet Union and the United States. Many whispered about World War III exploding out of the "cold" one, and the hatred was beginning to intensify.

"The extortionist doesn't want money. He wants my head on a platter, it looks like. Good old-fashioned revenge is what he's dishing out, and he's threatening a savage campaign against me in Louisiana," John explained.

"You know the blackmailer, John?" Her voice was calm, but her heart beat against her chest.

"Yes. He is that disreputable Governor Bennington Long," John said with disgust.

"Oh, my goodness. What does he want from you?" Beatrix thought of the current governor of Louisiana and the rumors of his abuse of power, uncivilized activities, crude humor, relationships with a string of high-profile prostitutes, mishandling of civil rights, deceptions with land purchases, and possible affiliations with the mafia. The list was long, and Beatrix knew for a fact that it was true, yet he had the charisma to get the votes of the wealthy citizens and muscle to coerce the poor ones. He was powerful, subject to bouts of outrageous emotional outbursts, and greedy for authority, or so it was said. Beatrix had been introduced twice through the years at Mardi Gras balls and then chose to watch him from afar.

"Why go after you, John?" Beatrix asked.

"This all has to do with something I *own*. I don't want to take up your time right now. I know you're probably expecting a patient. It's a long story. We'd best meet in person, Beatrix. Can you, Thomas, and the tot come for a visit? Or perhaps you should visit alone?" John asked.

"Yes, of course. Anything I can do to help." John Brockman was far from lily white in his dealings, but he'd saved Beatrix's life and helped her and Thomas immeasurably over the years. She's done things in her past that she wouldn't want published on the front page of the *Los Angeles Times* as well, and this might be one of the cases where she'd need to investigate while being ultra discreet.

"Good, thank you. Now, tell me why you called?" he asked.

She took a long, quiet breath and said, "You know my good friends Josephine and Sam Conrad?"

"Lovely folks, and oh, I really enjoyed those kids when they were over for Easter. We need to have another family gathering," John said.

The notion that John Brockman, confirmed bachelor, felt that closeness with the Conrad family, a family of color, size, and volume, spoke of his generous heart.

"I just got a call from Jo. Sam's been arrested. For crossing some unofficial, convoluted, thug-organized picket line," Beatrix explained.

"What? Sam's all union, and as much as I'm for American greed at its best, I support the unions." There was silence for a moment. "I don't often talk about it; it's still too hard. You see,

Beatrix, my mother perished in the Triangle Shirtwaist Fire in 1911," John confided.

Her hand flew to her mouth to stifle the gasp. She had, of course, read about the horrible tragedy. The young Jewish and Italian seamstresses in the clothing factory were trapped in an old, wooden building right there in the slums. It was locked, supposedly to prevent theft, and when the fire started, they were trapped. Screams could be heard blocks away. The stench was unspeakable. They all perished. Burned to death.

"My father left us when my youngest brother was born. Mama had no choice but to go to work. She had no skills in the workplace, but she'd been a seamstress in Germany before she immigrated. It was up to us older kids to care for the baby and the younger ones. Six kids are a lot to feed, so Mama worked two jobs, taking in washing and ironing after she returned from a twelve-hour shift at the factory. I got pretty good at ironing men's shirts so that Mama had just a bit less to do when she got home. Over 140 women died that day. I was fourteen. And suddenly, the head of our household."

"I am so sorry. I never knew, John."

"The Triangle Shirtwaist Fire started the movement for unions, for job safety and better working conditions," John explained.

"Now I understand," Beatrix said.

"As for Sam, we're going to take care of it. I'll get my local attorney to head to the jail right now," John said with authority. "I have the means and the connections to do that. We need to get the man out and pay the bail. Then we can strategize on a plan."

"They can't afford much in bail money, John. I'll take care of it," she replied. On her way to pick up Jo, she'd stop at the bank.

"Don't even mention it. I'm still paying it forward for the help I received after that fire. Three kindly families in our tenement building took us in, kept our parentless lives together, and expected nothing in return. I knew Mama would have done the same for other families. I don't have to tell you, Beatrix, we cannot pay back favors. Nevertheless, we can help when it's needed. Sounds like this part of my new family needs me."

Beatrix blinked, and even with her hurting heart for Jo and Sam, the notion that John was there for all of them was of abundant comfort. She desperately wanted to know more about John's mother, his life as an orphan caring for his younger siblings, the families that sheltered them, and even possibly, if he would reveal it, how he became one of the richest and most influential men the American South—possibly in all the states east of the Mississippi. Most of all, at that second, why Governor Long was out to destroy him. Yet there was no time. Who knew what was happening to Sam.

"Her name is Mariam Goldman—best lawyer on the West Coast, Beatrix. When should I ask her to me you at the jail?" John asked.

"Will she drop everything on a Saturday morning for this, John?" But of course, she would if she was John's attorney.

"An hour enough time?" he asked.

"Thomas and the baby have just gotten home. I have an appointment to cancel, then I'm off to the Conrad house to pick up Jo. Yes, thank you so much, John. An hour will work. I am in your debt."

"Nonsense. Um, Beatrix?"

She waited.

"Now is not the right time, but I feel compelled to tell you. You're more than a friend," he stated.

"Likewise, John."

"Please. Just listen. I've been wrestling with telling you for a good six months, and this debacle with crazy Ben Long has made me feel my mortality. With your permission, I'd like to appoint you to oversee all my charitable giving as well as the other financial interests I have accumulated once I cross over and become reunited with my mother and all my siblings again. I'm bequeathing it all to you, my entire estate, so that you can evaluate current charities and set up new ones. I want you to establish worthy causes. I know you. I trust you. As executor and director, you'd be paid and have the opportunity to make a difference in this sorrowful world we've begun to contaminate. There'll be no going back in the future."

Beatrix blinked rapidly, and if she could decipher her own face as she might read another person's, she would have seen shock and surprise. "No, John, this is too much. John, we need to talk about the situation, your visions and dreams, and your incredible generosity. I'm honored that you trust me to do your wishes. I'm overwhelmed, too. Can we postpone talking about the bequeathment until we unravel why Governor Long is after you and the blackmail threats? More so, how we'll stop him and let you get on with life—for an *extremely* long time. I'll telephone you later."

She had no idea, couldn't even venture a guess, at the extent of John's sizeable fortune. She knew he owned a lavish home in New Orleans, the villa south of Santa Barbara, a penthouse in New York, and he'd mentioned a cabin in Maine. He owned significant properties all around the South, and he recently told her he bought a string of homes along the coastline south of town. She knew nothing of the other investments, yet John would have all the documents in order. When the time came, and she loathed the thought, it would be a massive amount of work, yet one that begged her to comply with his wishes.

She was wealthy in her own right, all thanks to him and his terrier-style determination to get to the truth as to why Beatrix's parent's estate wasn't directly bequeathed to her. It came about that her adoption papers had been misfiled—most definitely done to swindle Beatrix out of her vast inheritance—however, it couldn't be confirmed. It took John and his attorneys to unravel why the trustees of Beatrix's rightful fortune had perpetrated the deed. *What would I do with John's largess?* The answer was easy: *Do good for the people of this world. Educate. House. Protect. Love. Accept. Especially the forgotten, the subjugated, the maligned, and the orphaned. I could create opportunities for people to learn from each other so that there'd be less pain, less ugly hatred.*

Beatrix sat for a moment, still stunned and deeply humbled. "Now's not the time to ponder his generosity but to correct what's so wrong that Sam Conrad was beaten and then arrested," she said. She dashed up the stairs, slipping out of the gardening clothes. She couldn't meet John's attorney caked with adobe soil from the previous day's outdoor work.

With that thought and what she must do, which was anything legal, she scrubbed her face, applied lipstick, pulled a smart light gray trouser suit from the wardrobe, and stood even straighter. "I've faced ogres, kidnappers, and serial killers," she told the reflection in the bedroom mirror. "I can do this."

In another part of the house, Thomas circled his hands around his mouth and called up the stairs, "What's happened? Bea, are you all right?"

"Oh, Thomas, it's dreadful," came the breathless reply. "I'll be right down. Are you and Birdy okay?" She raced from the bedroom to the second-story landing, pulling at the cuffs of her blouse and straightening her jacket. "It's Sam. He's been beaten and arrested."

CHAPTER THREE

THE NEXT TWENTY MINUTES INSIDE THE STATELY home felt like a tornado hit, at least in Beatrix's mind. In a string of breathless sentences, Beatrix told Thomas about the phone calls, the blackmailing, fanatical Governor Long, and how Sam had been arrested, although she couldn't imagine why. She told him about meeting the attorney in thirty minutes.

She telephoned Dr. Rayne and rescheduled her counseling session and then dashed to Birdy, cooing in her pram. She lifted the little one and held her close to her neck, breathing in the comfort of the milky perfume of her skin blended with Johnson's baby shampoo. Beatrix kissed the baby's fingers and nose, whispering how much she loved the girl. Then she turned to Thomas and said, "John is insisting that I accept, when he dies, to manage his estate."

Thomas took the infant from Beatrix's arms and asked, "Do we need his money, Beatrix?" Thomas gingerly placed Birdy in the bassinet in the kitchen, one of many strategically placed around the house. That was Thomas' idea so the little one could be with them wherever they were. "Scientists are chronically poor, but the university is grateful I'm here. We have your inheritance. Our family will always be comfortable. Won't we?" He wrinkled his forehead. Thomas had a head for complex scientific calculations but not their bank account or financial planning. His only luxury was fancy shoes, which he admitted to having too many pairs.

She grabbed his hand and slipped it around her waist. "It wouldn't be for us to spend on ourselves. We have more than plenty. I see us changing the world for the better with it." She pulled away and kissed his palm.

When they'd decided to restore the house, it was crumbling around them, and it had cost a small fortune. Now they had hot and cold running water in the kitchen and all the baths, clean ceilings, and comfortable furniture, although picked up from second-hand shops, and Beatrix was working from her office on the main level. That first floor had the living room, foyer, library, a bath, along with a spacious kitchen and functional mud room at the rear that led to the garden patio, which, in the summer, would be alive with geraniums, butterflies, and scrub jaybirds. The second story held six bedrooms and two more baths. The third level was unfinished but would eventually have two more bedrooms, a bath, and a playroom. At the beginning of the month, Thomas had inquired about installing an elevator to make the upper floors more accessible when his parents and grandmother visited and to allow the house to be a forever home.

As the couple rattled around in the huge house, it was Thomas's mission to "fill those bedrooms," and he was going about it as only a scientist could: wading through mountains of red tape to speed potential foreign adoptions—especially connecting with agencies about war orphans—while contacting any reputable organization inquiring if they'd qualify as adoptive parents. Because of an illness in his twenties, they knew that conceiving in the old-fashioned way might be impossible. Hence, they made certain to be on the active list for fostering and were told time and again that they were the only ones asking to foster and adopt children whose race was not known.

Beatrix grabbed her purse, a cross-body black leather bag, from the closet near the front door, kissed Thomas again, and headed to the garage. Thomas walked her to the back garden and stayed there as she sprinted to the carport. *I hate seeing her go out to save the world, but that's why I love her, admire her, and respect her. She's unafraid to do so,* he thought, but called to her as she was halfway out the back door, "Home for dinner?"

She turned. "Depends what you're cooking?" She'd made a New Year's resolution to learn to cook at least a few edible offerings. It was March, and her abilities now included potato salad, all kinds of sandwiches, and blueberry pancakes. "You'll be okay with Birdy? Lillian is at the Conrad home if you need an extra pair of hands. I don't know how long I'll be, and if I can, I'll telephone you."

He stood on the back patio and chuckled. He bent his elbow and patted himself on the back. "Well done, mate. I was born to be a dad." For about five seconds he languished in how clever, how brilliant he was, swaggering around and back into the kitchen. Then the whimpering from the bassinet underneath the kitchen window turned into a full-scale sound, much like a fire engine's siren on the way to a four-alarm blaze. Thomas rushed to the tiny girl's sleeping basket. "Birdy, sweetie, calm down." Her face was puckered, her eyes squeezed shut, and a wail that rattled the windows came from the twenty-pound child.

He lifted her from the bassinet and pulled her to his chest. "I'm worried about your mum and our friends, as well, but you don't hear me crying." He sniffed at her nappy. "All clean and dry there." He found her favorite teddy and waved it at her. She cried louder. Then he bounced her on his shoulder, kissed her forehead, and thought about retracting the notion that he was a natural dad. He did a silly wiggle walk around the house that always had done the trick to quiet her, continued out into the garden, then up and down the sidewalk in front of the house. Finally, Birdy quieted. They sat together on a wicker porch swing, and Thomas sang "Twinkle, Twinkle Little Star" until his throat was parched and his knees were fatigued from bouncing Birdy.

"Brilliant, Birdy, good girl, smile again for your dear old dad. That's a girl. Now, let's see if you can return to your bassinet, or as your British grandmother would call it, your Moses basket. Which term do you prefer, Birdy?" he asked the final question in Cantonese, flopped down again on a wooden kitchen chair next to his now cooing daughter, and rubbed his hands over his face.

"Mummy is going to be fine. Just fine, and you are not to worry, my precious jaybird girl. Mummy always loves to go on dangerous, um, helpful adventures. This time, she's just assisting our friend Auntie Jo. You know Jo. They'll bring Uncle Sam home from the nick—that's a jail to you and your mummy — and she will be back by the end of your afternoon nap. Then she'll be home with us, and everything will be right as rain." He knew he was talking too fast, and the words came out in puffs as he was trying to convince himself that Beatrix was going to be okay. *What could happen?* He thought. *Anything. This is Bea, mate.*

Thomas looked at his watch in what seemed like five-minute intervals and even wound it thinking that it was running slow. Only an hour had passed. Why did he have this gut-wrenching feeling that somehow Beatrix would once more face another peril?

Construction crews were repairing the street not two blocks from Sam and Jo's tidy bungalow on Garden Street, and traffic was frozen. If she could have pulled out of the mess and parked, she would have. However, there was no hope of that.

Beatrix drummed her thumbs on the steering wheel of the

bulky Ford Woody station wagon. One side of the road was gutted with a trench. A worker in a hard hat and orange safety vest twirled a "stop" sign, and there was a massive dump truck in front of her, so she'd had to lean out the window to see the road crew. She took a few calming breaths and replayed the memories that she carried about everything that had happened. With her stellar ability for recall, she blinked and "saw" in her mind the information she needed. It had been 1946. Thomas was at the university, and she wandered into town for coffee and a *Los Angeles Times*. As if she were there again, she watched herself reading the scorching headlines about the vicious strike, recounting each explosive detail.

There had been pandemonium, with turmoil and anger reaching a boiling point as union after union and the outspoken and powerful John L. Lewis, president of the United Mine Workers, and his colleagues crippled the country. Their objective, Beatrix knew, was noble: retirement plans, money to cover accidents and medical bills, better working conditions, and more pay. That meant that they were attempting to achieve rights for workers by confusing strikes and walkouts. Both sides faced unending riots. There was brutality by the police, especially so in Oakland, California, where the riots lasted for days, and causalities were horrific. All told, Beatrix recalled, a series of strikes involved over five million people from the end of 1945 and into 1946.

On January 19, 1946, at more than one thousand mills across the country, eight hundred thousand steelworkers walked off the job. There was a telephone strike, a meat packers strike, and a strike at General Electric, the largest power company in the States. On April 1, 1946, Mr. Lewis called a nationwide coal strike, and coal ran the factories and heated homes and offices. At the same time, a railroad strike was looming. Negotiations had been dragging on between railway management and twenty different unions, with Labor Secretary Lewis Schwellenbach acting as President Harry Truman's mediator. The president invoked the Railway Labor Act, providing for a sixty-day mediation period.

The pulsating blast of a car horn startled Beatrix. She felt a hysterical bubble of laughter in her throat, knowing instinctively she pushed harder on the brake and clutch; otherwise, if she'd hit the gas, she'd have become part of the massive steel dump truck inches from the Ford's hood. She shook to shoo away the memories of what could have been and focused on driving a few inches rather than on the terrifying strikes of the past. She put the car into first as now she was the problem stopping traffic. She waved out the window, yelled "sorry" to no one in particular, and slowly continued on to the Conrad home. She had just pulled to the curb when Jo flew into the passenger's seat.

"So sorry, forgot to tell you they were fixing water lines on my street. What are we going to do, Beatrix? I'm so frightened." Her chocolate brown skin glowed in the sunlight, and although the day was warming to a mild seventy, Jo pulled a red sweater across her bosom, the same red as the strawberry pattern of her cotton dress. Her hair was tucked into a fat black bun at the back of her neck, and Beatrix was pleased to see she had put on lipstick.

"First off, you need to be strong. I know people always say that in an emergency. It's intolerable to do. Yet, your husband needs to see you calm and capable. Sam's probably sick with worry, unable to get home to you and the kids. He might even be fearing that you're in danger, Jo. You are not, by the way. Mr. Brockman's attorney, Mariam Goldman, will know what to do. She's meeting us at the jail, and if John thinks she's a crackerjack lawyer, then that worry is off the table. Sam will be able to be released with bail after the charges are relayed to him and the lawyer."

Jo clasped and released Beatrix's hand.

"I need both hands to drive this bulky car. Let's go."

It seemed forever, but the jail was just five minutes from the Conrad home. Beatrix pulled into the parking lot of the county courthouse with its impressive Morish-Spanish revival architecture and rolled up the driver's window. Jo did the same. They both got out and stood looking at the imposing building with its massive emerald-green lawns and swaying palm trees. The jail was concealed in the basement of the stately, white stucco, four-story building with its majestic clock tower.

Beatrix turned to her friend, who suddenly seemed unable to let go of the car door handle. Jo wrung her hands and said, "I ran to the bank after you called and withdrew all our savings out of the bank. Will $200 be enough?"

"It depends on the charges, Jo, and what the court's judge has set. It hinges on factors we don't know about. Money is not an issue here."

"Yes, it is, Beatrix. Mama can't help. As a Black nurse, she barely made enough to pay rent on her little house. I don't know what we'll do. I know she was already having to dip into her savings with inflation as it is. My brothers have big families, and I cannot take money from them. And Louisa, my baby sister, is going to medical school in Chicago and working two jobs."

Beatrix bent down, grabbed her purse from the bench seat of the car, and walked around to where Jo was frozen in fear. "Chin up, girl. Good job. You need not worry about the bail. John told me that you and Sam and the kids are better than family. When John says this, he means it, and he insisted he's paying any and all court and legal-related expenses."

"Beatrix, can I let him do that? He's a fine gentleman, and I would never want him to think we were in any way taking advantage of him. I know he's rich—that house, his cars. We'll never be able to repay him. If the $200 isn't enough," she gulped, "Sam will have to stay in jail, or worse yet, they'll send him to the desert."

"John is wise and careful and a good person. You're right.

When we get you and Sam home, I'll explain why John feels compelled to help. You just put worry on the back burner until we talk with Miss Goldman. Wipe those tears, girl."

They walked through the courtyard and the massive arch. Beatrix watched as men and women scurried with purposes of their own like mice moving in all directions. "Miss Patterson?" came a voice behind Beatrix and Jo as they focused on the sign directing them to the police registration desk.

Beatrix turned to see a woman in a smart black suit, designed to be tucked nicely at the waist, with a crisp, white silk blouse in a style Beatrix had admired in a fashion magazine. There was a jaunty red scarf knotted around her neck. She was about as big as a minute but with the posture of an army general, and Beatrix guessed she'd been in the military, probably in the war.

A tiny scarlet carnation was slipped into a diamond pin in the form of a miniature vase on the lapel of the attorney's jacket. She put out her hand. "Mariam Goldman, and so glad to finally meet you. John speaks highly of you and your husband. You," she turned to Jo, "must be Mrs. Conrad. Thank you for being prompt." The attorney was confident and enunciated her words with care. That visibly made Jo relax just a shade, and she loosened her death grip on Beatrix's forearm.

Beatrix looked at the lawyer's shoes. They were black, sturdy, and flat, made for walking and not to attract attention. She remembered how her husband insisted that one could tell a lot about a person from their shoes. *No nonsense and efficient. This woman gets things done,* Beatrix thought.

"Thank you for coming on such short notice, and please tell John how much we appreciate this," Beatrix said.

"I have been John's friend since, well, since neither of us had gray hair." She touched her sleek bob where a sparkle of gray strands caught the sunlight. It made her more striking.

"John and I met in Manhattan. I got him out of a few scrapes in New Orleans, and when I moved here to Santa Barbara just before the war, I wrote long, inviting letters. I had hoped that the descriptions would convince him to vacation here one day. Then, when all hell broke loose, I volunteered to work with the army's court of appeals. John and I corresponded, and he surprised me to no end when he bought a home just south of the city. Now to business, ladies."

"Ma'am, what should we do?" Jo blinked back tears, and her lips became a straight line.

"We'll go into the police station, which is just down that flight of stairs." Mariam pointed to the door. "Please let me talk with the duty sergeant and find out what the charges are and if bail has been set." Then the attorney explained what would happen at the arraignment. "The arraignment is the first time the defendant appears in court."

Jo and Beatrix nodded, and Mariam continued. "At the arraignment, the judge tells the defendant what the charges are, what a person's constitutional rights are, and that if he or she does not have enough money to hire a lawyer, the court will appoint a lawyer free of charge. The defendant may then respond to the charges by entering a plea. Common pleas include guilty, not guilty, or no contest, also known as nolo contendere." Mariam pulled at the cuffs of her white blouse, adjusting them so that only a half inch of white was visible between her jacket and her wrists.

"I assume Mr. Conrad will plead not guilty. That means he's saying he did not commit the crime. Sometimes, defendants enter a plea of not guilty as a strategic decision during plea bargaining or because they want to go to trial and force the prosecution to prove its case beyond a reasonable doubt.

"If Mr. Conrad pleads not guilty, the judge will do one of three things. I'm hoping the judge will release Mr. Conrad on his own recognizance, promising to return to court on a specific date. The judge might set bail or—and I will not let this happen

—the judge may refuse to set bail, and Mr. Conrad would return to jail. This is a misdemeanor, and Mr. Conrad does not have a criminal record. His military record shows stellar service, including that Purple Heart. Yes, I've already checked."

"He never talks about the Purple Heart." Jo looked at her wedding ring, then said, "Thank you, ma'am, thank you for explaining that." She lifted her arms as if to move in to hug the lawyer, then stopped and added. "Whatever you need me to do, I'll do it." Jo looked at Beatrix, then said, in a whisper, "About bail—"

"Mrs. Conrad, John told me you might fuss about his largess and instructed me, flatly, to ignore you. I work for John, so you do not have a say in this. John wants this matter to be taken care of, and that's what I will do"

"Thank you," Jo whispered and grabbed Beatrix's hand for support.

"Ready? Good. Posture, ladies. We are heading into a police station, not a lion's den. There's nothing to be afraid of, dear. I've faced bigger giants and dragons than these," she chuckled at a private memory.

Just as they approached the station's glass doors, they were opened, and Beatrix's friend and colleague Detective Stella Rodriguez looked up from the manilla folders she was juggling. "Beatrix? Jo? Oh, no, tell me that your husband was not in that fracas at the railroad depot this morning?"

"He was, Stella," Beatrix said. "May I introduce Sam's attorney?"

Detective Rodriguez nodded, "No intros needed. Mariam, didn't know you were a champion for the union workers? Thought you did corporate and estate law, clean and expensive lawsuits and trials."

"Stella, good to see you. I'm a defender of any underdog around here. You know that."

"If you'll give me a minute to return these files, I'll get you through the red tape. I assume you will be making bail?" Detective Rodriguez asked.

"Mr. Conrad's been arraigned? Good. Yes, Stella. Thank you," Mariam replied.

It was obvious that the attorney and the detective were no strangers. *But are they friends? There is distrust on Mariam's face,* Beatrix thought. *Why? Probably because she gets her job done. Well.* After an initial and formal handshake, each looked away, a telltale sign that this might be a respected yet complex relationship.

Beatrix, ever curious about how microfacial expressions and body language always told the truth, filed the meeting away to talk about with Stella sometime when they were alone. Right now, getting Sam out of jail and stopping some bureaucrat from shipping him off to a federal prison was her main concern. She looked at Jo, who was clenching her jaw, and placed her arm over her shoulder, whispering, "We'll get him out."

CHAPTER FOUR

MOMENTS LATER, BEATRIX, JO, AND MARIAM WERE sitting in hard, wooden chairs that were possibly at one time white but now showed a crust of ochre-colored grime from the sweaty hands of visitors. They studied the starkly furnished police waiting room that wreaked of a strong cleaning solution. Beatrix remembered reading in one of her university classes how, in 1889, a German chemist named Gustav Raupenstrauch created Lysol. During this snake-oil era, where charlatans created fake medicine for all sorts of conditions, the early owners marketed Lysol as everything from a household cleanser to, more troublingly, a feminine hygiene product.

The stench clung to the back of Beatrix's throat. She knew the odor was rubbing off on her freshly laundered slacks, possibly forever, by the strength of the fumes burning her nose.

"Whatever they're killing germs with is about to make me vomit," Jo said, then looked both ways and ran toward the women's restroom.

Jo returned to the chair next to Beatrix and slipped her fingers into her friend's hand. Jo's palms were clammy.

"When is the baby due?" Beatrix smiled.

Jo whispered a chuckle. "Not even funny, Bea."

"Remember, I'm your best friend, so I can read your cues. A family of five kids, then?"

"Sam and I wanted a big family, three or four at the tops, and if this pregnancy produces yet another set of twins, that husband of mine is sleeping on the sofa until I'm eighty." The words sounded tough, yet Jo's face was rounder. She patted her middle. She always became even prettier when she was pregnant, more serene.

"Mrs. Conrad? Miss Patterson? I'm the duty officer, Fred Ford. I'm in charge of your husband's arrest. I understand bail has been posted for disorderly conduct, threatening an unarmed security officer, and verbally attacking a business owner."

The three women immediately stood up, and Mariam looked the officer up and down, stepping closer to him, physically and mentally signaling that she was in charge. "I'm representing Mr. Conrad. Mariam Goldman, Esquire." She nodded and handed him a business card, yet not her hand.

Beatrix liked the lawyer even more. "When will Mr. Conrad be released, officer?" Beatrix asked, feeling Jo's hand slide into hers.

"About a half hour. Ma'am, I am pro-union but will deny this if you repeat it: I think the dust-up was a ploy to get the press and the public angry with the railroad union," Officer Ford said.

"Were others involved arrested?" Mariam asked.

"No, just Mr. Conrad. I heard from one of the officers who arrived first on the scene that he was heading to the depot to clock in for his shift. Two local hooligans, whom I've dealt with before, apparently had been hired for the sheer purpose of stirring up trouble and picking a fight. Get their cause and faces into the city newspaper. Whatever their reason, the goons didn't seem to know it. At least that's what they've told me and their court-appointed lawyer. They are tight-lipped about who hired them. They'll probably will get a bonus if they don't rat out the leader. A few nights in jail because they can't make bail will soften them up. At least it has in the past."

Beatrix nodded.

Mariam looked to the women and then at the officer. "You've been honest and helpful."

"Was my husband badly hurt, officer?" Jo asked. The question ended with a quiver.

"If this has to do with police brutality, officer, I want you to know it will not be tolerated." The small woman ground out the words. There would be no denying she was powerful and capable.

He looked at the attorney and quickly added, "No one in our police department touched him, ma'am. I promise you that. Crap like that might happen in Los Angeles and did up in Oakland a few years back. Round here, we all grew up together. I met your man here in Santa Barbara High the summers he stayed with his grandpappy. We played a lot of football and got shipped off to boot camp on the same day. Bet you remember that."

"I do remember. Thank you for your honesty," Jo said, reaching out and patting his arm. "Glad you made it back from the war safely as well."

The beefy officer smiled now and looked down at his shoes. "Just have to have a release form signed, and Sam will meet you right here in a few minutes. Are you aware of the conditions of bail, Miss Goldman?"

"Not my first rodeo, officer," she snapped and then smiled. "No worries about me killing the messenger. I have been through this before."

"Yes," Beatrix replied. "Thanks to Miss Goldman, we understand."

A few minutes stretched into ten and then twenty, as Beatrix imagined some egotistical, low-level officer making what should have been a quick signature and then out the door into a lesson in frustration.

A squeak echoed. All heads turned to the door at the end of the long corridor. Sam Conrad, in his striped, oversized blue and gray ticking overalls, typical of train engineers at the time, walked out. He took a deep breath of freedom and gratitude, and seeing his wife, relief flooded his face.

Beatrix noted a limp, the gashes on his forehead and chin, and then his smile and kind eyes.

Jo ran to him. She buried her face into his chest and silently sobbed. She held him back and started to touch the lip that had been lacerated and saw the gash above his right eye, then stopped, shaking her head, whispering to her husband.

There was blood—his, most likely—splattered on his blue denim shirt and the front of his uniform.

Sam circled his tiny wife with his arms and, if possible, pulled her closer. Then he looked up to smile and nod at Beatrix. "I knew you would help us, Beatrix."

Beatrix gave the couple a few moments and then said, "Sam, thank goodness. We didn't know how bad it was."

Husband and wife pulled their friend into the little circle. "It was bad, Beatrix, and I got this," he waved a hand in front of his face, "for not fighting back. Hired thugs. Kids actually. Not more than early twenties. Boys who think they're men and have just messed up their futures."

Beatrix introduced Sam to his attorney and then inquired, "Any idea who might be behind it and why?"

Sam looked both ways and then said, "I'm betting they were employed by the owners of the railroad. The unions are pushing more workers to join. The owners are afraid they're losing power, but more so, losing money. Greed is my guess."

"Mr. Conrad, I believe you are correct," Mariam said. "May I call at your house, and we can talk later," she looked around, "in private?"

Beatrix patted Sam's arm, and he winced. "We need to get you stitched up and checked out. I saw that limp. We'll stop at Cottage Hospital. Don't want to scare your little ones with how this looks."

Just as they were heading to the courthouse's massive brick steps, Detective Rodriguez called out, "Beatrix? Have a moment?" The officer served in the military police force, and Beatrix could easily see when Stella was agitated. Something was causing her serious distress. Her posture was ramrod straight.

"We're on the way to the hospital to get Sam patched up," Beatrix answered.

"It's important. I've called Sam and Jo a taxi, if you all don't mind, folks. It'll be here in five minutes. There's something you need to know, Beatrix. Can we take a walk and talk?" The detective slipped her arm through Beatrix's elbow and guided her away from the courthouse and prying ears and eyes.

They found a park bench in front of the city's public library. "Not like you, Stella, to be this cloak and dagger-ish."

"Something has come to my attention, having to do with the strike, Beatrix, that ruffles my feathers, frosts my cookies, and upsets my apple cart."

"You have just murdered about a boatload of cliches in the process," Beatrix smiled, impatient for her friend and colleague to get to the point. The March sun was bright, but the breeze from the azure Pacific and the cold Japanese current in the ocean, just blocks from where they were, pulled any comfort away.

"It's murder I wanted to talk with you about. One of the vice presidents of the Union Pacific Railroad, Grayson Welsh, was found dead this morning."

"No. Where?" Beatrix asked.

"A neighbor of Mr. Welsh, who was out at sunrise walking her dog, spotted a black sedan creep through the neighborhood a few times. It parked a block away from Mr. Welsh's home. It stayed there for about a half hour, according to the woman, who seems to keep a written account of everyone in the swanky Upper State locale." Stella opened a small black notebook. "Her name is Antoinette Du Bois. She'd just walked Fido—or Fluffy or Flopsy—a nippy toy French poodle.

"When I interviewed her at the scene, the dog kept heaving its body at me as if it wanted to eat me alive. Luckily, she snapped up the little monster and tucked it beneath her arm. I swear it continued a low-level growl during the entire interview. Lordy, every minute or so, it would emit a volley of barks, a bark that could shatter crystal, I swear, and for the twenty minutes I was speaking with the witness, the creature did not stop. Mrs. Du Bois seemed oblivious to how annoying that was. To top it off, it had one of those haircuts with the pom-poms on its butt," Stella said.

"I'm taking it you don't care for poodles or the fancy haircut some impose on them?" Beatrix asked.

"I'm a hiker, Beatrix. That dog wouldn't last a minute on the trails where I go, not with the coyotes. They'd lick their lips and have it for lunch. Sorry, I just got distracted."

"Did the neighbor, Mrs. Du Bois, by chance, see the assailant?"

"No. When she saw the sedan again, she put the harness on Flop Dog and pretended to take another walk. She was on her front porch, according to her statement, when she saw the car once more. She said she was writing down the car's license plate when she heard a click."

"Not a gunshot?" Beatrix asked.

"No, and that's the weird thing," Stella said.

"Silencer?"

"Weird again. Yes, he was shot, but with a weapon that is used to sedate large animals. It tranquilizes them. The coroner,

Dr. Rayne, hasn't completed the autopsy yet, maybe not until tomorrow or Friday, but that was her best guess."

CHAPTER FIVE

"WAIT? WELSH WAS SHOT, AND A TRANQUILIZER ended his life?" Beatrix's mind was already in the investigation, knowing that the detective would not have made her privy to the details unless it was about being hired as a police consultant again.

"That'd be too easy. Dr. Rayne's conjecture is that Mr. Welsh was left paralyzed. He was, it seems, outdoors, on his driveway when the assault happened. Mrs. Du Bois discovered him lying on the pavement in his robe and slippers, newspaper clutched in his hand."

"Not to be indelicate, but no pajamas?" Beatrix asked gingerly.

"Nope, and everything was out for the world and your grand-mother to notice. Not something I care to see again with his rotund and hairy body exposed. The responding officer was new, or she'd have at least covered the victim with a blanket from the trunk of her patrol car." Stella shook her head as if attempting to shake away the image.

"What, then, caused the fatality?" Beatrix asked.

"Good question. Heart condition? He was a smoker, Mrs.

Welsh told us, and when I arrived on the scene with two other officers, he smelled heavily of cigar smoke. He was seriously obese, and his face was puffy. Broken capillaries on his bulbous nose and chunky cheeks. I'd guess it was from an alcohol addiction. He would have been fifty next month."

"Why are you sharing this with me, Stella?" Beatrix pressed.

"I am apologizing first. I know Baby Birdy is the love of your family life, and I know what I'm asking has the potential to be dangerous."

"Get on with it, please, and then let me say no if I'm uncomfortable with the request."

"This isn't as simple as interviewing the family and watching their facial expressions to see if they're lying like you've helped with in the past. Or grilling anyone who disagreed with Mr. Welsh's business ethics, which I've heard were malleable depending on what he wanted or thought he had to achieve. According to another cop who recently pulled the deceased over for drunk driving on the San Marcus Pass—crazy to even think about—the man was a bully. Started a fistfight, if you can imagine, with the officer—mid-day and on a blind curve, no less." She laughed and shook her head in obvious dismay. "From the little that I've been told, the current Mrs. Welsh is one of those free spirits who lives half the time in that questionable group of folks, Nature Boys and Girls, up in the hills."

"Current?" Beatrix asked.

"You don't keep up with our local newspaper gossip column, do you, Beatrix? Yes, Kay Welsh, age twenty-seven, according to the Department of Motor Vehicles, is wife number five. I dug up a wedding announcement published last June, and it said that the future Mrs. Welsh had at one time been a stenographer for the Union Pacific Railroad in LA and that she last worked with some of Hollywood's biggest names. Didn't mention any of the movies she'd been in or that she was actually an actress. Might be a stagehand for all we know from the newspaper. In the newspaper photo, she was pretty, towering over chunky Mr. Welsh's frame. Even when I met her at the crime scene, she was one of those women who just looks together. You know what I mean?"

Beatrix thought of the age difference and backgrounds of the couple, including that there'd been four previous Mrs. Welsh's.

Stella flipped past another page of notes in the small notebook. "She's a member of the group that resides on Mountain Drive. I've heard there are dozens more men than women, boys and girls, and plenty of babies. We have received a score of irate and cranky complaints at the station from folks who think we should run these free thinkers out of the county."

Casually and out of curiosity, Beatrix had been following the unique community that was quickly becoming a legend throughout the West, a group of what the city called misfits and rebels, often accompanied by expletives. The community started with tents and yurts and then, right after the war, began building shelters on the steep hillsides above Santa Barbara right. Some members were lost souls, wanderers, and others were returning veterans, she'd learned, who were disenchanted with the economy, Capitalism, all things to do with the government, the expensive housing market, dead-end jobs, and probably the price of coffee in Brazil was their platform for being disenchanted with society. These were folks who felt marginalized and opposed to the mores of conservative society, and the flock was growing. The combination of a landscape of rare and rugged beauty and freedom from convention allowed the blossoming of a lifestyle that was quickly becoming utopia for some and a warning of ballooning debauchery to the straight-laced citizens in the city. There were, supposedly, naked rituals, communal hot baths, groups sitting in circles, and horror of horrors, playing guitars, singing songs, and dancing.

Drinking and drugs? Beatrix wondered, but the articles didn't say anything about that. *Sounds like the group is rather reminiscent of modern-day vagabonds*, she thought, recalling a newspaper interview with the mayor and a few business executives complaining of rude and rowdy festivals and uninhibited sexuality with multiple partners. "At the same time," the mayor had said. That made Beatrix all the more intrigued, especially as she recollected that one prominent citizen who'd been interviewed was Grayson Welsh.

"Grayson Welsh was hotly vocal about the cult and all its depravity, and yet, his wife is a member?"

Stella shook her head. "I've given up trying to understand the dynamics of married couples."

"An unfaithful spouse, a love triangle, a public affair, and somehow connected to the union?" Beatrix thought back to an essay on the movement of free thinkers and those who wanted to live off the grid and were rebelling against society. The essay was a bit hazy on their manifesto, and still, she could have shared it verbatim. It had read: From the beginning, men and women wore their hair long and had highly tanned skin from reverence of nature and the sun. They preferred simple clothing, when they wore it. Author Jack Kerouac mentioned them in *On The Road*, and now, while he was traveling through Los Angeles in 1947, he'd see "an occasional Nature Boy saint in beard and sandals."

Beatrix finished processing her thoughts, and then it clicked. "You want me to go undercover with the railroad and find out who might have hated Welsh enough to stun him, kill him, and leave him naked in the driveway. And why? What about the wife and Mountain Drive? Will you have someone follow her there or infiltrate the community?"

"Geeze, Beatrix, you're like a hundred miles ahead of my words that I hadn't even formed into thoughts to convince you to do this. I was merely, yeah, dangerous as it would be, merely going to have you hang out at the depot and ask some questions. I had thought, perhaps, you could be hired by the Welsh estate as a maid to get the scoop on the family's inner workings. Sending you to the depravity of Mountain Drive? Nope." Then she chuckled. "I plan to do that myself," she said, rubbing the palms of her hands together.

"As Thomas would say, that's cheeky of you."

"Okay, bad joke. My captain at SBPD would have a heart attack if he thought I was going to join that commune. My parents?" She laughed, one of those contagious ones that was big and loud, and continued, "I'm nearly forty, and you know what? I don't even talk shop when I'm at their house, even though Dad was a beat cop in San Diego his entire career. They still think of me as their baby girl, and that's Dad's nickname for me. I'm the oddball daughter in my big Hispanic family. I've been trying to find a way to tell them about Milton Westchester III, my pretty serious beau."

"You've moved to 'pretty serious'? Why the secrecy, Stella?"

"My family came from Mexico City in the late 1890s. Migrant workers. Milton wasn't born yet, of course, but his father and grandfather were strong leaders of the AFL who hired the muscle to keep foreign workers, us Mexicans, Blacks, and Asians out. Dad told us stories about being roughed up. I know they'll think that Milt agrees with his family, with whom he's not close to due to his religious convictions, but that couldn't be farther from the truth."

"He's attending seminary, right? You're dating an *almost* priest? Isn't that about as scandalous as it gets?" Beatrix asked.

"He is not going to join the priesthood, Beatrix, and you know perfectly well that's true. He wants to teach at Bishop Garcia Diego High School next year if they'll hire him. The war threw a monkey wrench into his plans to play professional base-ball, as did the shrapnel in his shoulder he got thanks to a Nazi bomb when he was fighting in France."

"It'll work out, my friend, and I'm really happy for you and Milt." She squeezed the detective's hand and knew that her parents were not going to be over the moon about their only daughter marrying into the family that had violently opposed their uncles, fathers, and brothers.

"You'll hold my hand when I introduce my parents to this tall, skinny, *really* White guy?" Stella pleaded.

"Tell you what," Beatrix said, smiling at her friend. "Let's get the clans together at our house next week for a party, and you can start to refer to him as your guy, boyfriend, beau, whatever."

"Yeah, that could work, stave off World War III with me in the middle. You'll frisk my dad at the door, right, in case he brings a gun? Okay, we've got to get off my love life and back to Mountain Drive and why I pulled you into this secret conversation. Imagine that they'd go crazy if they knew I love Milton and then found out I was cavorting with wackos on Mountain Drive. They'd drag me home by the ears. Probably have our priest do an exorcism before letting me past the front porch. Kidding. But you've met them."

"Let's not discount going undercover. It's a viable option, but I have another idea. I need to be hired by the railroad here in the city. I need to become invisible so I can nose about, ask questions, and listen. That's the best way to find out why this made-up strike and the rumors of more violence are surfacing."

"Can't you just waltz into the station and pretend you're writing an article for the newspaper or something?" Stella asked.

Beatrix smoothed her hands over the thighs of her trousers. "No. The railroad is strictly a male domain, and I'm far too straightforward to try feminine allure. Does your Milt have connections with the labor union, discrete and all?"

"Must I implicate him?"

"Not at all. He's probably a terrible liar, with all the religious training and such. What if I pose as a conductor in training?" Beatrix suggested.

"Fat chance, Beatrix. They'd never let a woman be a conductor. It might have worked during the war when our guys were overseas. Now, as we both know, us women are expected to return to our roles as domestic goddesses, breeding and keeping the kitchen clean. The few gals that are at the station sell tickets, clean the toilets, scrub gum from under the wooden benches, and mop grimy floors."

Beatrix jumped up from the bench. "I need to talk with Sam Conrad. He'll want to help. About a month ago, Sam, Jo and the kids were having dinner with us when he talked about an apprenticeship program for returning vets to encourage them to learn the rail trade. That could work. Sam will be straight with me, especially when I tell him why I'm doing it."

"Who is going to believe you're a man with your beautiful, long auburn hair? Besides, you have a girly figure, my friend." The detective's hair was a mass of crinkly black curls, and she ran her hand through it, pulling at a lock of her own hair. "This I gotta see."

Beatrix patted her waist, "Maybe a sofa cushion will make my bust look, well, less chesty. Come by the house tomorrow afternoon. By then, I should have all the props needed. There are a few wrinkles that could ruin the plan, but I should be able to work them out."

"I hope that one of the wrinkles is telling your husband. I'm no expert on men, although Milton is close to helping me learn, but I've heard that they feel pretty protective when their wife dives into danger where someone has *already* been murdered."

Beatrix thought of Thomas, and yes, he was one of the wrinkles. "Who told you that?"

"Might have been my colleague, Detective Maria Davies, who went undercover as a hooker. Or was it you? Didn't you tell me some version of that and how Thomas nearly went berserk, panic-stricken with worry once, when you were kidnapped by Nazi sympathizers in New Orleans? Or was it when you exposed a crazed and murdering entertainer? Or unscrambling that evil cult leader who tried to steal your man, and then there was our last caper dealing with war criminals."

"Point taken. By the way, any chance that Maria might be able to get a job in the railroad depot so I'd have a contact there?" Beatrix asked.

"Now that's a winning idea. She was just saying this morning that shuffling paperwork was not her cup of Earl Grey," Stella answered.

The two said goodbye, and Beatrix briskly walked to the Conrad home on Garden Street, blocks from city hall. Beatrix headed to the back garden after hearing Sam and a child's laughter. Sam was pushing ever-energetic Gracie on the rope swing that hung from an ancient California oak tree limb. Sammy, their six-year-old, was at school for another hour, and the twins Jefferson and Jackson were nowhere to be seen.

Sam shouted hello and waved a greeting as Beatrix opened the waist-high white picket gate to the backyard. Gracie screamed in delight and flung herself from the swing when it was at least five feet off the grass, tumbling twice and finally throwing her tiny self into Beatrix's outstretched arms.

"Gracie, darling, that was unsafe," Beatrix chided.

"I like to fly through the air, like Superman. Right, Daddy?" the little girl hugged Beatrix.

She kissed the child's cheeks, fearing that, with Gracie as a role model, when Birdy was that age, she'd probably do the same. "Sam, this is why I'll have gray hair raising my children."

"Yep. Look at mine already. That girl does that all the time. Bounces pretty well." He gave Beatrix a one-armed hug. "Kids are great. You and Tom need more. I'd have nine if Jo would let us, but don't tell her that."

"That's the plan for us, not you, I suppose." Beatrix twisted the five slim gold bangles that Thomas had bought her, which also represented good luck in his Chinese heritage. The two had a quiet moment, watching Gracie do cartwheels and summer-saults on the grass. "Your face looks sore. Know what you're going to tell Sammy when he comes home from school?"

"The truth. What else is there? Sammy is going to grow up, I pray, in a world where he'll be free of this kind of hatred, but I can't shelter the boy. I refuse to do that but won't scare him either.

"Now, please. Come sit in the shade. Jo's putting the twins down." The big man's face grew somber, and the bruises looked nasty. "Beatrix, I've been through some harsh times growing up in South Central LA, the dark days of the railroad laying track with no safeguards and little money for hazardous work. Some worse during my time in the South Pacific with the Corps of Engineers building bridges that the Japanese bombed out as soon as they were done. Back then, and maybe because I was younger, I knew I'd survive.

"Today, I thought my luck had come to an end. Don't know who hired those thugs, but they were out for my blood. For a short time," he whispered, "I feared I'd never see Jo or the babies again. I cannot thank you enough and never will. Never will forget you or Mr. Brockman for bringing in the calvary. Miss Goldman said there'll be an arraignment where the judge looks into the charges. She insists that this was not my fault after hearing about how I was provoked. There are witnesses, too."

"That's a huge relief. It's still messy and doesn't answer who hired the hoodlums. Sam, I don't mind if you tell Jo everything we'll talk about, as you would anyway. The police are really taking this incident and others—accidents, things thrown on the track, dangerous mishaps like tons of freight not being tied down properly—seriously."

"Yeah, at first, I chalked it up to the new crews, the veterans that are being hired as soon as they hit town."

"Is it more?" Beatrix asked.

"Heck of a lot more."

"You know my friend Detective Stella Rodriguez? She has been asked by the mayor and chief of police to solve this, and that starts by discovering who or what's behind it. The police believe the minor riot led by the thugs that cornered you is somehow connected with the death of the railroad's vice president, Grayson Welsh."

"Welsh, the bigwig? Dead? Hmmm, I don't see it, but I'm not good at solving mysteries. I met Welsh a few times, and he was a pompous and self-important prig, but I always had the feeling it was a bluff. Bullies, and I've met my share, are that way."

Beatrix took a breath, knowing she could and must trust Sam. "The police want me to go undercover as an employee and see what I can find out. Talk around, listen, and watch."

"You'll never hear anything as a ticket seller or if you scrub the floors. The guys I work with are tight with each other. Newcomers, especially pretty gals like you, are to flirt with and maybe more, but not to share rumors or secrets with."

"That's why I'm here. You mentioned a pilot program where returning vets, especially those who had been injured in battle, are hired as apprentices and mentored into a full-time job. You said other cities are considering this as soldiers, sailors, and marines trickle back into society."

Sam started to rub his forehead and then flinched when his finger met the gash that had been stitched. He pulled his hand off his face and said, "You're not big enough to be in the engine with me, Beatrix." He flexed his biceps, and they bulged.

She nodded. "I probably couldn't hold on to the controls, Sam. I would need a disguise. Like I said, I could become a conductor in training."

"Women can't hold those jobs. It's the law."

She smiled. "All worked out. Just get me hired. You can pull strings and get me a conductor's uniform for someone about my size. Mr. Rosenbaum, the tailor on State Street, can make alterations. I'll do the rest."

Sam looked at his friend and shook his head. "You know this is crazy, right?"

"Sometimes we have to accept that crazy is the best option."

"If you were my sister, I'd forbid this. But, I've known you since I came back from the war. Know you care, know you're worried. This small squabble could be the flash point for troubles that could cripple the nation again, like in 1946. Now I'm just scared silly that when Tom finds out, he'll become more alarmed than usual when you go out to solve the crime. You've told Tom, right?"

"Not yet. I'll explain the situation. He'll understand. Thank you, Sam, thank you for putting yourself out there for the good of others, to help the union get fair wages, pay medical bills, put money toward a retirement fund, and even more needed, better safety."

Jo walked down the cement steps from the kitchen. "I don't like what I'm seeing—like you're plotting the overthrow of the galaxy. Heads close together and whispering." She sat next to her husband and smoothed the hair on his bare forearm.

"I've got to run, Jo," Beatrix hugged her friend. "Sam will explain. No worrying, honey. You just take care of Sam and the family. Love you."

Jo grabbed Beatrix's hand, and the grip was tight. She kissed it. "Be careful. I don't think I'm going to like what is going to happen." She released Beatrix's fingers and then bent over Sam, touching his stitched forehead. Her face clouded with fear.

CHAPTER SIX

BEATRIX WALKED MORE SLOWLY RETURNING TO THE courthouse to pick up the car and then drove to the home on Anapamu. She knew that Thomas would think much the same as her friend Jo. Putting herself in potential danger was a terrifying idea, yet the reality of not stopping future chaos was worse.

She also realized her husband understood her need to right wrongs, help and protect people, and find the truth. But would he be okay this time when violence was part of the package, and they had the baby's welfare in the equation?

The house was empty when she climbed the steep front stairs to the lavish porch, where they spent many days and evenings. "Thomas and Birdy must still be shopping." Thomas had become the chef in the family, although he acquiesced about Sunday morning breakfast, and the pancakes that Beatrix made, supposedly, were light as feathers. She secretly thought it was because he knew she needed to feel like a homemaker, and that made her smile.

In the kitchen, she poured a glass of water, walked through to the back garden, and looked up at the tree-studded hillside behind their home. Thomas had hired contractors to construct a gazebo where they often took the baby and watched the Channel Islands and the Pacific sparkling in the distance. The sunsets were magnificent in yellows, pinks, and purples as the light faded across the ocean.

Is this the right thing to do? To Thomas? To Birdy? Beatrix thought of her friends on the Chumash Santa Ynez reservation and their traditions, how they stood by what was good and proper, having respect for one another. After she helped solve a mystery of missing Indigenous relics and once again had become close to the tribal matriarch she called Grandmother, Beatrix often thought of their traditional ways. "Grandmother would tell me to find the truth. Truth always matters," she said out loud, climbing the steps to the gazebo, sitting on the wooden bench in the outbuilding where the view was expansive.

She'd recently been told by Grandmother that their street's name, *Anapamu*, meant "rising place" and referred to the prominent hill upon which had once held, eons in the past, a shrine. It was perhaps, she considered, exactly where she was sitting and how the local Chumash gathered to worship powerful supernatural beings that inhabited the world above. The shrine was considered holy and quite possibly had been located where she was sitting. It was, according to Chumash legend, a place where concentrated supernatural power was located. At the time of winter solstice, Grandmother recalled, when prayers were offered to the sun, Santa Barbara's first people placed poles decorated with feathers on the summit of Anapamu. These poles were to remain for an entire year, to be renewed by village chiefs in and about Santa Barbara. Prayers for food, good health, protection from bears and rattlesnakes, and a host of other human needs and desires were conducted on the summit of such shrines.

That same need for protection would be required if somehow the dangerous thugs who attacked Sam and caused the death of the vice president of the Union Pacific were connected. Beatrix had no doubt that they were. She, Thomas, and the baby attended church with Jo, Sam, Lillian, and their children, but right at that moment, smelling the pungent eucalyptus leaves releasing their aromatic oils, she thought of her bond to this city and the Chumash. She raised her arms into the air and said, "Elders, thank you for this land, for the air, for the sky. Whatever happens, help me help others and find the truth." Would the Baptist preacher she listened to each Sunday think this was sacrilege? Not at all, as he was biracial, and from long talks over big pots of coffee, Beatrix felt certain that he'd agree: the more blessings, the better. At peace, she strolled down the steps, crushing a eucalyptus leaf in her fingers as she returned to the house.

She was at the kitchen table finishing a note to Thomas when she heard them return. She'd just completed writing how she was going to see John Brockman, the riot at the train depot, and why he might find long strands of her auburn hair scattered on the back patio.

Evidently, he hadn't seen her hair in the bin near the back door as he called out from the adjacent mudroom, "Love, we're home. Tell Mum what a brilliant baby you were and how we met some new friends walking around Alameda Park on Santa Barbara Street. The groceries for dinner are still in the pocket of the pram. Thought we'd have mashed potatoes, meatloaf, and you can make some kind of salad. You're amazing with salads, love."

Beatrix smiled at her husband and their child, "You're just trying to get me to help. I can see right through your evil plan to get me to cook. I don't think I'll ever be Betty Crocker or even a good sous chef."

More often than not, he'd tease her back, and she'd have a funny retort. "It is vocabulary foreplay," Thomas once told her with a wink. This time, he frowned slightly, his lips a straight line as he patted the inside pocket of his light cotton jacket in an aviator style that was currently all the rage.

His silence told her that his sadness had to be about ending his sabbatical and, therefore, his full-time position as a dad. *That has to be it.*

Still with his back to her, Thomas looked out the kitchen window and over the early spring garden as he bounced the baby on his shoulder, whispering in the child's ear some secret. Then he said, "You are right, Birdy. Clarence and his mummy could be our new park-walking chums. Perhaps we could start a dad, mum, and baby playgroup. Jackson and Jefferson Conrad could round out the little ones. We'll meet them again for a stroll and bring this up tomo—" Seeing his wife, he stopped mid-sentence, his body weaving slightly as if he might tumble over.

Beatrix looked up from the note and touched her head. The short hair bristled against her palm. "Should I have warned you? But how could I, as you and Birdy had disappeared." That sounded like sour grapes even to Beatrix's ears, and she wondered and then filed away the notion of if she was jealous of the attachment that father and daughter had.

Thomas gulped. "Blimey, Bea." He handed her their child and flopped into a kitchen chair, scrubbing his hands over his face. "I don't . . . The hair? What have you done? Why have you done this? This isn't one of those crazy fads from Hollywood? You look, um, like, um, a beautiful, um, boy."

"I was just finishing writing you a note to explain every-thing," she said, sliding it across the kitchen table and then continued to kiss Birdy's forehead as the little girl gurgled in her arms.

"Bloody hell," he said and repeated it five more times. "Why?" Thomas stood up and hugged his wife, sandwiching Birdy between them. "I am not going to like this, am I? We go out for our walk and a bit of a gossip with the other mums.

Then, I return home to find that my glorious wife now resembles a lad."

"Thomas, let me explain." He was pacing, seemingly unable to read her note detailing the explanation that was still in the middle of the table.

She now bounced the baby on her knees, and Birdy, ever the sweet little one, accepted and chewed on a Farley Rusk, a dry teething biscuit that Thomas procured from his family's favorite grocery shop in their London neighborhood as his grandmother denounced anything except Farley's.

"Damn it to hell. You're alarming me." He swallowed hard. His wife had put herself in terrorizing situations before, but whatever this haircut had to do with their future, he did not like it.

"It's going to be okay. The hair will grow back."

"You look like a bloke, and how did you get such a robust belly in less than three hours?" Thomas asked.

Beatrix had taken one of Thomas' dress shirts, stuffed a pillow in the front, and tried to emulate what it would feel like to be a young, out-of-work veteran who would be hired by the railroad. She unbuttoned the shirt and pulled out the gray, striped cushion.

"This is about the fighting at the rail station. Sam was attacked by a gang. When he tried to defend himself, he was arrested for causing it. It was as if a few cops were waiting just out of sight. It's all not true. Sam would never cause trouble. Then some judge, who I think might be on the take, is conspiring to get Sam out of town because of his position and influence with people of color in the union. They were going to arrest him and send him directly to a federal containment center in Arizona. It's a pack of lies," she said, even more loudly than she expected. "I called John, and with his help, Sam's out on bail, and a doctor stitched up his lacerations. There's another problem, Thomas. It's all connected somehow, but I do not know the details.

"An executive, Grayson Welsh, with the Union Pacific in the city, was found murdered this morning. A sedation dart that might temporarily paralyze a wild animal was shot at him. The dart wouldn't have killed him; something else did, as he was unresponsive and cold with the morning's newspaper gripped in his fist when the police arrived.

"Coincidences like this do not happen, especially when most people in the labor union knew that Welsh was vehemently outspoken—at one time, totally against unionization, opposed to the strikes of '46."

"You chopped off your hair in protest, Bea?" Thomas asked.

"John's been a good friend. Loyal, compassionate, and honest," Beatrix explained. "And that's why I was about to go to his villa and get all the details. As we briefly talked about this morning before I dashed out, the crooked governor of Louisiana is trying to blackmail John. John's past is far from lily white, but the man is accusing him of crimes he could never commit— although I don't know the details yet—and will follow through unless John relinquishes some property and supports Long. Long apparently wants to run against Truman in the next election. If that happens and Long wins, our country will be at the mercy of a liar, a crook, and a criminal. Washington will be filled with criminals whose leader is known for corruption and greed."

"You are planning to be seen in public dressed like a bloke?" Thomas asked.

"Figured I would give this disguise a test run. I need to speak with John about the threats. John does not scare easily, as we both know, and I could tell he's rattled."

"Want us to go with you?"

"Not this time. We'll have some lunch, put Birdy down for a nap, and I'll be back before she wakes up," Beatrix said.

"Now, on a totally different topic," he began and then stopped. "This all points to you going undercover."

She nodded and smiled, but he didn't return it. "You are brilliant. Yes, I'm going to be working on the railroad. Thought if we were going to add to our family, we could use the extra cash. Sorry, love, bad joke."

"Cruel indeed, Mrs. Beatrix Patterson-Ling." He shook his head, fear obvious on his face for what his wife was about to do.

"I really don't see much danger, darling. I'm going to become an apprentice conductor to ascertain, if I can, why thugs are disrupting the railroad, threatening union workers with vague hints of violence, and throwing disparaging reflections on why it's wrong to join the union. It'll be for a day or two or a bit more. I'll probably be home at night. Stella has insider contacts with the railroad, as does Sam, of course, so I'll be conducting on the Santa Barbara to Los Angeles run that goes to Union Station in LA. I've arranged for Jo's mama to help you. Lillian volunteered when she learned what I planned to do and especially after she saw what the ruffians did to poor Sam." Lillian took every opportunity to care for the tot. She loved being the nana to four, plus assuming the role of nana for Birdy.

"Want me to read the note you were going to leave for me, if you left before we returned?" Thomas asked. "Might you tell me more before I have a mental breakdown as my imagination is speeding down a highway well above the legal limit, Bea?"

"Well . . . Stella, whom I bumped into when getting Sam out of jail, brought up the topic. The department has hired me as a consultant, to try to locate who or what's behind the accidents on the tracks, the small-time delays, and misplaced or stolen cargo, and why this is happening in the city. She fears there's a connection between someone on the city council and perhaps even California's governor and the upheavals with the railroad. When I questioned her, she admitted that she had found no hard evidence, but it could be an unhappy employee spreading rumors. The railroad runs the country, and it makes me wonder if this is happening in other cities in the state. Wait, Thomas, I agree it sounds outlandish. Stella is a dedicated cop, and yet, sometimes, I think she sees conspiracies where there are none."

"You'll be on your own?" He wrang his hands. "Don't get me wrong, I support your daring-dos, begrudgingly if the truth be told. However, I'm your husband first, and sometimes you frighten me to the core."

"I understand, Thomas."

"Wait, I have more to say. We must think of Birdy. If she finds out that her mother is putting her life in danger—again— she'll fret more than she is now."

"Nothing will happen to me. I'll be invisible in the uniform that's being altered to my size."

Thomas tried to believe his wife, but in the pit of his stomach, the sourness shouted otherwise. A bitter ball lodged in his throat, the same one that showed up at other times when his beloved had faced danger. Yet this time, the stakes seemed higher, more treacherous. His apprehension made his breathing shallow as fear crept into the hidden worry spots of his heart. *I'm getting paranoid,* he thought but said, "You're assuring me that you'll be surrounded by people who take care of one another, union members, not some wacko with a grudge and out for blood? There'll be nothing risky?"

She smiled and clasped her hand to his while feeling Birdy soft breath on her neck. "That is exactly the plan, and while I cannot and will not predict the future, by this time next week, I feel certain the entire mystery of the supposed riot and the death of Welsh will be part of our past."

CHAPTER SEVEN

BEATRIX INCHED THROUGH MID-DAY TRAFFIC, THEN south on Highway 101 to Montecito. John's home had been the residence of a fabulously rich and scandalous silent movie star from the 1920s, in a style more apropos of a brothel. They often wondered if they'd be shocked if the walls could talk. With the right architect and interior designer, it now felt like less of a mansion and more like a home.

She parked the bulky station wagon next to an early model silver Delahaye, the ridiculously popular French car that must have been imported before the war as that luxury auto factory had been destroyed during the conflict. The car was pristine, and Beatrix was puzzled about who the owner was and why John had invited that person there.

Yuri, John's chef and housekeeper, opened the door before Beatrix climbed the flagstone steps. "I heard you drive up, Miss Beatrix. Good day to you." She bowed slightly, and her entire face smiled. Yuri was a slight woman, but everything she and her husband had been through—losing everything when the American government decreed that all Japanese Americans must be rounded up and placed in internment camps—had made her stronger. If the woman was shocked by Beatrix's transformation into the clothing and haircut of a man, her face didn't reveal it.

"Good to see you, as well, Yuri. Is Mr. Brockman in his study?" Beatrix walked into the vast foyer. The architect had redesigned the home to bring it into the current style and was able to capture the stunning view of the Pacific and the Channel Islands. When John bought the home, he updated it with furniture that was sleek and modern and nicely counterbalanced with original art from his Garden District house in New Orleans. Beatrix always stopped to admire the work of Chagall, Matisse, Picasso in his early period, and the small framed magical landscape attributed to Van Gogh but never authenticated.

"Yes, ma'am. Please go through."

Beatrix stood at the open door. John was behind a pristine desk and across from him was Mariam Goldman. She knocked on the door frame. "A good time to interrupt?"

John blinked, and his lips formed a one-sided smile. His forehead wrinkled as he sat back in the desk chair. "Well, I declare." Mariam turned and stared as well. "This is not a look I ever imagined for you, Beatrix. Is this the height of fashion in Paris? London? Muncie, Indiana?" He looked more curious than alarmed. "Come, sit and tell us why you are wearing this attire and what happened to your hair."

Beatrix sat in the chair opposite the attorney. "Mariam, good to see you again so soon, and my true appreciation for taking care of Sam this morning. Thank you, John. If you hadn't brought Mariam in, I fear Sam would be on a bus right now, getting lost in the dregs of the federal prison system."

John nodded, unusually silent even for a quiet man. The room felt too still, like ugliness had intruded and taken over the peaceful life the wealthy entrepreneur had created in the mountaintop home with its sweeping views. "Was Sam badly injured, Beatrix?"

"Stitches to his forehead. A bruised rib where he was kicked, and his knee was twisted when the thugs pushed him. Everything will mend, the doctors assured him. He'll be back driving the engine tomorrow—no time off apparently, and the railroad is short-staffed."

John bobbed his head just a fraction as Beatrix folded her hands on her lap, waiting, thinking, *What does the attorney have to do with this? The estate? Perhaps she'd cautioned John not to change his will?*

"Beatrix, it's come to my attention," John began and fiddled with the fountain pen he'd been twisting through his fingers, "that I'm getting older."

"Aren't we all," she smiled, and he seemed to relax.

"As you know, I have a heart condition. It's been treated, but there are no assurances of how long I'll be among you. I trust you, Beatrix. You've been a good friend, and you know more about me than anyone. Yes, even you, Mariam," he nodded to the attorney. "As I began explaining to you earlier this morning and now fully to Mariam," he extended his hand toward the lawyer, "I have revised my will and trust, making you full beneficiary of my estate, all my holdings, including stocks and bonds."

"Are you convinced this is what you want to do?" Beatrix asked.

"More certain than I've ever been. There is one stipulation."

Beatrix waited.

"As I briefly mentioned just a few hours ago, which feels like a month, my goal for you, and part of the conditions of accepting this role, is to not squander the wealth. Set up nonprofit organizations to help the disenfranchised, the hungry, the ones left in the margins of our society. That is who I was a million years back. I do not expect you to do this on your own, because you have a career, but to hire others and oversee the organization."

"Those were my initial thoughts as well. John? You are

certain?" His facial expression made the repeated question moot, yet she asked.

Mariam looked between the two. "Beatrix, if I may interrupt, John told me of this plan about a year ago. Please don't be offended, but I have investigated you and your husband and know, without a doubt, that there is no one John could choose who would be better suited for this task."

John sat back and folded his hands on the desk. "Now that matter is settled, I must be candid. You see, Governor Long has threatened to expose me as a Communist and plans to make that fact known in every media outlet in the country."

"Why, John? What do you have on him that he's so afraid of?" Beatrix asked.

John sighed, looked momentarily defeated, and then squared his narrow shoulders. "In the 1930s, Long and I, by chance, met at a meeting that was to be about social reform. It was to honor the heritage of the South. It sounded like something a businessman like me should be aware of and possibly support. Remember, the South was extremely racist at this time, so I was cautious, to say the least. Long and I decided we'd attend another meeting of the group the following evening. I was all about networking, building contacts, and working to achieve acceptance. I liked Long. Most everyone did. Although, in retrospect, I am a terrible judge of character, as I would learn shortly thereafter.

"Long was shrewd and well groomed, and his pedigree was one of the best in the state with his ancestors arriving in Louisiana in the early 1700s, which almost made him New Orleans royalty, or so he still likes to announce to anyone who will listen. Did then, and, as I understand, does now. I was a hustler, more experienced at that than legitimate business dealings if the truth were then told. I wrongly thought some of his polish might rub off on me.

"He'd been injured in the Great War and walked with a

significant limp, yet the man had a smile, charisma, and temperament that could dazzle even Ebenezer Scrooge. He had clout as an up-and-coming politician and mover. He is a Presbyterian, but I didn't hold that against him," John produced a crooked smile, which for him was the equivalent of a boatload of laughter.

"What happened at the second meeting?" Beatrix knew there were communist and socialist cells secreted, for the most part, around the country—some even thought there were full-blown groups ready to bring war to American soil.

"I'm not proud of attending. It was there that I learned more about a hidden movement. It was the German American Bund, a pro-Nazi group that in the 1930s had scores of chapters across the US, representing what many believe was a real threat of fascist subversion in the United States. They held joint rallies with other radical groups and also ran summer camps for children centered around Nazi ideology and imagery, melding patriotic values with virulent anti-Semitism."

"Yes, John, I've read about this pro-Nazi faction. It was frightening."

He continued, "The Nazis were gaining power in Europe, as you know. The ideals of home and family seemed to be truly American to this faction. Long joined the group that night."

"You did not." She knew that her friend was Jewish, although he followed the less conservative ways.

"I did not. I could not. Furthermore, and as you know, I'm one to think over my actions, as mistakes can be costly. About a week later, I was handling some business dealings in the Lower Ninth Ward there in New Orleans, on Claiborne. It was close to midnight. There was an assemblage swaggering down the street, and I'm repulsed to even have to say this, they were dressed in what seemed to be white flowing gowns, white sheets . . . "

"The Ku Klux Klan? Oh, no. Oh, John." Beatrix thought few things in the world could shock her, but this was not what she'd expected. She'd lived in the South long enough during the war years to fear this murderous alliance. Sometimes rumors got out of hand, but when it came to the KKK, everything was typically true and nauseatingly worse than accurate.

"Bennington Long was leading a procession, carrying an ugly and flaming torch." John closed his eyes and scowled at the memory. "I knew that limp anywhere because of the twisted way he walked, but there's more. I stood in shock, repelled and mortified, near the side of Claiborne Street. Ben Long stopped dead straight in front of me and said something like, 'It's not too late, John. Come join us and fight for the rights of White men.' I was disgusted and afraid. Apparently, Long didn't know I was a Jew, or he would have spat at me."

"He denies he was or is part of the group?" Beatrix asked. "I never read in the newspapers while living in New Orleans that he was in any way connected."

"I think, but this is pure conjecture, that at the time, he had something evil to hold over the editors at the newspaper, and my money is on that he still does. There was never a breath of his being with the Klan. He contacted me the following morning and said there would be another march through the Lower Ninth Ward that evening. They were walking through the poorest neighborhoods, panicking everyone who lived there, innocents the bunch, huddled in their houses. Good working families, most of them people of color. I told Long I'd think about it and maybe stand on the sidelines again."

"Tell me you did not join them," Beatrix whispered.

"I need not, as I did not. I was repulsed. I did go to Rampart Street and waited. This time, Henry came with me. Henry was about thirteen at the time and became part of my inner circle. I trusted him then as I do now. I had him hide near one of the houses, in the shadows. As Long came toward me, taking off the head piece with his right hand and holding the torch in the left, Henry took his photo, looking like just a kid with a camera.

There were crowds of photographers around. Long smiled at them. I was horrified. I know Long never considered that I might have photos that could ruin him."

John straightened a few files on his desk, aligning them, moving them around. Then he said, "I had Henry follow Long and the degenerates. About a half hour later, Henry caught up with me, breathless. He'd snapped photos of Long straddling a Black man, punching him. Henry was terrified, as a couple of Long's goons had run after him. Henry hid until it was safe. I knew someday those photos could be valuable. I never thought they'd be used against me."

"Long wants the negatives. That's why he's attempting to blackmail you?" Beatrix asked.

"Yes, when in the late 1930s he decided to run against Roosevelt for the presidency, I told him I had these photos. A mistake, but I could not even entertain the possibility of that happening. Now, there's talk in the city that he's planning to throw his hat in against Truman for the presidency," John said.

"John, please don't get me wrong, but would rumors of you being a Communist sully your reputation?" Beatrix asked. "Seems to me you've been accused, even in the press, of much worse."

John looked to his attorney, and she gave a nearly imperceptible nod that anyone other than Beatrix would have missed. Whatever the next comments were, they'd already discussed the ramifications. John rose from the desk and walked to the floor-to-ceiling window in his study, turning his back to the women, choosing his words with care. When he turned, grief showed in his face. "There's more."

"You'd better just tell me, John, as, like my husband, I'm excellent at jumping to conclusions."

"Long is ruthless. He doesn't care who he hurts," John stated.

"What do you need to do to stop him from hurting others?"

John paced the study, just one lap, and said, "He will tell the world that you and Thomas are Communists as well. That's his threat. It would ruin both your careers, ruin the opportunity to adopt more children, ruin your lives. This Red Scare baloney is *real*, Beatrix. Americans are terrified of the Communists, and you'd lose everything. Even with your wealth and that which you'll inherit when I pass, it won't make a difference if you're not safe."

Beatrix slowly sat back in the brown, leather, overstuffed chair.

"Now it's clear, and I am so sorry," John said. "I don't know how he knew we were close."

"It's obvious that Long learned we were friends after our 'adventure' of destroying the Nazi terrorists in Louisiana. I'm sure he has minions who report details he could use. He was good at that, as I remember hearing when I lived in that city."

"I am at odds with what to do, and that is why Mariam and I wanted you here, to tell you everything. I do not see an easy answer. Either I relinquish the damaging photos and a known racist, a member of the despicable KKK, makes a run for president of the United States, or you lose everything in your life. Truman, as you know, is not that popular, and Long and his family have been leaders in the South for hundreds of years. My gut feeling is that this bast—this unscrupulous and cruel man would throw our country back to the evils that were stamped out in the Civil War. More lynching, further segregation, hatred in the workplace, in the unions, in the schools."

Beatrix closed her eyes. "What you've said is true, John. Being condemned as a Communist, Thomas would quickly be dismissed from the university, halting the crucial research he is doing with clean energy and the energy produced by the ocean's waves. As for me, please know, I'll survive. It's about Birdy. If, as Birdy's parents, we were accused of un-American activities, she'd be ostracized. It'd cost innocent Birdy the stability in learning, growing, and perhaps her own safety. That's so unfair. It would stop Thomas and me from adopting other children."

Earlier that week, Beatrix had read an opinion column in the *Los Angeles Times* about how Hollywood was being suspected as a hot spot for "Commies," as the writer called the group. "The Red Scare is like a terrible virus, and it's sweeping the country as we learn more about the Soviet Union and the United States. It happened before, John, as you well know, during the Great War. The Red Scare, this time, I fear, will lead to a range of actions that have a profound and enduring effect on the US government and society.

"Federal employees are already being interrogated to determine whether they are sufficiently loyal to the government, and the House Un-American Activities Committee, as well as US Senator Joseph R. McCarthy, are investigating allegations of subversive elements in the government and the film industry. All unfounded so far, but gossip and rumors are getting hotter and spreading wider."

"I heard McCarthy is insisting that we boycott movies because actors are all Communists. He's spreading lies that the Communists have infiltrated Congress, gotten into public positions and the police force, the armed services, and universities," Mariam said. "The man is treacherous and seems to attract, like a magnet, others who are fearful of anyone who isn't a true American. Whatever that means."

"That's what Hitler did, scaring people about Jews and others, and look where that ended up," John added. "It's a mess, Beatrix. Mariam and I do not see any logical way out. Damned if I do, and damned if I don't. Damn it, you'll be hurt either way."

Beatrix folded and unfolded her hands and squared her shoulders. "I know whatever you decide, John, will be for the best. I do not see a happy ending to any of this, but if I may, I'd like to talk it over with Thomas. He's part of the equation, and it would be unfair of me to usurp this discussion from him."

Driving back to the city, Beatrix mulled the options. She could not let John give up on the moral duty of stopping Long. With the governor a racist, Americans needed to know before the bid could gather enough votes for the nomination. If John relinquished the incriminating photos to Long, could he live with himself? If she and Thomas were accused of being Communists, it'd ruin their careers, even though it was not true, nor could it ever be proved.

I'll talk with Thomas. This isn't only my decision, she decided as she pulled the Ford into the carport, next to a newer model Woody with its unique baby car seat. Thomas had invented it so that Birdy would be safe and not bounce around should there be an accident. He'd just installed another in the car she often drove.

"There you are, darling," Thomas approached, balancing Birdy on his hip and greeting Bea at the kitchen door. "Detective Rodriguez is in the living room. We were about to make tea and wait for you." He looked at her face, put the baby in her playpen, and took his wife's hand. "Something's wrong. I can tell."

"There's a bit of a situation, Thomas. John needs to make a life-changing decision that also involves us." She briefly told him about the damaging situation and conversation she'd had with John and Mariam.

"I say, this is the dog's dinner," Thomas stated.

"Is that good or bad?"

"It's a mess. My first reaction is to tell John not to cave into a despicable politician." Thomas patted the pocket of his shirt. "We've weathered worse."

"It's not you and me. It's Birdy. This could ruin her life, her future, everything that we have ever dreamed of for her. Gone at the hands of a crook and a racist."

CHAPTER EIGHT

THOMAS HANDED BIRDY THE STUFFED TEDDY BEAR she'd thrown out of the playpen, and she at once threw it out again. "We need to do what's right in the face of this kerfuffle." He poured hot water into a hefty white ceramic teapot, swished it around, tossed that into the sink, and added loose tea leaves and the water that was boiling in the kettle. "Go chat with Stella. Let's put the other discussion aside for now and talk after you two make up a plan to find out who's in back of the riots and accidents at the railroad yard."

Beatrix had faced evil eye to eye, but now, with their child's welfare in the mix, the weight of what to do burdened her. She corrected her posture, tried to smile, and met the detective who was thumbing through the current issue of *Life* magazine. "Sorry, my trip to Montecito took longer than I hoped."

"Well, I'll be darned, without the lipstick and in that railroad conductor's uniform hanging over the chair in the corner, I think you actually might pass for a man. A pretty one, but a guy."

"Was that a compliment, Stella? I'll try to scowl. How's

this?" She pulled down the corners of her mouth with her index fingers.

"Good start. Try on the jacket. I can't wait for this."

Beatrix slipped into the conductor's jacket. After the alterations expertly done and then delivered by the tailor earlier that day, it was just her size.

"Thanks to your inside contact and Sam Conrad, all of the arrangements for me to travel the line from Santa Barbara to Los Angeles have been smoothed, and I'll start tomorrow. As a supposed young veteran in the apprentice program, I hope to listen more than talk but also ask questions. It's been my sad experience that railroad porters, like food servers, maids, and men and women of color, are often overlooked and discounted. I've always found porters to be especially kind and a chatty group, or that's been my experience when I traveled by train."

"Good thinking, Beatrix. Maria Davies will be at one of the ticket windows. The plan is she'll ask if you want a cup of coffee, and that'll mean she has gathered intel, gossip, etc., from being in the ticket booth and working with the other two ladies. If you need help at any time or you feel vulnerable, go into the ladies' restroom. In locker number 10, you'll find women's street clothes and a wig." She passed Beatrix a key to the lock." I've left money there for you to get a taxi home and to call me at the police station. By getting out of the uniform, it should make you less obvious rather than looking like a Union Pacific worker on the run."

"Thanks, Stella. That'll make Thomas feel a bit more at ease, and me, too. I don't know with whom I'm dealing, and a Plan B is always a relief. The schedule has the train running through Santa Barbara at 10 a.m. and arriving at Union Station in LA at 1 p.m. Then I pick up the two o'clock train north and get off here at five. Pretty straightforward."

"Don't seem too inquisitive, okay?" Stella stood up but didn't leave the room. "About Mrs. Welsh, her alibi checks out.

The guy who cleans their swimming pool saw her leave for an ocean swim just before five thirty. She wasn't there. She's an ocean swimmer and goes to the beach like clockwork each morning. Welsh was hit with the tranquilizer pellet and subsequently bounced off the cement driveway, I'm guessing, and his watch was smashed. Unless he lived longer, his time of death was 6:13, when the watch stopped."

"I thought that only happened in mystery novels. Didn't Agatha Christie use that in one of her Miss Marple books?" Beatrix asked.

"You're right, but I cannot remember which one. Okay, back to our dead guy. If the man who maintains their swimming pool can be believed, I see no reason why there would be any doubt. Unless, of course, Mrs. Welsh drove away and then circled back in a different car. However, the neighbor by then was out and taking notes when the officers arrived. The pool guy was still at the house when I interviewed Mrs. Welsh. Kind of handsome in a he-man way, and I did notice even with a dead, naked executive on the driveway."

"Think this pool man is involved? Perhaps a hired gun—or a hired tranquilizer gun?" Beatrix asked.

"A contract killer? In Santa Barbara?" Stella laughed.

"This is a stretch, but could it have to do with the members of Mountain Drive? I read in the newspaper that Welsh wanted them evicted, and one story said that Mrs. Welsh was a frequent visitor there. The people who live up there couldn't have bought that land and maintain such a lavish lifestyle without money. I failed to ask the man where he lived," she slapped her forehead.

"I'm sure you can get contact information from Mrs. Welsh or the company she hires to clean the pool," Beatrix said.

"Here's just a theory, if you don't mind me throwing this out at you," Stella said. "Welsh finds out that Mrs. Number Five is giving money to the misfits up there, one in particular or the entire group, and supporting them or whatever. Perhaps she's even planning to divorce him. She wouldn't get a nickel, I'm betting. She explained that there was a prenup, which is a moot point as now she inherits everything. That at least is the *Reader's Digest* version of what I got from Welsh's estate attorney this morning, who had already met with the 'grieving' widow."

"The amount of the estate?" Beatrix asked.

"The attorney hasn't calculated it fully yet. The property on the posh Upper State location, along with other holdings, gold bullion, and stocks, probably will come in at a cool and tidy fortune—one where the wife would never worry about her finances again, even if she funded do-gooder stuff like the Mountain Drive folks for fifty years."

"Hmm, that much?" Beatrix wondered.

"Yes, *more* than that much. I've got to go put an escape wardrobe in that locker for you and then get back with the coroner. Could you gather some clothes and a cloche hat to disguise your manly haircut? Did you use an electric razor to get it that precise? Not that I want it." She sat back, and for the first time since she arrived, the detective seemed to relax. "Okay, Beatrix. I'll take care of everything else. By the way, have you, by chance, seen a change in Dr. Rayne? More somber?"

Beatrix would never compromise her client/patient relationship with the coroner to anyone, including Stella. They were making progress with the battle fatigue she was carrying, sleeping better, not spooked at loud sounds, and that was an improvement. "When does her husband come back from the naval air station near Pearl Harbor?"

"You didn't hear this from me, but she was sitting at her desk crying when I walked in on her yesterday. She was blindsided. Never saw it coming, apparently. Between sobs, she said he'd confessed to falling in love with a *wahine* surfing champion and out of love with her. This was according to the letter she was ripping into shreds. His new girl's local, and he'd apparently been unfaithful for the last six months."

"They're ending it?" Beatrix asked, shocked.

"If it were my guy and I were that nuts about him, I'd head to Honolulu, hire a muscled beach boy, get hubby's attention, and drag him home. I am so sorry for her." Stella frowned.

"Me, too, and especially as every time she talked about the guy, she glowed. Childhood sweethearts and all. I'll have a quiet word with her," Beatrix said, knowing that their next session would be Friday afternoon.

"Okay, off to solve crimes and apprehend fugitives, or something like that. Stay safe, Beatrix Patterson. Who knows what that husband of yours would do if things fall apart."

"That's my goal, too. I plan to stay safe and keep Thomas from coming undone."

The weather had changed overnight, and the fog felt claustrophobic as Beatrix looked out the second-story window toward the ocean. Drops of dew clung to the willow tree, and the grass sparkled when the fog parted enough to let in a ray of sun. She slipped into the required navy wool trousers with their sharp press marks and the white, well-starched dress shirt. She snatched a small throw pillow from the bed and stuffed it between her bra and the shirt, flattening her breasts and making it appear that she had a bit of a belly.

"Here, Bea, let me tie that for you," Thomas said adjusting the neck of her shirt, slipping one end of the blue tie under the collar, and running his finger around to make sure it was flat. Then, in an instant, he was finished, and he stepped back.

"I never realized how complicated that could be," she said. "Thanks for not tying those fancy knots. I need to look like an everyman."

"I don't see how you're going to pull this off if you ever need to take off the vest and the wool jacket."

She looked down, and while the shirt was stiff, it didn't conceal her breasts as much as she hoped. "Then I won't." She sat at the dressing table and dabbed on cream-colored makeup, then applied some red lipstick as dots on her chin and cheek. She made her lips a pale cream color from another pot of makeup. By then, Thomas had returned to their bedroom with Birdy freshly diapered.

When Birdy saw Beatrix, she reached out her pudgy arms and clearly said, "Mummeeee." Punctuated, at the end, with a giggle.

The couple's mouths dropped. In unison. Then opened, yet no words came out as their eyebrows shot up.

"Blimey. That's not cricket. I've been trying to get her to say daddy, and now she even knows it's you when you're looking like a bloke." But Thomas laughed, Birdy laughed, and Beatrix did her best not to cry.

"I smell the same, and she doesn't care what we look like. Never having been a parent before, that's my unqualified guess."

All the time Thomas was coaching their child to say daddy first, Beatrix encouraged him and Birdy. Never once making it a competition. Yet, inside, something stirred with her intense love of being a mom, and she'd never be the same. This she knew.

What danger would she tumble over that day, dressed as a slight man with a limp, a war injury? She blinked and took a deep breath. "I'm going to have some toast and yogurt and then head to the depot." As she turned to give Birdy a kiss, her lips remained longer as if they were trying to memorize the softness of the baby's cheek. *Not a time for lingering doubts, Beatrix,* she said to herself. "Come on, family, let's get some food. Mummy's got work to do."

The railroad depot was quiet. Passengers wouldn't arrive until at least an hour before the Los Angeles to Santa Barbara at ten. Beatrix limped up to the ticket window where Detective Maria Davies was working undercover as a ticket agent.

"Morning, sir," Maria said and smiled and waved a welcome. "You're the new guy, right?"

If the other women could read micro-expressions, they'd have immediately seen that the two knew each other.

Lowering her voice an octave, as she'd been practicing for hours, Beatrix said, "Yes, ma'am. Charles George. Folks call me Chuck." She'd learned by chance that if one wanted to be quickly forgotten, first and last names that were typically first names did the trick.

"You'll want to check in with Sam Conrad. He's in the office right behind me," Maria motioned to her left. "He's the union steward around here and our engineer today." Then she said more loudly, "You are union, right?" The two other women looked at the newcomer.

The older one spoke up and had a slight southern accent. "We don't want none of the union problems like what happened last year."

"He'll want to see your union card," said the third, a pretty younger woman, wearing far too much foundation and mascara, with heavy, penciled eyebrows like Ava Gardner.

Beatrix patted her right breast pocket. "All in order." She limped her way to the office, where Sam did a double take at his newest union member. "Charles George, reporting, sir."

The women stopped working, nodded to each other, slid along the way, and crept close to the open door. The youngest one whispered, "He's kind of cute. Think he's married?"

Maria wanted to laugh. Oh, yes, Beatrix was definitely married. "I think he's too old for you, honey," she said instead as they strained to hear more about the new conductor and Sam's questions for the man.

Sam spoke loudly, "Good to have you aboard. You'll report on the train to whichever senior conductor is on duty. That can change, although most of the crew like to keep a regular schedule. Just saying, don't get attached to any of the fellows."

"Yes, sir."

"Follow them around. See how they handle any problems. It could be a kid getting lost, someone falling, or a passenger stubbing a toe—or worse. On my first day following the training engineer, I was so focused on the mechanics of the huge old engine, so thrilled about getting the job, well, I didn't notice something quite obvious. The door was open, and I tumbled right out. Luckily, we were still in the station." Sam laughed, and Beatrix tried not to, as it could come out as a girly giggle. "I will never, no matter how many years I'm here, live that down."

"No, sir. Probably not," she said. "I'll try not to repeat your experience."

"Now, down to business." Then he switched to a whisper, "Everyone needs to think you're really apprenticing for the next few weeks here. I let the gossipmongers know you'd been in Seattle and Chicago, and the Union Pacific bosses are still deciding where you'll be needed permanently. It's a new program, so things are vague." Then, once again in his normal voice, "Couldn't help notice. You got a limp there, man. Not going to stop you from hoisting luggage around and helping little old ladies on the train, will it?"

Beatrix grimaced as she patted her knee. "No, sir."

"Where'd you get it?"

"Battle of Guam, near the end of the war, when we were there to liberate the island."

"Nasty business there. What do the docs say?"

"Get used to it."

"You look fit enough otherwise." Sam wrote a note and passed it to Beatrix: "You're doing great. Be careful out there."

After she read it, he pulled it back and ripped it into shreds before putting it in his pocket. Then he continued, "It got ugly for a lot of us. Yeah, I served with the Corps of Engineers. You know, Chuck, if I'd been there in peacetime, it would have been a whole different ball game. Probably a true tropical paradise. Now? Wonder if it'll ever recover." Sam sighed and then said in his deep baritone voice, "Okay, mister, let's get you introduced to the crew you'll be working with today, the porters and the conductors, baggage handlers, and who knows who else might be chewing the fat in the break room. It's time that they get a move on. The train will be here shortly, and I'm taking it to LA."

The women exchanged conniving looks, scurrying back to their desks, dropping their eyes to their counters, and pretending to be too involved organizing the ticket drawers to eavesdrop. When Beatrix and Sam walked out to the railyard, Maria said, "I like him. Too bad they'll transfer him once he's been here for a couple weeks."

The older of the two women wrinkled her nose. "There's something familiar about him. Maybe it's the blotchy skin. My brother came home from France with a skin rash that still flares up, especially when he's nervous. Poor guy."

Maria cocked her head. "Just another injured veteran. That limp isn't ever going to go away. Quite a war souvenir. I hate seeing our young guys disabled like that. Cuts me apart each time I know the sacrifices they made, and ladies, don't get me started on those who didn't make it home." She pushed a tear off her cheek. "Chuck's just a kid off some farm in Minnesota or Kansas. Now that he's seen action, farm life won't cut it anymore."

The younger one, Dora, said, "I'm going to figure out a way of starting a conversation when he and the crew bring the train back from LA." She smiled, and the dimples appeared, making her much more girlish than the makeup could cover.

Maria laughed. "Heard rumor from someone here at the station that you had a sugar daddy—rough around the edges, they said, but seemed to be nuts for you in a weird, possessive way. You need to pace yourself. Besides, with Chuck, I think you're spinning your wheels. He didn't even look your way when you were adjusting your blouse to show, um, more of you. Besides, everybody knows all the good ones are taken."

"Humph," came the comment, and then Dora said, "You're funny, Maria. I don't want a 'good one,' I just want one or two or maybe three. The sugar daddy is history after the embarrassment and things I would rather not remember. You weren't here that day, Maria. He snapped—not my fault at all—and became a demanding monster. Besides, I can always find a replacement. A girl needs some young, fun stud once in a while. I did meet a man a few weeks back, smart and cute, different from the highly polished guys I've dated. Asked me to be his wife—well, one of them."

"Now you're teasing us," Maria laughed. "Listen, Dora. An elderly friend once told me, 'The woman who's looking for a husband never had one.' I had one, and that was enough for me. Are you actually thinking of sharing a man with others? Is that called an open marriage or just plain crazy?"

Dora laughed with them. "More the merrier? Come on, ladies, you can't say you wouldn't be tempted if the man was as handsome as Clark Gable?"

Maria checked her cash drawer to get ready for the customers who were lining up waiting for the ticket windows to be open. "Now, if we're talking some hunk like Robert Young, ooh la la. I could make an exception for that man." She wiggled her hips and fluttered her eyelashes. The women giggled and began selling tickets to the queue of passengers.

CHAPTER NINE

THE RAILROAD PORTERS PACED BACK AND FORTH ON the wooden platform while the conductors adjusted their caps and straightened their jackets. Beatrix could tell that most of them had been in military service; many of them were young and fit. A gray-haired conductor yelled at one of the men to tie his shoe and another for leaning against a wooden crate. Obviously, he was or wanted to be in charge. Beatrix limped toward him and introduced herself.

The man barked, "You will be shadowing me, kid." He stuck out a callused hand. "Ken Purdue. Your boss for today and, if I read the schedule right, for all of the next seven days, too."

"Charles George, but they call me Chuck." Beatrix extended her hand and grasped the senior conductor's hand far harder than she naturally would have. She had to become Chuck.

"Good deal, Chuck. I didn't serve—too old, wouldn't have me—so I stuck with the railroad during the war. They give you a ticket punch? Tell you anything about how we handle rowdy passengers?"

Beatrix made sure to lower her voice as she tipped back her jacket to show the ticket punch laced to her belt, but not so much to disclose her breasts beneath her uniform. "No, sir. Do you get many boisterous types?"

"Nah, not on this run. Sure, there's exceptions, and if you need anything, need help, just holler. When I've been on the overnighter to San Francisco, kid, there are always drunks. These passengers are pussy cats, business folks, travelers visiting family, and some kids sent off to grandma."

"I can handle that, sir."

The senior conductor looked Beatrix over. They were the same height, yet his shoulders were square, beefy, and strong. "Walk through Cars 2 and 3 when the train pulls to a complete stop, and for God's sake, stand back from the train even if it's going slow. A rock could get kicked up and send you straight to the cemetery on your first day. That'd have our union and the bosses screaming at me, and I got enough grief at home, so I don't need more," Ken went to slap Beatrix on the back, and when she saw it coming, she bent her knees to steady her stance. "Here is the train. Show time, Chuck."

The behemoth locomotive squealed into the station, and Beatrix moved between the waiting crowd, the massive engine, and passenger cars. She stretched her arms out to each side as a warning not to get closer, as Sam had told her conductors did. She looked down the line, and the other conductors were doing the same. Her first test pretending she'd been a conductor in training succeeded.

A young boy was bouncing up and down right next to her, and his father could barely hold the kid's hand. Beatrix turned and said, "I was about his age when I fell in love with trains, too."

"We're visiting my parents in Pasadena. This is his first train trip."

"Here you go, young fellow," Beatrix pulled a tin toy conductor's badge from her front pocket.

The boy looked ready to burst. "This is swell," he said and

polished the tin replica on his sweater. "Thank you." He jumped up and down. "I want to be like you when I grow up."

Beatrix smiled to herself, knowing that the child meant a conductor, not a woman dressed as a man. She looked down the line, watching the other conductors pull open the passenger doors. She was strong, but the doors were heavy. She made sure no one was watching her as she had to grip the handle with both hands. Then the passengers exited the cars.

"Chuck," the older conductor called out. "Walk through and make sure you talk with the guys on the last shift. Find out if there were any problems. Pick up trash, look for forgotten items, the usual stuff."

She greeted the porters who would ride along the two-hour trip, climbed the steps, and surveyed the cars. There were newspapers, a greasy paper bag that contained someone's half-eaten breakfast, and a baby shoe. She jotted the time on a schedule at the back of the car, then spied a briefcase. She tossed the trash in a bin and asked a porter to take the forgotten shoe and the briefcase into the depot where the objects could be added to Lost and Found. Then she climbed back down the steps and yelled, "All aboard," as did the other conductors down the line. She'd punch their tickets once the train had left the station.

Back on the platform, Beatrix fiddled with the extra tickets in her jacket pocket that passengers were allowed to buy on the train. As she glanced down the track, she saw the senior conductor talking with the baggage handler, close to one another, sharing a joke as they were both laughing and then shaking hands.

It was the handshake that alarmed her. She'd never seen one, even during her time in New Orleans and other places she'd visited in the South. But she'd heard of it. She could have been mistaken with all the information that had bombarded her in the last few days.

She wanted to be wrong.

She wasn't.

As they shook hands, the conductor extended his index and middle fingers along the wrist of the scruffy baggage clerk. Time seemed to stop, and they stared at one another. While pumping their hands, if this truly was what Beatrix thought, each man would press their fingers into the wrist of the other. It was called the Klan handshake.

The second that they'd ended their encounter, Beatrix twisted her head away. *The Klan active in Santa Barbara? No, it cannot be.* Yet, she saw the truth and knew that the monstrous and notorious clan of racists were functioning in all parts of the country. Why not sleepy little Santa Barbara? Could this be the connection to the railroad bigwig murder? It seemed to have everything to do with the African Americans working on the rails and Sam's beating and arrest.

Beatrix's thoughts stopped for a millisecond, and she knew this was the way her brain worked until it instantly sorted the memories to the topic she wanted, to the right citation, the right experience, the right moment in time. She blinked, and it all came back.

It was 1925 in her mind. Beatrix was twelve, and the conversation occurred right after breakfast as her father finished reading the newspaper. She was nibbling toast with plum jam and knew shortly their chauffeur would drive her to the private school in Santa Barbara that she attended. Jennie, Beatrix's mother, looked up from her coffee and, seeing her husband's serious face, intuitively knew this was about the ruckus she'd also read about that had just occurred in Washington, DC.

The couple never concealed truths from their only child, but Jennie wondered if Beatrix really needed to know the repulsive hatred humans could inflict on others. "Billy," she put up her hand as if to stop him. Everyone else called William Randolph

Patterson "sir," William if they were close, or Mr. Patterson. Jennie used Billy as a term of endearment that always made her husband smile. Right then, his intended smile hesitated and then disappeared. "Beatrix is a sensitive young woman and I do not believe this is breakfast conversation," Jennie said.

"Jennie, darling. We must discuss the realities of our world at the breakfast table here with Beatrix. I believe the conversation we must have concerning right and wrong needs to be talked about at every breakfast, lunch counter, and dinner event in our country. This organization cannot be stopped by hiding it under the carpet."

"Tell me, Daddy, what you're talking about," Beatrix said. "I won't be afraid."

He patted his pretty, red-headed daughter's hand and watched as her eyes were drawn to the black-and-white photos in the newspaper that was lying on the table in front of her father's empty coffee cup. "What funny costumes, Daddy. Are they going to a party?" He turned the newspaper so his daughter could better read the article and see the black-and-white photos.

"Oh, Beatrix. How I wish that were true. You'd better explain, Billy." Jennie nodded to her husband.

"Beatrix, there is some information I'd like you to consider. If you have questions or if you ever have things you want to talk about, including why people are unkind, your mama and I will tell you the truth."

"Yes, Daddy," she replied. "I know that."

He finished his coffee, and the maid removed the breakfast dishes. "You're going to be late for school, darling, but this is important." William Patterson spoke clearly and watched his daughter's face for a hint of misunderstanding. She'd been thriving at the prestigious Blanchard-Gamble School on Valerio Street, which opened its doors in 1902. While the staff would certainly not discuss civil unrest with the girls, the students themselves might, and William and Jennie wanted to be the ones to talk to their daughter before she might hear rumors or a convoluted version of the facts.

William had always been a student of history, and while living in New Orleans, decades before Beatrix was born and well before he married Jennie, he'd been approached by a local civic leader to join a group of "like-minded" men. Learning of their true cause, he flatly refused to be a part of the madness. That tradition of the Old South had been one of the reasons he'd moved to California, where he'd met and married into one of California's original Spanish families.

"You know about the Civil War, is that correct?"

"Yes, we studied it a few years ago." She was a bright child, and her parents knew from the moment she could speak that her memory was powerful.

"After the war, a group, including former Confederate veterans, founded the first branch of the Ku Klux Klan. It supposedly started as a social club in Pulaski, Tennessee, in 1865. The first two words of the organization's name allegedly derived from the Greek word *kyklos*, meaning circle. In the summer of 1867, local branches of the Klan met for a big get-together, a general organizing convention, and established what they called an 'Invisible Empire of the South.'"

Calmly, the billionaire explained to his child how the leading Confederate general Nathan Bedford Forrest was chosen as the first leader, or "grand wizard," of the Klan. The leader presided over a hierarchy of grand dragons, grand titans, and grand cyclopes. They were—and Beatrix realized, still—active and serious about their objective, their agenda.

William waited a moment to see if his child had questions. Then continued, "They truly believe that they, as White people, are inherently superior to Blacks, Jews, and other minorities. Some leaders strived to turn the Klan from a racist organization, which it was in the eyes of the public, into something respectable and acceptable. That did not work.

"The reason why I'm telling you this, darling," he spoke in a confident tone and looked to his wife for a nod before he went on, "is that last month, on August 8, 1925, more than fifty thousand members of the despicable Ku Klux Klan paraded through our national capitol, Washington, DC. Some walked in lines as wide as twenty abreast, while others created formations of the letter *K* or a Christian cross. A few rode on horseback. Scores waved American flags. Men and women alike, the marchers carried banners emblazoned with the names of their home states or local chapters, and their procession lasted for more than three hours down Pennsylvania Avenue, which was lined with spectators. National leaders of the organization were resplendent in colorful satin robes, and the rank and file wore white, their regalia adorned with a circular red patch containing a cross with a drop of blood at its center." He flipped the page in the newspaper to see more photos from that date. They both solemnly scanned the grainy images.

Jennie cleared her throat. "Whatever has gotten into the editor of the *News-Press*? It's not enough that the newspaper covered the disgraceful spectacle once, but here it is again."

William solemnly nodded. "It's news, Jennie, whether we like it or not. Now, with more violence in Mississippi, Tennessee, and throughout the South, apparently, it was the editor's idea to rehash the sickening events."

Beatrix's father continued explaining how the Klan was easily at its most popular in the United States during the 1920s, and while Beatrix was just a child, her father explained the horrors of their philosophy and actions to his daughter.

During this time, he had clarified how the Klan reached out and grabbed the downtrodden, White underclass and any racists who had a minuscule view of equality. The members were disproportionately middle class, and many of its very visible public activities were geared toward festivities, pageants, and social gatherings. He recalled, "In some ways, it was this superficially innocuous Klan that was the most insidious of them all. Packaging its noxious ideology as traditional small-town values and wholesome fun, the Klan of the 1920s encouraged native-born White Americans to believe that bigotry, intimidation, harassment, and illegal, inhumane violence were all perfectly compatible with, if not central to, patriotic respectability."

"Can't good people stop this, Daddy? Mama?"

The couple looked at each other, and Jennie pushed a tear off her cheek. "In the future, darling, it will take kind-hearted people like you to prevent them from doing any more damage and repair the harm already done."

Seconds had passed as Beatrix's perfect memory recalled further details of the breakfast conversation from decades before. "Oh, my, why is this happening again?" she whispered as the older conductor waved to her, then bellowed, "All aboard."

Her heart felt heavy, and the scene she'd just witnessed incensed her. *This is bigger than what happened to Sam and the violence at the train depot.*

CHAPTER TEN

THE RAIL RUN TO LOS ANGELES WAS UNEVENTFUL IF one could overlook a small girl licking one lollypop after another and subsequently throwing up all over her mother's purple silk dress. Beatrix rushed in with towels and a cup of water for the child.

There was a frightened older gentleman who had called for her after losing his glasses only to find he had been sitting on them.

In the second car, she saw a returning Marine in uniform opening a letter and bursting into great fits of agony. When she asked if he needed some water, he gulped out the full scenario. The letter was from his sweetheart. He said to Beatrix, "She was saving herself for me all the time I was in France, all those three years. We wrote every day, or at least I did. I figured when I didn't hear from her for a few months that her studies were taking all of her time. She's going to be a teacher. Look." He pointed to the neat cursive writing on a floral printed page of the two-paragraph letter.

"Now she's up and married a boy from the college that she's

attending. It's in New York City. What am I going to do? I'm a farm boy from Glendale, a tiny town with wide open fields that reach to the mountains. I can't compete with some Lothario from the East Coast, probably a rich playboy, too. Suave and with slicked down hair." The "Dear John" letter quaked in his fingers.

"I'd like to tell you that there are more fish in the sea, young man, but that's trite, and we both know it." Beatrix made sure her voice was gravely and tried to frown, supposedly making wrinkles that would infer that she was older than her thirty years. "The truth is, you've got to get home to that farm, to your family. You said it was Glendale? That's where you live now. Get a job. Go to church, volunteer, meet new friends, and find the ones you went to high school with. I'm not saying you'll replace your girl. That doesn't happen, and my heart's been broken, so I speak from experience. I'm saying you'll restore your life. Is that what you'd tell one of your buddies if he got a letter like this?"

"I only want Penelope." It was a protest, but his voice was not quite as pathetic as it had originally sounded.

Beatrix placed a hand on his shoulder. "Penelope is out of the picture, my friend. You've seen the worst of the worst in the war. You know life somehow, whether we like it or not, goes on. Time to move forward and meet your own future. You're tough, or you wouldn't be wearing that uniform. Get on with your life." She pulled her hand away, suddenly realizing how pale and unblemished it was. She'd better start wearing the white gloves that came with the uniform, or she'd be found out.

"Thank you, sir," said the veteran, right after blowing his nose with a blast that made several heads turn. Beatrix coughed to cover her lips. She smiled as she limped through the railcar, studying the scenery as the train slowed, pulling into Los Angeles Union Station.

In the room for conductors, Beatrix unpacked her brown bag

lunch and settled at a staff table in the basement of the Los Angeles Union Station built in 1933. The building was still grand and had been the hub of hundreds upon hundreds of troop trains transporting service members throughout the war years. The staff room was clean but far from the glamorous façade above in the terminal. A few of the conductors were flipping through the *LA Times*, another was writing in a journal, and yet another was reading the Bible. She'd make a point of talking with the porters, all Black gentlemen, who chose, she hoped, to eat in a different location than the White conductors.

Beatrix finished her peanut butter and jelly sandwich and a cup of thick, bitter, and inky coffee from the pot on the hot plate. She pulled a weathered copy of *Gentlemen's Agreement* by Laura Z. Hobson from her duffle bag by her feet. While this had not been part of her plan, reading the bestseller would shout out to anyone who had KKK affiliations that the new, slight, and limping conductor would not be asked to any Klan meeting.

"Time to get moving, boys," Ken Purdue bellowed. Apparently shouting was his only level of communication. The men quickly gathered the papers and lunch wrappers, tossed everything into a bin, and headed to the tracks. "You doing okay, kid?" Purdue hollered and nodded to Beatrix.

Reminding herself to lower her tone, she said, "A lot quieter than when I was working in Chicago. On my first day there, a couple of the passengers got into a fistfight, and a teenager attempted to end her life by jumping out the window, a window she could not get open. She actually asked me for help." The story sounded good, and Beatrix had read about a train in the Windy City where, a few months prior, this had actually happened.

Ken laughed—an earsplitting cackle, of course. "Some folks don't got the brains they was born with. You, kid, been around the block a few times, I can tell," his head shaking in agreement with his words. "Wondered if you got lodging? Not staying in a flea-bag boarding house, are you? Wife and me rent out a room to folks."

"Thanks kindly, sir. I'm staying with a family I've known for a while, right near Santa Barbara High School. This is just a temporary apprenticeship, so I didn't want to get anything permanent."

"Now, if that changes, Chuck, you just talk to Uncle Ken. Like having young blood around."

Maybe she should have flaunted *Gentlemen's Agreement* more obviously, as she had a creepy suspicion that Ken Purdue might want to recruit her.

The return trip run was a breeze compared to dealing with the morning travelers. As the train headed north, stopping in small coastal towns on its journey back to Santa Barbara, Beatrix introduced herself, as Chuck, of course, to the porter who was serving coffee and offering water to the passengers. Somehow, she got the feeling that this kind-faced man could see through her disguise. Or? Wait. Had Sam told the porter she was a friend who was trying to find information about the ruckus that got him beaten and arrested? *Of course he did,* she thought. *It is just like Sam to know I might need a friend on board.*

The spritely gentleman stuck out his hand, "Happy to meet you, Chuck. You want anything to drink, coffee or water, just come to me."

"Thanks, Marcus. Been a porter for a while?"

"I tried to enlist at the beginning of the war, but the powers that be at the recruiting station said that fifty was too old. Too old to fight for my country? I'm proud to be an American, but I guess the recruiting board had a point. War is for younger guys."

"They have their rules." Beatrix patted her knee, where the supposed war injury caused her to limp.

"Yeah, suppose it makes sense, but us old guys are more expendable than youngsters like you."

"Anything I should know about the folks I'm working with right now, just to make it easier?" Beatrix asked, accepting a paper cup of water from the man.

He looked both ways and didn't speak until a passenger returned to her seat at the far end of the car. "Think a few of the conductors like to go out for drinks after their shifts. I'm not a drinking man, and besides, my color is all wrong to hang out with the White folks."

"No law against drinking, except if they plan to drive afterward," she said.

This time, his voice was even lower. He turned his back to the people on board, and she leaned into him to hear. "A few, including the one with the most seniority, Purdue, imbibe on the job. Not often, but I have seen it. You didn't hear that from me, and it's against the bylaws of the Union Pacific company and the union as well. That's how accidents happen. Fatal ones." He looked down quickly and fiddled with the gold pocket watch fastened to his navy blue vest. "Yep, that's right, sir," his voice was loud and clear. It was then that Beatrix saw Purdue entering the rear of the car.

"Appreciate you reminding me to offer passengers the newspaper of the day," she said, knowing Purdue was listening and probably had the other conductors trained to report back any gossip or rumors that could be useful. He was that kind of a person, she knew.

Purdue nodded at Beatrix and Marcus and exited the car.

Drinking on the job and then going out for more after the shift, she thought, and wondered, *Would they include a newcomer? Do I really want to be with men who are part, unless I was drastically mistaken, of the Klan? Was the Klan trying to destroy the union or the railroad? Or bully or eliminate anyone of color?*

She waited no more and caught up with Purdue in the next car. "Sir, I'm new in town and just wondered if there was a friendly tavern around if a man needed a beer after work?"

Purdue smacked Beatrix on the back. "Now we're talking, kid. The guys, just from this shift, all meet at Garcia's Bar and Grill, a little dive on Lower State. You welcome to tag along, good fellers, good for a few laughs."

The whopping chuckle sounded bawdy and offensive. Or was she imagining the message behind the laugh? "See you about six?" he asked.

Beatrix agreed and pondered the invitation as she left the train station that afternoon. She took a circuitous route as she walked back to their home in the posh neighborhood. It required an extra half hour, and she was tired, but she did not want anyone, especially the dodgy conductor, to see where she lived as Beatrix Patterson, Ph.D., and wife to the renowned scientist, Thomas Ling. As she strolled along State Street, turning west on Anapamu instead of the most direct way, she continued to stop and study the shop windows in order to see if she was being followed. Then, certain that this was not the case, she took back alleys to their Victorian home.

Thomas and Birdy were in the rear garden, a place where they often spent mild afternoons. While it was March, the garden was sunny, and he cradled her against his shoulder and swayed. Beatrix smiled, kissed him and the baby's head, and flopped down in the red striped, padded patio chair.

"I have the greatest respect in the world for those whose jobs require them to stand all day." She slipped off the manly boots and the black socks and rubbed her feet.

"Can you do it, Bea? Can you find out what happened with the riot at the depot that sent Sam to the slammer and the hospital?"

"Slammer? Oh, yes, the jail. You've been listening to too many episodes of Dick Tracy on the radio." She bent forward and rubbed the sleeping child's back and then Thomas's knee. "Weird things happened today, and I feel overwhelmed by where to start."

"How about at the beginning?" he handed off the snoozing baby and said, "Let me get you a cup of tea or lemonade, or something stronger?"

"Tea, please. A good cup, black as you can. I hoped this would be the end of the day for me, but I need to go out again," she looked at her official railroad pocket watch. "Two hours. I'm meeting a few of the conductors for beers at Garcia's Tavern."

Thomas stopped, dipped down his chin, and cocked his head. "One day on the job, and you're drinking buddies with strange men. Should I be jealous?"

"Be assured, you have no worries now or ever about my fidelity, especially so with these guys, one or more of whom might be part of the Klan."

Thomas felt his knees wobble. "The Klan? Oh, Bea, that's not reassuring at all. I should come with you."

"If they are with the Klan, having an Asian as a friend will instantly blow my cover, even though with you there, I would certainly feel less nervous."

Within five minutes, two mugs of steaming tea sat on the glass-topped table between them. Birdy was in her Moses basket, cooing and chewing on a teething biscuit. Beatrix's eyes were closed, with her head resting on the cushion. He knew she was not asleep but reviewing the memories of the day, cataloging them, making sense of them, and placing the concepts in the right groupings for future reference.

"Ah," she said, opening her eyes that were the color of emeralds in the late afternoon sunshine. "Builder's tea, also known as builder's brew or gaffer's tea, is a British English colloquial term for a strong cup of tea. It takes its name from the inexpensive tea commonly drunk by laborers taking a break."

"That I did not know, although I've been drinking the stuff

since I was Birdy's age, or maybe just a few years older. You are a cornucopia of significant quantifiable information, as I've always said. When you're ready, darling, tell me about your suspicions and how you're planning to be careful around these men." Thus, the details of the day were shared, and that helped her process their meaning.

Two hours later, with Birdy heading to bed for the night after a boatload of mummy's cuddles, Beatrix left the house by yet a different route into town, once more stopping at shop windows to ascertain if she was being followed. She'd made sure the railroad-supplied flashlight was clipped to her belt as it would be dark when she returned home.

The moment she left, Thomas was on the telephone to Sam's mother-in-law, Lillian Benson. "She's doing something potentially dangerous," Thomas told her.

"Again? I'll be right over and stay as long as you need me to be with Birdy. Thomas, you must keep an eye on her, even though our Beatrix can take care of herself. I've seen that with my own eyes," said the older woman.

Thomas changed out of jeans and a cotton dress shirt into black slacks, a black pullover, and a black jacket, snatching an inky fedora from the top of the closet on his way out of the bedroom. He was just tying his shoes as Lillian walked through the kitchen door. "My goodness. Now if your skin color was just as dark as mine, you'd practically be invisible." She gave him a hug. "Don't be stupid, young man. If the police have asked Beatrix to help uncover something concerning the trouble at the depot, then you can just telephone Detective Rodriguez, and she'll call in the troops. Our Beatrix is no fool."

"You are a miracle, Lillian, and I'll be back as soon as I can." Thomas dashed out of the house, pulled the Ford from the carport, and headed to town. He parked two blocks from the pub and walked the rest of the way. It seemed logical at the time. *Just being extra cautious as I'm on surveillance duty,* he thought, pulling his hat down to cover his eyes. He lurked in the shadows of the alley across from Garcia's when Beatrix walked by, not five feet from where he was hiding. In a second, he ducked further into the night.

A voice came from the distance, loud and clear. "Hey, Chuck, wait up."

It was a man with silver hair, and Thomas knew, from all Beatrix had told him, that this was the senior conductor. They shook hands and entered the tavern. Purdue slapped Beatrix on the back.

Beatrix walked to the table where the other three conductors who'd been on the same shift were already sitting. The barkeep was Beatrix's old friend, Gordon Blackfoot. She could tell he recognized her, even in the conductor's uniform, yet his face revealed nothing. The only change in his rugged Indigenous features was a raised eyebrow and a slight cock of his head that gave him away, but only to Beatrix.

"You guys want to order at the bar, or are you having food?" he called out. "Menus are on the tables. The short-order cook does a pretty fine hamburger. Now, what can I get you to drink?"

Beatrix, in her new, lowered voice, replied, "I'll take whatever is on tap, bartender. Have Rheingold or Pabst?"

"Pabst. You got it."

The others followed her choice, which inwardly made Beatrix wonder, *Is this what men do? Follow the leader?* She limped to the round table next to Ken, withdrew sixty cents from her trouser pocket, and handed it to Gordon when he brought over the round of drinks.

"Nothing to eat, fellows?"

Beatrix shook her head to indicate no, preferring to have the group think she was shy, fearing if she said too much, they might detect her feminine tones.

"Listen, boys, I brought you here for a reason," Ken looked around the group, catching each man's eye for a second.

Beatrix realized she wasn't breathing, waiting to be invited or bullied into attending a KKK meeting. She put both hands on the frosty mug of beer that had just arrived in front of her, a bitter drink she typically avoided.

"I have heard some rumors, and I fear that the union is going to be disrupted. No telling what group is planning to do the damage. Not yet."

Here comes his pitch, she thought, and then when he spoke, she knew there was surprise on her face.

"I'm banking it's those blasted Commies. Them Red devils don't like that our democracy works good and every man counts, every man can work hard and make a living. We don't need no dole like the Communists are doing to ruin every man's right to freedom. There are enough freeloaders in the world, in this city."

There was a chorus of "amens" and "right-t-o's" and Beatrix managed to growl an answer, still waiting for the racist conductor to push his bigoted personal agenda.

"Think that's what happened two days ago." Ken polished off the beer in two big swallows, slammed the mug to the table, and called for another round.

"Commies? Ken, does this sleepy town even have 'em?" she asked.

"You bet your sweet grandma's favorite apron there are Reds lurking here." He stopped talking when Gordon appeared over his shoulder with another tray of drinks.

"Nuf for me," Beatrix said and held her hand up. "Gotta long walk to get home and don't want to trip or something worse."

The other men grabbed the beers, and Ken fished two dollars from his jacket to pay the tab. Then he whispered, "You boys hear or see anything fishy during your shifts, come tell Uncle

Ken. I'll get the news to the bosses, and we'll stop them low-life Commies from invading Santa Barbara."

One of the men wiped his mouth with the back of his hand and said, "I heard there were bomb threats in Los Angeles right there at Union Station. You guys had to have heard about that big wig Welsh who got bumped off in his own front yard. Commies? That's what my money's on, too. Didn't like Welsh but thought he was at least better than the next guy, but killed in front of his house? Wrong, so wrong. Yep, gotta be Commies."

Beatrix slid her chair back, held the edge of the table, then asked in the most earnest, manly voice she could muster, "Ken, you think there are any other potentially violent groups wanting to disrupt service?"

"Nah, not in this town. Sure, we've got some folks of color, but they seem to know their place. None of them is going to make a fuss like the Commies will if we don't stop them. Stop them dead in their tracks, so to speak," he nodded in Gordon's direction, whose skin was the color of toasted bread and hair as black at midnight.

She wondered how good old Uncle Ken got along with Sam and the other workers, including her new friend Marcus, the porter on the day's train. How far would Ken's racist talk go? Did she actually want to hear more after seeing him give the KKK's secret handshake earlier that day? She felt nauseous, and it was not the beer. Time to get out and breathe fresh air that didn't reek of cigarette smoke and stale beer. *And take a hot shower,* she thought.

"Night, gents," she said, putting her regulation hat back on and nodding to Gordon, who knew exactly what was happening at the table in the corner and probably guessed why Beatrix was dressed like a man. She put quarters on the table for a tip. The idea of "Uncle Ken" paying for her drink or the tip was repugnant.

Instead of walking home, as was her original plan, Beatrix stopped at Woolworths Five and Dime, bought a pack of Wrigley's Doublemint gum, and after paying, walked back onto State Street. It was just 8:30 p.m., but the businesses were closing and traffic was nil. She popped a stick of gum in her mouth to get rid of the beer taste, walked twice around the block to make sure she wasn't followed and headed to the police department in the Morish-style and grand courthouse building on Anapamu.

Earlier, she'd called Detective Rodriguez and arranged to meet with her once she'd left the tavern.

Stella Rodriguez was at her desk, neat folders piled on the left and odd bits of paper in the middle. She was leaning back, feet up, reading the newspaper in the big bay area, and looked up toward the duty sergeant when Beatrix walked in. She called out, "I've got this. Let the man through. Okay, young fellow, let's go into interview room four and hear what you have to say." Her voice was all business, and if any of the ten or so officers in the bullpen suspected it was Beatrix Patterson, a regular consultant with the police force, they didn't seem interested enough to even follow the women with their eyes.

Stella closed the interview room door. "Let's make this short. You need to get home to Thomas and Birdy."

"Birdy's in dreamland already, I'm sure, and Thomas is probably reading, sitting by her crib, or glued to the radio for his nightly fix of cops-and-robbers programs."

Beatrix told Stella about the meeting with the other conductors and Ken Purdue's insistence that the Communists were behind Welsh's murder and the brawl at the depot. She told her about the secret Klan handshake and the feeling that the other men who were at the bar that evening didn't seem to be close to Purdue, although they were cautious and excitedly dangerous when talking about the Red Scare. "Like too many Americans, I fear, Stella."

"Yeah, and from what I hear along the grapevine, there's a senator who wants to prove that the Reds have already taken over the government."

"I don't have a shift tomorrow, so I want to talk with Dr. Rayne about the results of the autopsy."

"Not in this disguise, I hope," Stella said.

"My friend Lillian took some of the hair I cut off and magically weaved it onto a scarf, sewing it to a hat. I can wear the stylist hat, and no one will be the wiser that I'm sporting a crew cut."

"You know, Beatrix, you'd make an excellent police detective should your psychology business flop."

She laughed, "I do like to figure out puzzles and protect the underdog, but as a full-time gig, think I'll pass."

Thomas stood in the shadows outside the bar, finally sitting on a convenient bus bench. He smoothed the fabric on his black slacks, adjusted the black fedora and pulled the black wool jacket across his chest. He only took a full breath of air once he saw his wife leave Garcia's. Alone. He tried to conceal himself when she dashed into the five-and-dime, then walked forty paces behind her as she took two laps around the block.

He felt satisfied that she hadn't spied him or even known he was following her.

What surprised him was that she walked into the police station rather than coming straight home. He lingered against a wall and waited, again hopeful she wouldn't look his way.

He was stretching his arms when fingers connected with his shoulder. He froze as adrenaline coursed through him, and at once, he was in a self-defense position, one he'd practiced through years of martial arts. He knew the offender would be on the ground in less than a second, regardless of the opponent's size or height. His speed took the adversary off guard; he twisted, ready to flip the attacker and pounce on him. With a swiftness that comes with conditioning, Thomas grabbed the hand that had touched him, ready to break that arm if need be.

Fear didn't have a chance to question the attack, and Thomas knew he'd win.

He crouched in a battle position, and then the eyes he met made him gasp.

CHAPTER ELEVEN

"BULLOCKS, BEATRIX, I COULD HAVE TOSSED YOU INTO next Tuesday and hurt you without ever knowing it was you, especially in your conductor's uniform." He loosened the forceful grasp on her wrist, sobbed back an expletive, and yet held her at arm's length.

"Thomas, we need to have a conversation about you following me. It's happened so often that if you did not follow me, I'd be shocked."

He pulled her close. "Darling, forgive me. I have been fretting all night. I do not like the characters you were drinking with and know, yes, I know, this is what you do. You help people, you investigate, and you pretty near gave me a heart attack this time, sneaking up on me as you did."

She put her arms beneath his jacket and around his trim waist. "I did not sneak up. I was actually whispering your name, but you were looking so intently at the courthouse courtyard that your focus was off. I exited from the rear in case Purdue was following me."

"How can you blame me? I worry myself sick about you. I

thought I'd get used to your 'adventures' in crime fighting, but I have not." He pulled her closer.

A couple, who'd just turned the corner, abruptly stopped, nearly tumbling over the baby stroller that the woman was pushing. Even in the twilight, Beatrix and Thomas could see their eyes expand and their posture become ridged at the embracing couple on the sidewalk. They exchanged glances and stopped just after they'd passed, and Thomas and Beatrix heard the woman say, "Oh, what is coming to our city when men are openly coupling on the street?"

Then, the man made a production of spitting into the gutter.

"I have a good mind to walk right over to the police station and report them. This should not be happening. If they want to do that in private, that's fine with me, but not in front of our children," the woman huffed.

Beatrix and Thomas stepped apart. "Perhaps we should go home and continue this," Beatrix said, slipping her hand behind Thomas's elbow. "Then," she said in an even louder voice, "you and I can make wild love until dawn if we want to without rude comments from disrespectful strangers."

Thomas laughed and whispered, "Darling, you are boorish, and I love you even more for this rebuke."

"Let's get home." She kissed his cheek and then looked back at the shocked couple's faces, etched in the horror of it all. Beatrix pushed her face into Thomas's jacket to stifle the laugh and she could feel him chuckling as well.

After hugging Lillian goodbye and thanking her for being the at-ready babysitter, Thomas and Beatrix sipped chamomile tea, sitting up in bed. She told him all that had gone on inside Garcia's, how Purdue was worried about Communists, and the fact that the other conductors had been agitated but not enough to do anything. It seemed to be all talk. She told him about Purdue's racist remarks and made a mental note to ask Sam about any outward hatred Purdue had ever shown toward people of color at the railroad yard.

"What would the Commies," Thomas asked, placing the empty mug on his nightstand and stretching out in bed, "have to do with the executive's death and from an animal tranquilizer gun?" He yawned. "Any idea where one could get such a weapon? I doubt that Ott's Hardware downtown carries them."

"Perhaps a big game animal hunter would have the gun or someone who works with the Los Angeles Zoo?" She finished the tea, snuggled down, and put her head on Thomas's shoulder. "I'm going to meet with the coroner tomorrow and maybe have a better idea of who and why someone would use such a means to murder Welsh."

Another yawn could not be stopped as Thomas said, "There's something in addition to me stalking you that we need to talk about, darling Bea." Thomas pondered again, for the hundredth time, the letter now in his desk drawer. He thought of how, should John Brockman reveal the photos of the crooked politician dressed in the uniform of the Klan, and if he and Beatrix were accused of being Communists, it would wreck their careers and tarnish the future for their baby. He thought of how short life could be and the weight of being a good father, a good husband, and he fell asleep with his wife's hand to his lips.

Seconds later, and with a start, he woke again when Beatrix asked, "Can we wait to discuss whatever else you need to tell me? There are a few things to add to your agenda as well, Thomas. Darling, you really cannot keep following me. At some point, you'll have to let this go."

"Until tomorrow? Yes, of course. Forgive me for tailing you. Being the husband of a sleuth is new territory for me, I am not prepared and feel like I've taken a trip to the Arctic and only packed a swimming suit."

"Go to sleep, darling. You are not making any sense at all."

The next thing Beatrix heard was the gentle puffing of Thomas's snore.

Birdy sat in her highchair, pulled to the kitchen table, and was delightedly squishing a hard-boiled egg in her plump fingers and giggling. Once in a while, she'd pop a piece in her mouth.

Thomas was tempting her with sliced bananas that were facing the same execution. "My adorable child, we need to talk about childhood nutrition," he said, tickling her under the chin. "You may not be aware yet, however, babies and young toddlers should get about half of their calories from fat. Healthy fats are essential for normal growth and development.

"Consequently, it's wise to understand from my extensive research into your well-being that not all fats are created equal. Healthy fats like those found in avocado, olive oil, fish, nut butters, and dairy are good for a child like you, and for Mummy and Daddy. Unhealthy fats such as those found in fried foods and delicious treats, like my secret-recipe brownies, are fine in moderation. One day, Birdy girl, that recipe will be yours. You must guard it with your life—well, perhaps not your life, but don't just give it out willy-nilly. Have no fear, my sweet Birdy, while you've been napping each afternoon, I have been studying the history of the calorie."

Birdy nibbled the banana and a bit of whole wheat toast as Thomas continued, "Yes, I did find that it was captivating how the calorie was originally defined. I'm sure when you can talk, other than saying 'Mummeee,' you'll be as fascinated as I am. You see, a calorie was originally defined as the amount of heat required at a pressure of one standard atmosphere to raise the temperature of one gram of water by 1° Celsius. Since 1925, this calorie has been defined in terms of the joule, the definition since just this year, 1948, being that one calorie is equal to approximately 4.2 joules."

Beatrix stood just out of sight in the hall leading to the spacious and light-filled kitchen. She smiled, loving how naturally Thomas talked with their child.

"Good morning, my darlings," she said. "We need a dog, Thomas."

"Did you just hear what Mummy said? A dog? What a brilliant idea."

Beatrix waved a hand toward the floor. "A dog would keep the kitchen cleaner, don't you think?"

Thomas took Beatrix's hand and cocked his head. "You're not winding me up, are you? I've always wanted a dog, and," he looked at the child, "if you want a dog, throw more food on the floor."

The little girl took her left hand and swiped it straight across the highchair's tray, as she'd begun doing when she decided she'd had enough to eat. Then she reached her arms up and said, "Mummeee."

"A dog," Thomas repeated and got the broom and dustpan. "Labor saving, a good companion, and will help increase Birdy's immunity. A wickedly smart idea."

"Ah, Thomas, a dog is a long-term commitment. If we were certain we'd be staying here for a long time, it could work." She pursed her lips and said what was on both their minds. "Until we know John's decision, it is unresponsible to bring another creature into our home."

"Sit down. That's what we need to talk about." His face grew serious.

Beatrix bounced the baby on her knees as Thomas took a moist towel to the child's messy face and hands. "Are you ill, Thomas?"

He pulled a chair next to her and withdrew a letter from his crisp dress shirt pocket. It was folded in four, and he held it with the tips of his fingers as if it were dangerous.

"This letter," Beatrix said, "is the cause of your frowns and starts and stops of conversation about our family?" For someone who was ultra perceptive about other people, reading them quickly and correctly, somehow, it seemed that her love for Thomas clouded her vision.

"Dr. Albert Einstein would like to meet with me."

"Why, that's fantastic. What an honor. He's heard of your research on clean energy and wave power? Of course, he has. When will you meet?"

"I have not yet decided. There's more."

Birdy put out her arms, and Thomas took over the bouncing.

Beatrix looked at Thomas's eyes. "Tell me everything."

"You see, Bea, Dr. Einstein is currently working in New Jersey. At Princeton University. He's making the trip to California in June for the official opening of the Palomar Observatory in the mountains an hour northeast of the city of San Diego. This letter is an invitation to meet with him."

Beatrix took the letter from Thomas's hand and read it. "He wants to learn about your theories on global warming and how we must contain the use of fossil fuels. This is marvelous, oh, my goodness."

He handed her another folded letter. "Here's page two."

"Oh, he wants to have you consider joining him at Princeton. He'd supply you with assistants and a considerable grant to cover all our expenses."

"When I talked with Dr. Einstein . . ."

"You talked with him? On the telephone?" Beatrix thought, *How could I have been so involved in my own affairs that I neglected to communicate with my husband?*

"No, we transported our thoughts through the vapors, Bea. Of course, on the telephone," he laughed. "It's an opportunity of a lifetime. But our family, you, me, and Birdy, would be uprooted. You love it here. We have a big house ready for a bigger family. And, there's more."

"You'd better just spit it out, mister, as my days of being a fake psychic are long past."

"There is the new country, Israel."

"You've suddenly lost me. Yes, I've been following the formation of the country closely, a safe land for displaced Jews. John Brockman and I have been talking about it, and he plans to travel there in the future, possibly financing a university."

"Dr. Einstein, well, he's never been one to shy away from heated issues. He wants me to consider creating a laboratory at Princeton in New Jersey and possibly a satellite program in Israel once the fledgling country is stabilized. There are so many Jews, educated and thoughtful, that could help with the program and provide more permanency for the population."

"Thomas, darling, what do you want?"

"I want my wife and child to be happy." He looked like he might cry. "And a dog." He laughed.

"Any special breed that you're looking at?" She lightened her voice, knowing that the opportunity with the luminary was a momentous decision.

"There's a little terrier I've liked since I was a child and visited Wales. They're spunky, good with children, playful, and live a long time."

"Wait a second. Have you and Birdy been plotting to get a dog for a while?"

"Ever since she could sit in the highchair and throw food on the floor."

"When do we need to make a decision?"

"I'd say we get a dog as soon as possible."

"No, silly, you know I meant about Dr. Einstein's offer."

"He'll give me as much time as I need. I haven't discussed it with anyone but Birdy, not even my boss at the university. My additional concern is if John Brockman exposes the corrupt politician in New Orleans and we're accused of being Communists, would the offer still be viable? I know, because I asked, that Dr. Einstein considers the concept of clean energy more important than a person's political affiliation. He said he has been following my career since my early work at Cambridge." Thomas swallowed hard and shook his head in amazement. "That said, a number of the top administrators at Princeton are quite conservative, as you can imagine. They have been highly critical of the Communist movement."

"Is Dr. Einstein a Socialist or Capitalist? Or even possibly a Communist? I have read that he is a peace activist and a firm advocate of global federalism and world law."

"We must have read the same article," Thomas said. "I know he favors the principles of Socialism, asserting that it was an ideological system that fixes what he perceives as the inherent societal shortcomings of Capitalism."

"Have you made a decision, dear?"

"Yes, well, nearly, and it will all depend on what our friend John concludes and the direction of his moral compass."

Beatrix picked up a triangle of cold toast from the plate on the table, twisted it in her fingers, put it to her lips, and decided against eating it. She'd rightly concluded that the choice as to whether Thomas would work with world-famous scientist Dr. Einstein and possibly save the planet from ruin by securing unlimited clean energy was, in fact, in the greedy, filthy, and blackmailing hands of a corrupt, racist politician from Louisiana and his threat to destroy their lives. If John turned the photos over to the press, which seemed to be the moral choice, the governor who wanted to make a bid for the White House would lose.

Only in doing so, Governor Bennington Long threatened to destroy John. Thomas. Beatrix. Not to mention the life, safety, and future of their precious Birdy.

CHAPTER TWELVE

"We cannot let this happen, Thomas. Governor Bennington Long just might be controlling the fate of our very planet. This isn't about us anymore."

Thomas scrubbed his hands over his face. "We? How can *we* do anything?"

"We must help John."

Thomas tickled the little girl, and she snuggled into his chest, oblivious of the weight on her parents' shoulders. "What we need is a *skew-wiff*."

"Skew-wiff? Sounds like something I'd sweep off the floor."

Thomas shook his head. "British slang for scoundrel, racketeer, thief, crook. I do know a few expletives to add, but I'd offend myself and you and Birdy."

"We need to talk with John. There has to be another way of dealing with the Long than just giving into his diabolical demands."

"Hire a triggerman, um, a hitman? A sniper?" Thomas suggested.

"You really do like American cops and robber movies and

radio shows, my dearest. The answer is absolutely not. I'm afraid enough already. Mind if we put the adoption of a dog out of the equation for now and visit John?"

"We shall table this issue for now or until we find the perfect pet. I've got feelers out."

She glanced at her watch. It was just nine. "Before we go to John's house, I have a meeting with Dr. Rayne. I need to find out who might have owned a tranquilizer gun. The closest zoo is in Los Angeles, and I cannot imagine a local veterinarian needing one. Stella Rodriguez might know something about that by now."

"Want me to talk with John while you're at the police station?" Thomas asked, placing the baby in her playpen and handing her a favorite teddy bear, which immediately became a teething toy. "Or I could contact the two vets in town to talk about bringing a dog into our home and see what they know about tranquilizer guns."

"Thomas, you might want to rethink that, or they could imagine you'd use the tranquilizer gun on the poor little pooch."

"Blimey, I see your point. Bit awkward. How does one bring that up in a conversation?"

"One doesn't. The police or their consultant," she pointed an index finger at herself, "does."

"I'll take Birdy for our morning walk and perhaps stop at the two veterinary clinics in town. I must interview our future dog's personal physician before the adoption papers are signed," he quipped. Then he got serious. "Please, Bea, don't do anything that will frighten me or make more of my hair gray. There's far too much happening and troubling me already. I cannot worry about your safety as well."

Ten minutes later, her manly hairstyle concealed under the "hat with hair," as she called it, and dressed in a trim, black-and-white checkered suit with a slim skirt that hit well below the knee, a hip-length jacket with the current fad of shoulder pads, and black shoes with a small heel, Beatrix pulled the car onto Anapamu and parked in the city's public lot. *I need to see if Gloria Rayne has any more information after the autopsy, and then I'll visit Stella at the police station.*

Standing in front of the door marked MORGUE always made Beatrix take a breath. *This is certainly not the lifestyle my parents would have expected,* she thought, *but it is what I need to do. To protect the innocent and speak for the dead. Even if it's true that Mr. Welsh was unpleasant, his voice deserves to be heard, and his murder solved with the killer brought to justice.*

She opened the door and the young man she'd met while solving cult killings was there, feet per usual on the desk and a Superman comic book in his hands. He jumped up yet didn't let go of the caped crusader. "Just taking a break, pretty dead around here," he giggled, and his fair complexion and freckled face turned a light pink.

Beatrix shook her head and smiled. "That joke never gets old, does it."

"No, ma'am. I'm Rudy, by the way. Coroner Assistant Rudolph Mass." He held out his hand. "Dr. Rayne speaks highly of your deductive skills, Dr. Patterson."

"We met briefly when I was helping the police last year. Dr. Rayne told me that you're doing well balancing university classes and working here in the morgue. Planning to stay on after you graduate, Rudy?"

"Been living in Santa Barbara all my life, grew up on a farm just north of town. Why, this is heaven on earth, I couldn't find a better place in the country. Dr. Rayne is in a meeting but asked if you'd please wait. She won't be long." He motioned to one of the chairs in the small waiting area. "Coffee? Water? Comic book?" He laughed at his own joke.

Beatrix sat in the visitor's chair. "I bet you know a bit about everything that happens in this town. Are there any recent sightings of bears, coyotes, or large wild cats in the foothills?"

He sat down but didn't put his feet up. "Never seen a bear, except when the circus came to town, and that was long before the war. Guess you know I lost my foot in that farm accident. Got this prosthetic." He knocked on his leg. "So I can still hike the hills, and just a few weeks back, I saw a puma. Big guy, cunning golden eyes, a magnificent creature. Scared me spitless. I hollered something lame like, 'Your kind isn't wanted around here,' and the cat looked me up and down, possibly considering if I was worth his while. Then I swear he licked his lips just to scare me more before ambling in the other direction. Coyotes, on the other hand, ma'am, are everywhere, even seen them in the city a few times. Can't blame them. We're building houses, invading their domain."

"You don't want to mess with coyotes or the big cats, Rudy."

"No, sir-eee, ma'am. It is spring and there will be mama pumas with babies in the hills. I'm going to stay on regular trails from now on."

"One more unrelated question: have you ever visited or gotten close to the commune on Mountain Drive? Would there possibly be pumas that close to the city?" Logically, it made no sense to Beatrix, but the thought of the free spirits and Welsh's tirade kept circling in her mind.

"I'm twenty-five, but Mama would scalp me if she ever thought I had anything to do with that gang of nut jobs, running naked through the chaparral, having wild, um, romantic-like orgies in the buff." Rudy blushed. "And God only knows what they're drinking and smoking."

"Other than the commune, are there other wild creatures on Mountain Drive? Any hermits or camps of travelers?"

"Wouldn't surprise me if the crazies up there are making cougars into pets," he said as the telephone on his desk rang. He took the call with efficiency, said yes, the coroner could be at the address in a half hour, and finished by making notes.

At that second, Dr. Gloria Rayne and a couple, dressed head to toe in black and dabbing their eyes with handkerchiefs, walked through the door. "Again, I am truly sorry for the loss of your grandfather," she said.

The woman grasped the door handle, nodded, and smiled, dimples barely visible through the black veil cascading over her face from the hat on her head. The man with her touched his black fedora, never removing it, which made Beatrix curious about the two. Etiquette changed after the war, yet it was still considered good manners, although quickly fading, that men take off their hats inside.

After the two people left, Gloria said, "Some days are tough, and some are just weird. That brother and sister wanted to have some kind of astral-cleansing ritual done on their grandfather. They might look like typical citizens, but those two and their grandfather are part of the Mountain Drive clan."

Rudy had returned to the Superman comic book, but when he heard they were with the cult, Superman came in second. "Dr. Patterson and I were just talking about what goes on up there, in the yurts and sing-alongs and . . . other stuff." Pink returned to his cheeks.

"They wanted the grandfather's body and asked that you not send it to a funeral home," Beatrix said.

"Sometimes, Beatrix, you frighten me at how you know things."

"No trickery, it's just a matter of being observant and adding two and two that sometimes comes out five."

"Rudy, make a note please. They're returning this afternoon with the means to retrieve their grandfather. One of the options they're considering, and I didn't press it as I knew they'd lie to get him, was that they felt the need to transport the deceased to the mortuary personally, but between the three of us," she looked toward Rudy and said, "Mum's the word on this—right, my good assistant?" She waited for a nod before she continued, "I have the idea that they're either going to cremate him themselves or perhaps dig a hole and dump Gramps in."

"Dr. Rayne," Rudy's voice was a whisper. "Aren't both of those options illegal in the city?"

"You have been studying the laws. Good job. Yes, but it is not against the law to transport a loved one from the morgue to the funeral home. It's not our business to ensure that the departed get to a mortuary. There's no accountability or check-in process right now. Besides, if they really want to bury a body on their property in the hills, that's county land. We're city employees."

"Should I come and get you before I let them take the deceased, Dr. Rayne?"

"You bet. This is above your pay grade, Rudy."

"Oh, Dr. Rayne, you're wanted at the nursing home on Chapala. There's been a death. I told them you would be there by ten. Is that okay?"

"Yes, absolutely, and why not come along, Rudy? You need to learn what happens with calls to the nursing home and to private residences." She signed a form on Rudy's desk and turned to Beatrix. "Okay, enough local update, Beatrix. I have a couple of interesting facts to share. Please come into my office."

Beatrix followed Gloria and closed the door behind her. "Rudy's a trustworthy kid, trying to be a good future coroner, but I didn't want to have him learn the details of Mr. Welsh's death or the gentleman we were just talking about. Not yet, anyhow."

"They're tied together."

"Stop that, stop it. You can't know this stuff."

"Like I said, I'm just perceptive, Gloria."

"The elderly man in the refrigerator died of a wound that got infected," Gloria said.

"A wound that is the same shape and diameter as the tranquilizing bullet that stopped Mr. Welsh," Beatrix stated.

"If this is perception, you're an Olympic gold medalist at it. Does this all mean to you, like it's starting to with me, that we've got a berserk serial killer out there? I mean, really, Beatrix, what are the odds of two of the same types of wounds in one week?"

"Mr. Welsh was struck in the chest. And the grandfather in your fridge, where was he shot?" Beatrix inquired.

"Foot. Why on God's green earth he didn't get medical help is beyond me. He'd been dead twenty-four hours when it was reported, and I still don't know why the commune called me. The wound must have happened early last week. There's really no excuse for him dying this way—unless someone was hunting him.

"Geez. We're living in 1948, not the dark ages. It was sepsis that killed the old man. Sepsis occurs when the immune system has a dangerous reaction to an infection. It causes extensive inflammation throughout the body that can lead to tissue damage, organ failure, and even death. A lot of infections can trigger sepsis, which is a medical emergency."

"Other than being dead, did the autopsy show any organ failure?" Beatrix asked.

Gloria flipped open a manilla folder and ran her finger down the notes. "His liver was declining. Rapidly."

"Alcohol? Or a genetic cause."

"The drink."

"Could the man have shot himself in the foot while he was drunk and then ignored the wound?"

"It would have hurt a lot. The curious thing, Beatrix, is that this points to the Mountain Drive screwballs having a tranquilizer weapon in their possession. I do not like that, but I'm not the law around these parts, and for that, I'm thankful. I'm going to share this with Detective Rodriguez in my final report. She's the one who finds coincidences troublesome."

"As do I, Gloria. This is peculiar. Any other abnormalities I should know about Mr. Welsh and his death?"

"You were right about there being more to it. He would have regained consciousness, I think, although his heart was not strong, arteries were seriously blocked with a kind of fat called cholesterol. But someone attempted to do the deed—tried to smother him. Right there on the man's driveway, near the road, for all to see. There's also something odd."

"Odder than what we've been talking about?"

"I'll do the complete autopsy tomorrow, but there were a couple strands of black hair in his mouth. He was gray and balding. Mrs. Welsh's red hair, I was told, comes from the salon, not that there's anything wrong with that. The black hair? I don't get it. Like I said, I'll know more tomorrow."

The two women sat for a moment, processing their own thoughts.

"What traffic would there have been that early in the morning in his neighborhood?" Beatrix asked.

"Little. I made you a copy of the report." Gloria handed Beatrix a folder and said, "I need to make a confession. Do you have an extra minute or two?"

"If it's personal, do you want to wait until our next therapy session?"

"No, because I know you will not share what I'm about to say, and you can give me advice if I should talk with the city manager or the mayor, if that's what is needed." Gloria sat back in the swivel chair that loudly demanded it could use some machine oil. "It's more of a lie of omission. You know, I did serve in the Pacific in the war."

"You're suffering from combat fatigue and your mind is healthier than when we first began. You're smart, Gloria, lots of medical doctors who served, like you, would pretend everything was hunky dory. Suffer silently and numb themselves with drugs or alcohol."

"Yes, I was a surgeon. Saw more carnage than even my worst nightmares could conjure up."

"Now you're safe, and, I hope, we are friends."

There was a long silence before the coroner said, "Beatrix, I was also a spy. Before the war."

CHAPTER THIRTEEN

"For America?" Few confessions shocked Beatrix, yet this was one of them. The question tumbled out of nowhere. However, after meeting some Nazi war criminals in the past, she knew from experience that pure evil could easily be concealed.

Gloria squinted, "Of course. I was forced by our government to do a few things I'm not proud of, nothing horrible, but more like gathering intel and wearing listening devices. That kind of thing."

"Has something happened that made you want to tell me?"

"Yes, and this sounds . . . silly, and down-right crazy."

"I am good with crazy, Gloria. You can tell me in confidence. You are my patient, and I will not divulge details of our sessions, even if this isn't really one of them."

"I got a call at home this morning, from the San Francisco office of the FBI."

"Oh?"

"I was shocked, but apparently, there are rumors of a rogue group of the KKK setting up operations in Santa Barbara," Gloria said.

That confirms my suspicion. Beatrix nodded and waited for Gloria to continue.

"Wild or what? Now I'd expect this in the South where I grew up, but California? No way." Gloria fiddled with the stacks of papers on her desk, shaking them into neat piles. "The regional director knew I grew up in Pulaski, Tennessee, home to the vile Ku Klux Klan. Daddy was a farmer, principled beyond belief, and sent me, when I was about ten, to live with an aunt in Upstate New York. Said things were going to heat up in our town and I was not safe. Mama had died of complications with diabetes the year before and it was so brave of Daddy to send me away. To keep me safe." Gloria explained that her father was forced to join the Klan with like-minded neighbors or face the consequences. "My grandparents were Quakers and morally opposed to the Klan, but they were gone, and Daddy was, I know, trying to do the best." She rocked back and forth in the creaking desk chair.

"You still have a hint of the accent, and I think it's charming."

"The FBI's area director has come up with this scheme that I make friends with the supposed ring leaders of a pro-Communist movement here in the city, weasel myself into their confidences, and learn all I can. He says that the intel supports the scheme that the pro-Communists are trying to destroy the KKK and vice versa. Or maybe it's a rouse and they're coming to join forces. In our state? Have you heard of this? Is it nonsense?"

"It is rather like a gang turf war, then?" *Did the police know this?* she wondered.

"You're right, Beatrix. I didn't realize it."

"Have you made a decision?"

"I got the full-blown 'America needs you' sales pitch, but these folks, as you and I know, play for keeps. There is a growing fear about the Red Scare, and the area director told me there's a senator, McCarthy, from Wisconsin, who has a vile idea that Communists are lurking everywhere. Especially in Hollywood.

"The area director says that McCarthy is potentially dangerous. Even if one's named in the same sentence as a known Commie or a pinko, it could mean being blacklisted."

"A pinko?" Beatrix raised an eyebrow.

"Yeah. New term for someone who isn't considered a die-hard Communist, as in a Red, but with inclinations toward that. Hence, they're a lighter shade of Communist and thought of as a pinko."

Beatrix sat back. *That way of discrediting people is the same scheme that Governor Bennington Long is trying with John.*

"The contact at the Bureau—if you can answer—what are they asking you to do?" Beatrix said.

"They have managed to create a surgeon's position. Close to the glamour, I've been told. It's at LA General, and I would not, I have been assured, work as a surgeon. I saw way too many surgeries during the war and vowed not to do that again. My hands are no longer steady enough." She stretched her fingers, and they trembled. "Just thinking about cutting open a live human does this to me. When they're dead," she motioned around the morgue, "I know I cannot hurt them." She massaged her hands, attempting to reduce the pain caused by emotional trauma, not from war injuries.

"I'd be there in name only while I'd hobnob with celebrities and report back if they're about to overthrow our democracy. They've designed a phony background for me, supposedly as a doctor for the rich and well-heeled in Atlanta, so I can immediately get connected with producers, directors, movie stars, and the folks with the money behind it all. They say I'll be invited to all the in-crowd parties. I just have to be fun and chatty and a good listener so I can hear the gossip."

"Could you still stay on here as the coroner?"

"I'd have to take a leave of absence, and actually, that's

where you come in, Beatrix. You are a licensed psychologist and could recommend that I need some time away, a respite from death and all I saw during the war."

"That would be the truth, Gloria. You really could use a respite from body counts and autopsies."

"It does sound attractive, Beatrix, but do I need to rest badly enough to pass this up? I don't want to leave the therapy we've been doing. That's what is holding me back. I feel that the work we've done in your therapy sessions has helped me become mentally healthier than I have been in years. I'm afraid." She stood and walked to the window, which looked out onto the mid-morning traffic on Anapamu Street. "Supposedly this gig would last six months, and then I was told I could be here, back at work."

"Must you accept?" Beatrix asked.

"That's what is frightening. I love this country. I also fear that acting as a spy, even in this capacity, would slap me right back into the nightmares and panic attacks I was having before we started our sessions. I do not know what to do, Beatrix."

"When do you have to give your answer, Gloria?"

"By the end of the month." Gloria picked at a fingernail, typically highly polished from a professional manicure. Now they were ragged, the paint chipped.

Those bitten nails shouted the truth of the conflict inside the coroner.

"How will this affect your marriage? Yes, I think all of Santa Barbara by now has been told the story of your wayward spouse."

"Figured when I told Rudy a week ago, without asking him to keep my confidence, it'd get around like wildfire. That's what I wanted because then I don't have to tell anyone."

"It could work for you, you know. You could tell the FBI's area director that you must go to Hawaii to talk to your husband first."

Gloria stood again, walked across the room, and opened the window. "Suddenly the room feels too hot. Before I started coming to you for therapy, the heat meant a panic attack was about to strike. You've taught me how to breathe and count. The truth about my spouse? That ship's sailed. My husband, what's the polite term, always had a 'wandering eye,' and I've been told, wandering hands too, by some of my women friends before the war. I denied even thinking of the possibility. Denial is stupid. We both know that."

"What's the level of danger if you *do* go to Hollywood?" Beatrix felt torn for her patient and friend. *The government needs to see if there is any validity to the Communists invading Hollywood, but is Gloria emotionally strong enough?*

"A heck of a lot less than thrashing around the Pacific while trying to perform surgeries when the background noise is a Kamikaze pilot taking aim at the ships I was on. I don't have to apprehend anyone. Just gather intelligence and report to my supervisors. Famous last words, but this seems almost too good to be true. What do you think, as my therapist, Beatrix?" When she turned to face Beatrix, her forehead knitted together, and she clasped her hands.

"What's your gut feeling?" Beatrix noticed that the gold wedding band on the coroner's left hand was gone.

Gloria suddenly smiled. She looked more engaged than Beatrix could ever remember. "I love it here in the city, low key, monotonous in a great way, yet . . ."

"You're missing the experience of not knowing what the next day will bring?"

"Is that wrong, Beatrix? Unhealthy? This spying job, well, half of me is scared to death. The other half shouts that it'll be a holiday, an adventure. The agency will provide housing in the ritzy Santa Monica area, a sizeable salary, with a budget for the glamorous clothes I'll need in order to fit in with the rich and famous. There's even a car and driver. *Me?* Imagine me, a little scrawny White girl from Pulaski, Tennessee, having a chauffeur. If Daddy weren't in heaven with Mom, he'd be speechless. That's a lot—that man could talk paint off a car."

"Is Rudy ready to take over as the coroner?"

"Absolutely negative. He's not yet performed an autopsy. I'm going to suggest to the mayor that the retired coroner come back."

"They didn't tell you when you were hired? That man is a menace and an alcoholic," Beatrix explained.

"Oh, no. I did hear he left quite suddenly. They'll have to recruit another coroner then. The agency said if I agree, they'll handle the details of the situation here in Santa Barbara."

"Sounds like you're needed and wanted."

"Am I ready emotionally?"

Beatrix smiled. "There are plenty of psychologists in Los Angeles. I can make some inquires."

"Could I still keep seeing you? I can drive from Los Angeles or take the train once a week for our therapy sessions."

"Fridays at two? Or we can work around your glamour gal schedule in Tinsel Town. Seriously, we'll make this succeed."

"Thanks, Beatrix. For that and for being a friend."

"Sleep on your decision, Gloria. Let it stew in your mind a bit. If you start feeling inner discomfort, then it's not right. Sure, we all get anxious about new situations, yet you've been through too much to slip back to where you were."

"That's my main concern. Do you really suppose I could discover the Communists are invading Tinsel Town and even our city, which is where the stars come for weekends and private romantic getaways? I know the answer, as you would tell me, if I do not try."

"This Senator McCarthy? Does he pose a danger? Will he discredit people without any evidence, without due process?"

"From what I've learned and been told, he's hot-headed and likes to point fingers at anyone who isn't a 'true' American.

That's a slippery slope. Name calling, as we found out when Hitler did it, is powerful."

"As with both world wars, lots of folks accused each other of being a menace to our country. I am in the middle of another investigation that deals with similar issues."

"Then that's it. I'll wait as long as I can, and then, please, can we talk before I make the final decision?"

Beatrix left the morgue, found out Detective Rodriguez wasn't available, and stood on the steps of the massive building. She wrinkled her forehead at whom she saw across the street from the courthouse. It was Thomas pushing the pram, and she assumed Birdy was safely tucked inside. She was lifting her arm to wave when they disappeared into a photographer's studio.

Odd, she thought. *Thomas hadn't mentioned anything about having a photo taken. Maybe he's arranging it. Or a current photo of Birdy for his parents. She's growing so fast. Of course his parents must have more recent photos of their California granddaughter. He's so thoughtful.*

Beatrix headed to the traffic signal, waiting for it to turn green so she could cross. *I hope this is not a surprise for me because I'm about to ruin it,* she thought, opening the door of the studio. A young woman looked up from filing her nails as Beatrix came to the reception desk, inquiring about Dr. Ling.

"Oh, he and the baby are in a studio," she said. "They won't be long. Want to wait here?"

"I'm Dr. Ling's wife and the baby's mother."

"Oh, of course, my apologies. I just assumed since Dr. Ling and the baby are Asian . . . um, go right down the hall, ma'am. Second door on the left." She barely looked up and continued to file her sharp, cherry-red painted fingernails.

Beatrix walked down the hall, and when she opened the door, Thomas was sitting on a straight-back chair, and Birdy was in the middle of his lap with his fingers around her middle so she wouldn't tumble. A photographer stood in front of a large, professional camera as he fiddled with the knobs, moving the lights.

Thomas straightened Birdy's legs in front of him and then looked up. Thomas's mouth dropped open. Words did not come out. His eyes shifted to the right and left as if he wanted to run to avoid whatever explanation was forthcoming. "Oh. Bea, darling. What a surprise." He definitely looked stunned and fought not to seem guilty.

Why is he hiding this from me? she thought and said, "A surprise for me as well, Thomas." She turned to the photographer. "Would you mind if my husband and I have a few minutes alone?"

Sensing a domestic situation, the photographer stood, hesitated for a moment, then flicked off a light and exited with the speed of someone late for an appointment. "Excuse me, folks, I think I just heard the telephone."

"Let me explain, darling. It's not what it seems, not how it looks," Thomas began.

"I really can't fathom what it seems. This is certainly not a family photo." She stood in the doorway, imagining why he and the baby had secretly come to have their photos taken and in such a rigid pose.

"I was going to tell you."

"When?" Beatrix asked.

"At dinner, unless I saw you earlier today?"

She tilted her head. "You'd better illuminate me."

"Sit here, Bea." He got up and pulled another chair close to where they'd been seated.

"Your reason is so dreadful that I must sit? Thomas Ling, tell me what's going on."

Birdy reached out and Beatrix grabbed the infant out of her husband's arms.

"It's this accusation by the crooked governor in Louisiana

and the rotten situation it puts John in, and then there's Dr. Einstein's offer."

Beatrix stood closer. "You know this isn't making sense unless you tell me why you're here."

"Birdy might need a passport," he blurted. "Oh, Beatrix. If things go 'south,' as they say in the mobster movies I prefer, we must have everything ready to dash off to Canada quickly or even return to England where the idea that one can be a good person *and* a Communist—as we might be accused of—still exists. Getting a passport can take weeks and months, I've heard, and as reactionary as it sounds, we might not have enough time."

"You're that afraid?" She stood and pulled him close with the baby between them as if Birdy were peanut butter and jelly and they were the protective slices of bread.

Beatrix's mind raced with details of the current global situation. She knew it was not the right time to discuss politics or pessimistic thinking with her agitated and troubled spouse.

But, she thought, *In 1945, British author and journalist George Orwell published the essay "You and the Atom Bomb" and the novella* Animal Farm, *an allegory of a world living in the shadow of a nuclear war. He called it a cold war.*

The first use of the term to describe the specific post-war geopolitical confrontation between the Soviet Union and the United States came in a speech by Bernard Baruch, an influential and wealthy advisor to Democratic presidents, was just last year, 1947, she thought.

Thomas sensed that his wife was organizing her thoughts, making decisions about their family. He said, "This fearmongering could last for years, decades, unless America or the Soviet Union decides to blow the other to smithereens with the horrific nuclear bomb and us with it. Billions of dollars and millions of lives could be lost in any clandestine fight."

"What a world for our baby to inherit. Were we wrong to become parents, to hope and pray for more little ones?" She looked at her hands, flipping them over to examine the palms as if this might supply answers.

"Darling, my father once told me that he and Mum were criticized soundly for conceiving me and my siblings, knowing even then that the Great War was imminent as it was in the wind."

"I never knew that."

"Beatrix, I am afraid for us." His lips made a straight line, and his brow was furrowed. She could tell he tried to smile, but there was only apprehension on his face.

"I am concerned greatly. We've lived through some brutal times. This, however, feels far more frightening. It's like the enemy is walking among us, and we don't even know who to accuse or who to hide from. This is a war of misdirection, of secrets, of fear peddling, of racism, and of hate.

"Oh, if it were just possible, I would like to take you and Birdy and head off to 1925, in a suburb of England where I grew up. It was safe and friendly, and the worst-case scenario was that my mother planned to cook dinner. Never a good idea. I've told you she was on friendly terms with the fire brigade in our town as we often had oven fires. When my sisters got old enough, at the age of ten, they took over the kitchen, and the fire chief, a kindly man, came to the house with bouquets for Mum as he finally got to retire."

Beatrix loved her mother-in-law and chuckled at the story. "It couldn't have been that bad, Thomas. Yes, 1925 sounds wonderful, except I'd be twelve, and you'd be seventeen. Romeo and Juliet?"

"Just in my wishes, Bea, where we'd settle in a rose-covered cottage, and Birdy would grow up next to her cousins and their cousins. We both know that whatever happens with this war between John and shifty Governor Long, the results will change our lives. We must be prepared for the worst."

CHAPTER FOURTEEN

AFTER THE PHOTO SESSION, THOMAS LOADED THE pram into the back of their station wagon, belted Birdy into her safety seat, and opened the driver's door for his wife. "I've been through a lifetime of discrimination, Bea, in England and in my travels. I've finally felt free here in California, where the Chinese, since the war, are now trusted. This whole Red Scare fiasco could turn that around. You need to know—"

"That you attended Socialist meetings in England?" Beatrix predicted.

"Did I tell you in a drunken frenzy?" asked Thomas.

"First, I've never seen you drunk or in a frenzy, except when you dashed off to England because you'd been drugged by the leader of a murderous cult. And second, I figured all university students would have, at one time or another, been to a meeting. I have."

"You have? What else do I not know about you?" He got into the car, always preferring that Beatrix drive since he tended to forget which side of the road was right in America.

"There is a whole lifetime of things I need to tell you. Now, as for the passport, Thomas, if you're really feeling this much pressure, we need to make sure we have cash in the house, a suitcase of essentials packed should we have to leave unexpectedly, and a file of legal papers, like our house's deed and Birdy's adoption certificate."

He took her hand. "I'm quite skilled indeed at jumping to conclusions, but I don't like all that's been happening. There's been the murder of a man in broad daylight right there on his driveway, and someone you may have had to talk to about the fracas at the railroad could be involved. There are the goons who attacked Sam, and there's still no reasoning about who is behind that madness. Then there's the little matter of the KKK and the secret handshake you observed. Not to mention—but I will—that John's situation is in an abysmal and immoral quagmire. We've been trapped in it, too."

She massaged his hand and said, "Somehow, along with all of this is a commune called Mountain Drive. It's involved, and I need to get to the library to research its organizers and visit the newspaper archives to find out if they've had any conflicts with law enforcement."

"Rather than following you at your conductor's job tomorrow, would it help if I did the research on Mountain Drive? It would make things go more quietly, right? I am a researcher by profession, after all. Additionally, the Dewey Decimal System and I are old friends. We Brits use it. It's not just for Yanks."

She turned the ignition and pulled the car into traffic. "Would you mind doing that for me, Thomas? I'm on the railroad tomorrow throughout the day and won't get back home until after the library closes.

"On another subject, Lillian mentioned that she is tired of all the politics and grueling shifts as a hospital nurse. Further, you remember that she was recently made redundant, um, let go from her job?"

"What a smart man you are," Beatrix said.

"It's impolite to read my mind."

"Thomas, you are transparent, at least to me, and at least a good measure of the time. With your sabbatical coming to an end and the heavy issues of our country, along with Dr. Einstein's offer, do you suppose she'd consider being a live-in nanny to us, to Birdy?"

Beatrix turned to Thomas, touching Birdy's plump little fist on the way. "I doubt it," she said, answering her own question. "But it would be amazing. If Dr. Einstein expects you to work at Princeton, it'd break her heart to leave Jo, Sam, and her grand-children."

"Would it be awkward for us to ask her?" Thomas wondered.

"She knows us well enough that she'll make a decision that is best for everyone," Beatrix said.

"Maybe Dr. Einstein, once he visits the university campus here in Santa Barbara this July, will see that I am a complete thick-o."

"This is one of the reasons why I love you, and you certainly are not dumb." She laughed. "Thick-o? That's a new British slang word. The crushing issues we're facing will work them-selves out, dear. Someone said, 'It'll all work out in the end. If it hasn't worked out, it's not the end.'"

"I must remember that. Would it be appropriate for me to contact Lillian about being Birdy's nanny? How is she paying bills now that she's been let go?"

"She rents the little cottage, and Jo told me that the landlord was raising the rent. We can ask what she made as a nurse at Cottage Hospital and triple it. We have the funds, and she and Birdy love each other."

"Will I still be able to take the baby for a spin each day?" Thomas asked.

"Silly husband, of course. By the way, did you bring an extra bottle for Birdy?"

He turned in the seat to check the child. "She's sleeping. She always falls asleep as soon as I strap her in her safety seat and the car gets going."

"I noticed. I think we should head down the coast right now and talk with John. We can also see if his passport is up to date, too."

"Is yours, Bea?"

"Always. My father told me that a valid passport is our right as Americans, and besides, he said something like, 'Bea, now if you should ever commit a crime and need to skedaddle the country, you must never let a passport expire.'"

"I would have liked your father, darling. I certainly like the way he thought. The photo of Birdy will be ready on Friday and I'll apply for her passport at once. God willing, everything will remain calm so we can prepare if we need to 'skedaddle.' What a brill' word."

They drove through town and headed south on Highway 101. At the turn-off for Montecito, Birdy woke and let them know either her nappy needed a change or she was hungry. "Probably both," Thomas said. "I'll take care of that when we get to John's if his housekeeper Yuri will let me."

"Birdy certainly has a boatload of bonus grandmothers."

They were welcomed with open arms by the housekeeper, who spoke to Birdy in Japanese before whisking her away for a change and a bottle. Thomas had, as always, packed small squares of cheddar cheese, whole wheat crackers, and sliced grapes for the child's lunch.

John was at his desk reviewing a stack of documents as they entered the study. Thomas hesitated and looked at his wife, who seemed surprised to see a woman in one of the visitor's chairs. "Ah, my friends. Mariam, Mariam Goldman, I'd like to introduce my friend Dr. Thomas Ling, Beatrix's husband."

The diminutive woman stood up and nodded. "John's told me about the adventures that you've had. My goodness, Dr. Ling, you all do have a history of finding trouble."

Thomas smiled. "That's typically been the realm of my wife, and I am dragged into the fray. You are the attorney who got Sam out of jail, I assume? Beatrix told me. Thank you for your quick response."

"We'll find out who is in back of the attempts to have him imprisoned or have him quit because of the danger. I'm working on some leads now."

Beatrix sat in the second visitor's chair, and Thomas stood behind her with his right hand on her shoulder. "Any progress on the blackmail, John?"

"I've known Bennington Long years, he's a bully."

"John, what if you took your side of the issue to the press and exposed him as a racist?" Thomas asked.

"My word against the popular politician?" John cocked his head. "Even with the corruption he's known for, in a weird quirk, he upheld the civil rights of some Black farmers, which was totally out of character for Long. He's got to be working a new angle, some kind of scheme."

"Maybe he has turned over a new leaf?" Thomas offered.

Miriam laughed. John smiled, which for him, meant that he was chuckling, too.

Mariam nodded. "Whatever he's up to—and it's no good, I can assure you—Long knows the photos John has are in safe keeping and not here in the house. Otherwise, he'd burn the house down. Those photos, if revealed, would rightly annihilate any chance of him running against Harry Truman in the next presidential election."

"Are the photos truly safe, John?" Thomas asked.

He blinked, and Beatrix knew he was going to tell the truth. "Is your house safe?"

"Our house?" Thomas inquired.

"I put the photos in a box and slipped it into the top shelf of your kitchen's pantry. It was last fall. Feel free to look at them, but be warned, you'll see the hatred etched on the faces of the Klan's men who were marching through the Ninth Ward that night and of Long's fists pulverizing the Black man he'd attacked."

Thomas and Beatrix exchanged glances, and Thomas asked, "John, is your passport current?" Then they explained the fears they'd previously shared about their safety.

"I've been alive a heck of a lot longer than you two. The Great War, the Depression, the Dust Bowl, crazy schemes, and stupid things, and I've given up worrying. I still, like you, Beatrix, want to protect good people and great causes." John rifled through a desk drawer, pulled out a passport, and showed it to them.

"Are you saying, old chap," Thomas said, "that we should ignore global unrest?"

"Not anywhere close, Thomas. I just recommend that you don't let it eat you alive."

He's working on a plan to have Governor Long removed from office, Beatrix thought. She'd seen that confidence in her friend before. Suddenly she realized that what he said was true. There world would always have wars and rumors of wars, dishonest leaders, and natural disasters. *More than ever, I've got to find out who instigated the riot at the train depot,* she vowed.

Driving back to the city, Beatrix shared her intuition with Thomas. "Did you pick that up?"

He was holding sleeping Birdy on his lap, and her eyes were starting to droop. "What I caught, actually, was the knowing looks between the attorney and John."

"I think they're an item."

Thomas turned to his wife, who was merging the car into afternoon traffic. "An item? Oh, like chemistry, like a spark? How marvelous is that?"

"I have wondered if John thought he might be too old for romance. I am so glad I was wrong, but let's not say anything. He'll tell us when he's ready." She patted his knee. "I'll never forget the day I happened upon you lurking outside my office in New Orleans, and it was love at third sight."

"Yes, I remember trying to convince you I was a laundry worker, and you saw right through that act."

She pointed at his shoes. "Your one indulgence. Laundrymen do not wear expensive wingtips. Didn't take a fake psychic to decern that."

They got into the house and were snuggling Birdy down for her afternoon nap when Beatrix said, "I'm going to pay a visit to some of Grayson and Kay Welsh's neighbors, pretending to be a reporter. There's an older woman, Antoinette Du Bois, who had the wherewithal to jot down the license number on the car she insists had the shooter with the tranquilizer gun in it."

"Antoinette Du Bois? Sounds like a movie star's name, and I bet she's a looker. One with smoky eyes and fire-engine red lipstick. Has to have a French accent with a name like that."

"I'll report back with all the glamorous details of the lady. I'm betting that she's probably eighty-five years old, wears barrels of heavy perfume, and dotes on her poodle." She laughed, knowing he had been kidding.

"Oh, possibly oodles of poodles. That cinches it. I want a full report. Go get ready, and I'll call Lillian to see if there's any interest in being Birdy's nanny. I may just throw out the idea that she's just blocks away from the Conrad home, so she'll be able to get all the kids together for playdates at a moment's notice."

"And?" she said ten minutes later, checking to see if the hat with

THE CONDUCTOR

the hair scarf was adjusted well. "It was a long shot about Lillian. Was it awkward?"

He kissed her. "Lillian was pleased, even before I offered her three times what she was getting nursing. I didn't realize those angels in white were paid so little. However, she wants to be our nanny yet turned down the offer to live with us. She said, 'Honey, now that I'm going to have all that dough, I can pay the rent here in my cottage.'"

"I figured as much, but she'll be here for us, and Birdy?"

"Our dear Lillian was chuffed. Said the offer was an answered prayer."

Beatrix put a steno pad and pen in her messenger bag and slipped the leather strap over the shoulder of her brown light wool suit. "Plans for the afternoon?"

"Thought I'd read until Birdy wakes, and then we'll walk to the mission. Well, I will, and she'll be in her pram. Tomorrow, I'll spend the day at the library with Lillian here for Birdy. I've always wanted to know what goes on in a commune. All those naked parties. Righty oh, must look into that," he teased.

"I'd start with books and then slowly, as the weather warms, move into naked outdoor parties, Thomas. It's always a bit cooler, and the wind is stronger up on the hillside. Just my suggestion."

Waving goodbye to his wife, wishing her luck on the fact-finding trip to the dead man's neighborhood, he thought, *At least this feels like action with any help I can give her, rather than fretting about nuclear bombs, the Red Scare, and John being blackmailed. Oh, and the long, ugly reach of the KKK.*

Born with the tenacity of a terrier, Thomas couldn't let the idea go and knew they must be prepared. He brewed tea and sat on the porch, making lists of things he would need to do should they have to leave California and flee to England. "This is not improving the level of my worries," he said, ripping the paper

135

from the tiny notebook, always in his pocket. "What would Beatrix do?"

A heartbeat passed. *Blimey, why didn't I think of this before? Beatrix is doing it right now, pretending to be a reporter to get information. I'll do the same. It's not the first time. When we met in New Orleans, I'd taken the disguise, serving as a courier for what turned out to be a rubbish treaty, which didn't seem useless at the time. I was supposed to be a sailor and then a laundry man.* He smiled, and in his mind, he was at once a Hollywood star about to play a critically acclaimed film role.

Would the Mountain Drive gang allow an Asian in their group? Could I pretend to be that lost, that needy? A little field trip, a short visit with the members might tell me how they live and see if I can ascertain if, in fact, they own a tranquilizer gun. Wonder how I'll bring that up? Thomas swept the kitchen floor, and thought once more, *If we had a dog, she'd eat all the crumbs that Birdy throws to the floor. A symbiotic relationship if I ever knew one.*

Then he said out loud. "I need a costume if I want to visit the commune, and this time I won't wear natty shoes. Beatrix saw right through my costume as the laundryman because of my spiffy wingtips." He dashed upstairs to their bedroom, pulled open the closet doors, and stared at his shoes. Every pair shouted, "Expensive." Then he remembered that in their tool shed, he'd left army boots covered with dirt and mortar that he'd worn when he was attempting to fix the garden path. "They'll do the trick, especially if I want the folks having naked orgies to believe I am a vagrant who needs a handout. Now for the rest of the disguise." He touched each of the crisply ironed dress shirts he wore daily, even though he was on sabbatical. Then, randomly, he yanked out a long-sleeved white shirt and began distressing it with the scissors he found in the desk. He unraveled the edges with the points of the scissors, bunched the starched shirt in a ball, and stepped on it, grinding the cotton into the carpet. However, it still looked too clean. He snipped off the two top buttons, and yet it still didn't satisfy him. "Tea. There's still some in the pot. I'll splatter it with tea and maybe add some catsup."

He dug through the closet again and discovered an already stained and torn pair of khaki trousered he'd worn in the garden when he tried to help the crew that built the gazabo on their hillside. He'd meant to throw them away months back but was glad now that he hadn't.

On the shelf above where his fashionable suits hung was a baseball cap he'd bought last season when the farm team in Santa Barbara played. He and Sam Conrad hadn't missed a game, although truth be told, Thomas still didn't completely understand the logic of it or the rules. The beer, hotdogs, and popcorn, however, made the outing worthwhile, along with watching his friend enjoy it. He fumbled with the hat. "It's a sacrifice, but I'd do anything to help Beatrix and keep us safe. Let's see, maybe sandpaper to the bill to make it look old. Maybe grind in some dirt. Then I'll be ready. By cracky, going undercover at the Mountain Drive commune will be a piece of cake.

"What could possibly go wrong?"

CHAPTER FIFTEEN

BEATRIX PULLED THE FORD TO THE CURB BENEATH one of the clusters of stately eucalyptus trees that lined the quiet neighborhood known as Upper State, about four miles from Beatrix's home and the busy downtown. It felt like an exclusive world away. These homes were solid, as if they sprung from the earth, not of wood and stucco. Each was unique, but the theme appeared to be flaunting red tile roofs and Moorish influences. When Beatrix's parents built their home in the center of Santa Barbara, the plan was they could walk to the theater, the shops, cafes, and restaurants. Here on Upper State, it was as if the residents even asked the birds to tone it down. Apparently, the wind had been warned not to rustle the leaves in the giant trees. *It's spooky it's so still,* she thought.

Beatrix had vowed never to lie again when she left the fake life in New Orleans. However, telling strangers that she wrote for the local newspaper wasn't a lie as she often wrote editorials about mental health and those services in the community. Still, she wasn't keen on the plan, yet there seemed no other way to ask questions. She certainly didn't want to say she was a consultant with the police.

"It'll have to do," she whispered.

She noted the Welsh's home and walked to the neighbor on the left. She rang the bell, and an older woman in a black uniform with a frilly white collar answered. "Yes?" The woman didn't smile and only looked out a crack in the door. Made sense, especially since there'd just been a murder on the street.

"Hello. I'm with the *News-Press*. I'm asking all Mr. Welsh's neighbors if they'd seen suspicious activity or strangers in the area recently. Did you note anything you can remember that was out of the ordinary before, um, the accident or even the last two days?"

"No, ma'am. I'm the maid. I don't live in, and the police were already blocking the streets when I walked to work that morning. I was terrified that something had happened to my employer. She is quite frail."

"Might I talk with her?"

"No, ma'am. She's napping." The maid started to close the door. She held the frame, changing her mind about whatever was on it, and opened the door completely. "The lady across there," she pointed to a two-story, rosy-pink stucco home, with a tidy walk and manicured lawns. "She might know. She sits at that bay window all day and watches what happens. It's unsettling, like she's a secret spy or something, and when she's out walking her dog, she does this slowly, stopping to peer into any windows where the drapes might be pulled back. My madam asked me never to open the front drapes again. She saw the lady staring at her and writing down something in her notebook. Not even a bit of embarrassment for getting caught snooping." The maid slowly closed the door. "I've said too much. I'm sure Mrs. Du Bois has a good reason."

"Thank you, you've been most kind. I'll see if I can interview her. Is that the lady's name?"

"Du Bois. Mrs. Du Bois. I've never talked with her—not my place—but I heard her talking with our letter carrier the other day when he delivered a package. I wasn't nosy, ma'am. I was upstairs, and the windows were open. Mrs. Du Bois must be hard of hearing. She was shouting at him, something about walking on her lawn."

"You've been generous with your time. Thank you again."

Beatrix turned and heard the door shut and the deadbolt click even before she was down the broad steps toward the sidewalk.

Okay, a deaf lady who minds everyone's business. She's also the woman that Stella talked with, who'd copied down the license plate of the suspicious black car. For the first time in days, Beatrix felt that the investigation had made a bit of progress.

Approaching the door, it swung open, and a small black dog ran at her like a mechanical toy that had been wound too tight. The thing yapped and jumped and barked and turned around to see its owner on the porch, which she was. "Most likely, she won't bite you," the full-figured woman said. Her posture was ramrod straight, shoulders back and chin up. She towered over Beatrix.

She was wearing an unfortunate shade of yellow, not sunflower yellow or egg yolk. It was on the green side of the color. Her tweed skirt, the yellow twin set, and a long string of yellow pearls matched exactly, making dark stockings and gray orthopedic shoes a contrast that was not flattering. The outfit, even more than her wrinkled face, showed she was living in the past, still wearing the styles popular a decade before the war. She was openly suspicious of Beatrix. The dog took a position at the woman's feet and growled.

Beatrix stood still and said in a louder-than-normal voice, "I'm with the local newspaper and looking into the death of your neighbor, Mr. Welsh."

"Come closer, or better yet, come inside. I'm Antionette Du Bois, and you are?" She looked down her Romanesque nose at the stranger on her front porch and then once more swept her eyes up and down, inspecting and judging what Beatrix was wearing. Her face clearly indicated that she disapproved of Beatrix or her trousers. Or both.

"The dog? Is he all right if I come? Oh, I'm Beatrix Patterson. Would you perhaps rather put him inside, and we can talk on the porch?"

"Foofoo is a girl, madam. Foofoo would never be a boy's name. That's absolutely ridiculous. Come now, Foofoo, heel." The dog miraculously obeyed and trotted right after Mrs. Du Bois' ankles without any hesitation. As the dog crossed the threshold, it turned and bared its teeth, cocked its demonic head, and scampered after her mistress.

The living room, with the large bay window, was, indeed, a perfect spot to monitor the comings and goings in the community. The furniture was dark wood, which did not surprise Beatrix. However, it smelled of citrus oil, and there was a large bouquet of pink roses on a low coffee table. Clustered on the built-in bookshelves were decorations of spectacularly carved, blackened wood statues of warriors, quite likely from trips to the African continent. On other bookshelves were more elephant figurines than Beatrix knew existed on the planet. She stopped counting at twenty. Among the precious pachyderms was a five-by-seven framed photo of two smiling men, arms over each other's shoulders, massive rifles by their sides. *Thank goodness, no dead animals.*

"Your collection is fascinating." *Definitely fascinating if one wanted four hundred little elephants everywhere and on every flat surface.* She pointed to the photo, which was obviously old from the style of their safari clothes to the brownish tint of the paper. "Are these family or friends?"

Mrs. Du Bois touched the frame as if caressing a loved one. "My late husband and my brother, Frankie. You may have heard of Frank Buck. He's celebrated, a legend around the world, you know. He's working with the San Diego Zoo these days, humanely transporting endangered species to zoos that can help preserve them. He's quite famous, and Frankie and my husband often trekked to Africa in the early days. Oh, my manners. Please sit down. Tea?"

"No, thank you. Are those tranquilizing guns by their sides?"

"I suppose so, although I never went on safari, and I'm deathly afraid of all firearms. I served as an ambulance driver in the Great War and never ever want to see a gun again. Oh, and Africa," she shivered, "all bugs, dirt, and frighteningly large creatures." She wrinkled her nose as if she were smelling something repugnant.

Beatrix took a chair facing the window, and Mrs. Du Bois sat opposite. She had to move a cluster of pillows that seemed to cling to the furniture as moss does to trees in a forest. There were stacks, and Beatrix counted ten squarely on top of one another. A pillow skyscraper. "I'm talking with the neighbors about the incident two days ago. I understand you have been interviewed by the police?"

"Oh, what a terrible business." The little dog positioned herself on her mistress's lap and bared her teeth, squinting at Beatrix in what seemed to be loathing. Since Mrs. Du Bois was petting the dog's back, she couldn't see the warning, the menace in the canine's eyes. Or the teeth.

"I believe you told the police you saw a car that could have been involved in the situation."

"Murder. Why not just say murder? He was shot. Everyone knows that, and besides, it was in two-inch headlines in your very own newspaper this morning, young lady. Shame on that editor you work for, Miss Patterson. The news story even gave Mr. Welsh's address. Upper State doesn't have incidents like this. Ever. Well . . ."

Beatrix nodded and waited. She scribbled in her notebook, which was a prop, but all reporters carried one. With her super memory, it wasn't necessary to take notes, but people expected it. It also gave her something to do when waiting for the person she was interviewing to fill in the awkward silence with information they often had not planned to offer.

"A few weeks back, I was walking Foofoo here, and an open-bed truck with the name Lowy Brothers painted on the side stopped in front of the Welsh home. Mind you, Lowy Brothers is a," she hesitated and pursed her lips as if something tasted bad, "it's a discount shop with used things and old appliances. Why would anyone in Upper State buy from that store? Buy cheap trash?"

"Did you see the driver make a delivery anywhere?"

"As a matter of fact, he wished me good day, tipped his hat, and walked up the slight incline to the Welsh home."

"I know you weren't watching," Beatrix said, knowing full well that she had been. "However, did you see the driver go inside or who answered the door?"

"Are you getting all this down in your notebook, dear?"

Beatrix made some scribbles on the page.

"It was about eleven. Mr. Welsh always left the house precisely at 7:00 a.m. He would have been in his office. He was an influential man with the Union Pacific Railroad, you know. It was his current wife who opened the front door. Shocking bright red hair, always wearing green. That day, it looked like she had on some flimsy erotic emerald-colored kimono. Why, that was probably all she had on," she huffed. Foofoo turned her head as if agreeing and then returned to baring its teeth at Beatrix.

"You were friends with Grayson Welsh? What was he like?"

"Oh, I wouldn't say friends. He'd nod periodically if I was on the sidewalk with my precious Foofoo girl." She petted the tiny poodle, and it cuddled closer to her thigh, emitting a low snarl.

Beatrix wasn't sure if Mrs. Du Bois was oblivious to the dog's aggression or did not care. "Did you have a neighborly interaction with Mrs. Welsh? I'm trying to get a feel as to his personality, you understand." Beatrix tilted her head and waited.

"There were countless wives over the years, Miss Patterson, I gave up after number three. Although the current spouse does like dogs. She said one day that in the future she'd love to get a standard poodle, and Foofoo just adored her. Why, my goodness, I cannot say that for her husband."

"Oh?"

"You see, I'm a responsible pet owner, and when Foofoo, well, takes care of business on our walks, I always clean up, um, you understand."

"Mr. Welsh took offense at that?"

"Yes. Can you imagine? I was bent over one morning, before six, I'm certain, and getting ready to clean it up. I hadn't noticed him as my back was to their driveway, where I suppose he was picking up the newspaper. Why, I was mortified. He had the audacity to swat Foofoo with his newspaper. I was stunned, more so as his bathrobe flapped open and he was unclothed." She put the hand not petting the dog over her eyes, like a Victorian schoolgirl. "Oh, so distasteful.

"My little girl was terrified. She flipped around and went after his ankle. Well deserved, I say. How could I blame her? I was in shock. How would you, Miss Patterson, feel if you were casually taking care of business and a giant human being swatted you?"

That concept stopped Beatrix for five seconds, and she hoped it didn't require an answer. "Did he ever talk to you about this incident?"

"No, my little, precious pet and I scurried off. I wrote him a stern letter and mailed it. After that, I always wrote down the times when he would get the paper so I could avoid seeing the wretched individual."

Beatrix felt she had a better idea of the type of man Welsh was. "Now, about the car, if you can remember, that was driving around your block before the incident?"

"My memory is excellent, I'll have you know, young woman."

"Oh, that's not what I meant. I appreciate that you have a busy life, so much to do."

"Right you are. I did copy down the license plate number and gave that to the police. I even stopped at the police station yesterday to find out if the detective, a woman, mind you," she snorted, "with some Mexican-sounding name, found out who owned the car."

Beatrix made sure her eyebrows didn't raise at the racist remark. "That would be my friend Detective Stella Rodriguez. Have they found the car or who owned it?"

"She was busy and had one of her underlings shoo me out of the police station. Here I am, mind you, a lady of quality and social standing, a taxpayer and citizen of the city for thirty years. It's outrageous. I came right home and wrote her a stern letter as well. Such disrespect."

Her face reminded Beatrix of an apple left on the tree too long.

Beatrix started to get up as Mrs. Du Bois put out a hand. "Do you want to know about the pool service and the fancy man who frequents the hussy's house?"

CHAPTER SIXTEEN

"IS THERE SOMETHING THAT YOU KNOW ABOUT THEIR pool service?" *Possibly this was the connection, and Welsh was killed by a jealous lover.* Beatrix settled back into the bilious, floral-printed chair. *No, that doesn't feel right.*

"I'm not one to gossip, mind you," Mrs. Du Bois said, yet her eyes glittered with excitement about doing just that. "Mrs. Welsh often meets the pool maintenance fellow on the street with a cup of coffee for him. I am scandalized. One should never mingle with the help. Don't you agree, Miss Patterson?"

Beatrix wanted to laugh out loud and thought, *A snob and a racist,* but she covered her mouth with a pretend cough. "How often do the servicemen come? Is it always the same gentleman?" The questions were specific because she knew Mrs. Du Bois probably kept tabs on the times.

"Once a week, and that is what is so outrageous." She withdrew a lace-edged handkerchief that was tucked inside of her garish yellow sweater's sleeve and dotted off her cheeks in quite a theatrical way, enjoying her role as the provider of information.

Beatrix realized she was staring at the older woman. "What is that, ma'am?"

"It was different men, well, not the same one week after week, then quite without notice, the same man started coming. He came regularly as if he were waiting around the corner and saw when Mr. Welsh left for the office.

"Even worse, Miss Patterson. It is improper for a married lady to entertain tradesmen when her husband isn't home." Mrs. Du Bois stood with such force and speed that the little poodle flipped off her lap. Neither seemed surprised. The dog bounced, found her footing, and barked furiously, but not at Mrs. Du Bois. The poodle seemed to be blaming Beatrix.

"You've been most helpful," Beatrix said, knowing this was the end of their chat. "I may need more information in the future. May I call on you again?"

"I rather doubt, young lady, that there are any more details you'd be interested in. You have heard all I plan to tell you. Now, if the police would return and ask pertinent questions and value my opinions, I might be able to remember further information."

Beatrix opened the front door, and Mrs. Du Bois was by her side as Beatrix said, "If I see the detective on the case, I'll let her know. Good afternoon, ma'am."

The door shut, but not before the dog glared and growled. Beatrix sighed. She hadn't met such a complex person in some time, and while she wasn't one to judge, she hoped she wouldn't have to cross paths with the woman again. However, the photo of her husband and the former big game hunter Frank "Bring 'em Back Alive" Buck, as he was nicknamed by the press and adoring fans, was a loose end. She would definitely share that with Stella.

Beatrix talked to a few other neighbors, and found that the residents, unlike her part of the city near the high school and the Santa Barbara Bowl, were not sociable. One woman said that everyone kept to themselves except one. She nodded toward Mrs. Du Bois' regal home.

Slipping the steno pad into the messenger bag, Beatrix drove back into town, pulling to the curb at Garcia's Bar. "Fingers crossed that Gordon Blackfoot will be in." She checked her watch. It was just before four.

Luck was on her side, and the tavern was empty except for Gordon. They'd stayed friends after meeting at the Santa Ynez and Chumash Indian Reservation during a previous investigation.

Gordon smiled when she came in and sat at the bar. "Coffee?"

"Do I look that browbeaten? Just had a long, convoluted conversation with a neighbor of the executive from Union Pacific who was found dead on his driveway two days ago." Beatrix accepted the steaming mug gratefully.

"I figured you were undercover the other night when you showed up looking like a pimply-faced man-boy," Gordon said, joining her with coffee.

"Thanks, Gordon. I took a chance that you wouldn't give me away. The police have asked that I consult with them and try to find out who is in back of the troubles with the railroad. That really is one of the reasons I'm here today."

"What do you need to find out, Beatrix? I'm like an encyclopedia of useless information because, well, us bartenders hear more gossip than anyone in town except maybe a hairdresser. Definitely more than the local priest."

"Did you know Grayson Welsh, the man who died?"

Gordon put down the mug, looked at a customer who had just come into the bar, and waved, calling out a greeting. "Let me get this regular a beer, Beatrix, and then we'll talk."

Beatrix fiddled with the handle of the mug and thought that while she'd learned that Grayson Welsh was not a model citizen, there was still no clear reason why anyone should shoot him with a tranquilizing dart and another, or perhaps the same person, attempt to smother him. *Is Mrs. Du Bois to be believed, and why should I doubt her? But I do. I need to put aside her contemptuous racism and condescension and think of the facts. She saw a car, although the police have yet to find it. She didn't like Grayson Welsh, but whoever killed him didn't either. What is the connection?*

Gordon refilled her now empty coffee cup. "The guy's as deaf as a post, but we should keep our conversation quiet." He nodded to the bearded man in the corner, staring out the window.

"What do you know, Gordon, about that executive from the railroad, Grayson Welsh, who was killed two days ago?"

"Shot and then smothered. I read that in the paper."

"It's not known if there were two assailants or one that did both acts." She'd known Gordon for two years, trusted his judgment, and knew he was a confidant. "Did he ever frequent the bar?"

"Nah." He waved a hand around the neighborhood pub. "This place isn't chic enough for the likes of Welsh. It's a favorite, however, when Welsh wanted cheap digs for an event. The office staff always held a Christmas party here, and he'd show up, looking like the lord of the manor, in a three-piece suit. He made a big deal, theatrical actually, of handing out their bonuses as if he owned the entire railroad line. He passed out all the envelopes and then, as if he were the Pope or something, would say something like, 'Now open them up.' There were a few workers who scowled. I remember last year when they tore open the envelopes and looked at the money inside."

"This is a stretch, but did Welsh determine how much each got?"

"You're amazing at putting two and two together. A disgruntled accountant I was talking with that evening had compared the cash he received with a gal, a typist. The accountant held a far more prominent position than the secretary, yet somehow, he found out that the young woman received double what his bonus had been. Welsh called the shots on how much each office worker received, and it seemed it was a case of who he liked more, rather than if they were competent in their job."

"Motive for murder? Why wait all these months?"

"You're the detective, Beatrix. I just know people, and that guy was irate. I see him in here once in a while. Not a regular. He works for the county these days. Guess he did something proactive rather than go berserk, as I probably would have. Sure, that night, he was steamed. A lot of the employees were that evening, and their alcohol consumption didn't help. Had to cut off a few after Welsh swaggered out."

"The women who were here, likely all typists and secretaries, did they look pleased with the bonuses?"

"Honestly, and I don't like thinking this because I've been accused of crimes I didn't commit, but it seemed like the plainer, the married, and the older women didn't seem as jubilant as the ones decked out in skin-tight party dresses."

"That could be a motive. Welsh wouldn't be the first high-powered man to approach a female employee. Typically, women will not come forward, even those who have been abused, against a man of power."

"That's inexcusable. We both know it, Beatrix."

Yes, wrong, but it happens, she thought. *Happens too often.*

"Any other questions? Customers are going to be coming in soon," Gordon wiped down the immaculate bar.

Beatrix looked around and out to the street, where two women seemed to be waiting for a friend as they scanned up and down the sidewalk. "Thanks for the coffee." She put fifty cents on the bar, and Gordon shoved the coins back at her. "One more question, Gordon. By chance, did the current Mrs. Welsh ever come along with Grayson for this holiday party?"

"Always, glued on his arm, hanging like a parasite. Rumor has it she did something in Hollywood, so it could be she'd acted for a living. The good-looking women who work for Welsh didn't even approach the boss until the misses left that evening. I didn't catch what happened but remember she slammed down a sequined clutch purse, screamed an obscenity, and left."

"My goodness, okay, that's another bit of info I'll follow up on. Thanks so much, Gordon. And your grandmother? She's well?"

"Please join us again for dinner soon. Grandmother is still talking about your little Birdy and your charming husband. Think she's got a crush on your man."

Beatrix opened the door, and three women walked in, office workers ready for happy hour. She headed back to the car. She wanted to talk with Kay Welsh and somehow chat it up with Welsh's office staff. It was nearly five, and she needed to get home. She had a shift on the Santa Barbara to Los Angeles line tomorrow morning, and she'd need time to process all she'd learned that day. Yet rather than driving straight back to the house, she returned to Upper State, pulled her steno pad from the messenger bag, and walked up the curving driveway to the vast Welsh estate.

She was just about to knock when the door opened. "Oh, hello?" said a smiling woman in her mid-forties with shiny red hair in the current pageboy style. She was dressed in flowing black slacks and an emerald-green silk tunic, with at least six long necklaces strung in a dazzling rainbow of crystal beads slipped around her slim throat.

Beatrix returned her smile. For a widow of two days, the woman, whom Beatrix assumed was Kay Welsh, seemed quite composed, but everyone grieves in their own way. "Mrs. Welsh? I'm Beatrix Patterson, and I'm working with the police on the cause of your husband's death." With this woman, Beatrix felt no need to pretend to be a reporter as she had with the formidable Antoinette Du Bois.

"You'd better come in. If we're here on the front steps, that nosey biddy across the street will be taking notes. I swear she can read lips. Just between us, once a week, she writes me or my late husband a letter accusing us of everything from not raking the leaves in the gutter or my car waking her up if I return later than eight o'clock from a social event."

"Mrs. Du Bois?" Beatrix nodded and filed that tidbit of information away.

"A one-person vigilante committee, and don't get me started on her dog. And I love dogs." With the closing of the front door, the barks started, and this time, Beatrix was surrounded by small, bouncy black and tan terriers.

"Hush," Kay Welsh said in a normal speaking voice, and the three stopped barking. "Sit." They did.

"Wow, that's impressive," Beatrix said. "May I pet them?"

"Certainly."

Their fur felt rough, and their eyes sparkled with mischief. Tails wagging against the hardwood floors, they looked like they wanted to run circles around the house yet somehow stayed still, looking to Mrs. Welsh and Beatrix.

"I was a professional dog trainer for the movies before I married Grayson. Trained Lassie, Toto, and Rin Tin Tin, among other canine celebrities." She turned her attention to the dogs. "Come on, kids. Let's go into the sunroom."

Beatrix obediently followed the pack. "What type of terriers are they, Mrs. Welsh?"

"Welsh terriers. Yes, same as my last name. That's the only reason Grayson allowed me to have three dogs, another thing to pad his ego." The words, however, were said without malice, which made the situation even odder, especially from the rumors about her controlling husband. Yet, perhaps Mrs. Welsh was immune to his domination.

The woman hopped on a chintz-covered sofa, and the dogs followed her. She tucked her bare feet beneath her and motioned for Beatrix to sit in the overstuffed chair. The room was bright with late afternoon sun, filled with lush house plants and purple, white, and orange flowering orchids. The art that studded the walls was definitely Italian, and there was a decorative piece of gold-colored Murano glass sculpture in the middle of the coffee table.

"Now, how can I help you and the police?" Her face was free of makeup and she seemed comfortable as a woman in her forties to be completely herself.

Beatrix liked her a lot and hoped that she didn't have a hand in her husband's demise. She looked at the woman's face for any signs of tension, and there were none. *Odd. Very odd. With her husband's death two day's prior, shouldn't there be a hint of stress? Unless, the love was gone. Relief? Is that what I'm seeing?*

"Were you home when your husband was killed, Mrs. Welsh?"

"Kay, please. No, actually, every morning I go to the beach for a daybreak swim, just me and my swim instructor. It's never smart to swim alone, you know."

"Yes, of course. What time did you return?"

"The detectives have already asked me this, but I'm sure it's routine to have me repeat it."

"Exactly."

"My gentleman friend and I stopped for coffee and bagels at Stein's Bakery. We gossiped for a while, and I pulled into the neighborhood at about 7:45 a.m. There were police cars lining the street, so I left the car down the block. As I got closer, I saw the police around my driveway. That's when it hit me. I ran up toward the house, not knowing it was Grayson under the sheet in the middle of the driveway. Then I screamed. His legs and tatty old brown slippers were sticking out from the bottom of a sheet. A uniformed officer grabbed me, holding me back. I screamed bloody murder that I wanted to talk to his boss, demanding to know what happened."

"Then you met Detective Rodriguez."

"It was a shock. One doesn't go for a swim and normally return to find their spouse dead. I had to go to the coroner's office yesterday to identify him. Frankly, Miss Patterson, he looked more content dead than alive. Oh, that's a horrible thing to say, but it's the truth. He rarely relaxed, and his face was typically flushed—high blood pressure I assumed. Refused to go to a doctor."

"Your husband was unhappy?"

"May I speak freely?"

Beatrix nodded.

"I've come to realize that Grayson was only happy when he was on the hunt, chasing down a deal, making a score for the Union Pacific Railroad, finding his next female conquest. Thinking back, that was what initially attracted me to him, how he was single-minded about victory. I knew about his infidelities with his previous wives, but the fool I am, I thought I could be enough for him."

"Not so?"

She laughed, but there was no humor in it. "I gave up on our marriage about six months into it, and that was a year ago. We led separate lives, and he seemed to be content with that. Maybe five wives were the perfect number for him. I have no idea." She shrugged. "You're wondering why I stayed? Me, too. Although with Grayson's health issues, oh, this is wrong to say."

"That you thought he would suffer from a fatal heart attack?" Beatrix asked.

"In one of his girlfriend's beds, most likely. There, that's out."

"Did you mention this to the police? Perhaps it was a jilted lover who shot him?"

"No. It didn't seem to matter. He was dead. The marriage was over. The police asked me questions and then left. Yesterday, that same detective came back. I was wondering if maybe two people had a grudge against Grayson since one tried to shoot him or stun him to death. It was well known in our circles that he had a weak heart. Had a heart attack at work, about three months ago. Being smothered was really odd, however. I don't get that."

"The police are excellent at making sense out of random information. Did they ask you details about your relationship with your husband? Such as what you've just told me?" It was a line of questioning Beatrix wanted to dig further into.

"I told them it was fine. Fine and good, Beatrix, are two different things, as we both know. Grayson was all flowers and chocolate and romantic getaways before we married—when I tried to avoid him. He'd come to the movie studio or my dog training center in Hollywood and bring gifts, jewelry." She lifted her graceful wrist and let the sunlight play off a diamond bracelet heavy with stones. She smiled, as if admiring it while twisting it to capture the rays. "I was seeing someone else and had no intention of getting mixed up with him."

Beatrix nodded and waited.

"He oozed charm, with a suave personality like a short, fat Cary Grant. I gave in and cut it off with my previous boyfriend, a lifeguard I'd known since high school. It was the money, the thought of sleeping with this powerful tycoon, the social circles. I didn't grow up poverty-stricken, but there was never enough for fine clothing and expensive meals in highly regarded restaurants. And a driver for my car if I wanted one."

"Money can make us do things we never thought we would."

She laughed, and then Beatrix finally noted a hint of sadness in her features. "Marrying Grayson ruined my life. I've got all this, but I messed up royally."

"Were you planning on leaving him? And this?" Beatrix waved her hand around the professionally decorated room.

"Actually, no. I, well, I know some things about my late husband that I can still call leverage if need be. You see, Grayson was leaving me here in the house with my dogs because of that.

I have to thank Mrs. Welsh one, two, three, and four. They must have been far less cunning than I am, as Grayson was not open about his unsavory negotiations on behalf of the railroad. I just snooped, took photos, and kept some records he'd tossed into the trash. *He* was moving out. Not me. He owned some property around town, including a cottage on the beach, which I guess is now mine, unless he cut me out of the will without telling me. I would not put that past the man. I believe the apartments and houses were where he entertained other women. There was no way in hell he would ever again bring one of those floosies to the house, pretending she was a private secretary and they had 'business' in his study."

"When did the secretary visit?" Beatrix asked.

"You know? It was less than a month ago." Kay looked around the room, and when she spoke, her voice was edged with disillusionment. "Honestly, Beatrix, at first, I thought I'd struck it rich, and I had. I didn't realize the amount of negative energy, the lies, the cheating, the games that came with it when I said, 'I do.' Then, there was Grayson's fixation with perfection. I swear, the man expected me in full makeup and pristine hair and nails the moment I opened my eyes and called me names when that didn't happen. It is a relief to give up trying to protect his reputation. I'm certain that his current mistress was getting all the flack for being flawed."

"Any idea of who this woman might be?"

"I wondered that, too, so I got friendly with the office manager in the Union Pacific building. She loves a good listener. Before me, whom she called Number Five and, yes, said that to my face, he'd been with one of the typists. Young enough to be his daughter. The gossip was that this blonde beauty was demanding more and more attention, and Grayson was greedy with his time. He fired her for some made-up misdeed, or so the rumor has it. But ironically, she continued to stalk him even after she got another job. I'd have loved to have seen that."

Beatrix waited as Kay let the dogs out the sliding door to the patio and smiled as they tumbled and rolled in the grass by the massive swimming pool. *Ah, this is what the dog Thomas wants looks like. Smart, silly, and apparently trainable,* she thought, *but then again, Kay Welsh is a professional dog trainer.*

"I understand that stalker now works selling tickets at the depot. He likes—liked, them young."

Instantly, Beatrix recalled the women at the counter when she talked with Sam Conrad, her first day as a conductor. There was Maria Davies undercover. A gray-haired, stout woman who wouldn't have measured up to Grayson's young and pretty requirements for romance. Then there was the third. Beatrix saw her in her mind as clearly as if she were in the sunroom right with Kay and herself. She had blonde hair, overly processed by bleaching chemicals, and creamy white skin, although with too much black eyeliner, giving her the look of a startled raccoon.

Kay settled back on the sofa. "I can dig a bit more if it helps. But could a girl that age do harm even to a self-centered, secretive, ego-maniac lover?"

A knowing smile came to Beatrix's lips. "I've found, Kay, that one should never underestimate the wrath of a jilted woman. Women may not murder as often as men but don't discount them for their gender. The circumstances of your husband's death didn't require a muscled man. It could have easily been planned and committed by a woman."

"You know I'm not sad about his death. It's messy, but my attorneys are pouring through the details. I had to sign a prenuptial agreement, and now," she waved a hand around the gorgeous room, "it worked out."

Could I be wrong? Was all that she'd receive from the estate be worth murdering her husband?

CHAPTER SEVENTEEN

THE DOGS WERE MILLING AROUND BY THE SLIDING door. "Do these Welsh terriers make good companions? Are they well-behaved with kids?" Beatrix asked.

"You have children?"

"A little one, nearly a year old, and my husband, who is British, was just talking about this breed. I swear he is going to dash off on the spur of the moment to buy one from a breeder in Wales if I give the thumbs up."

"Puppies are demanding, but an adult dog could work well." She let the dogs into the house, and one with an inky black saddle of fur and light tan legs and intelligent chocolate-colored eyes sat at Beatrix's feet, looked at her, and then oh, so gently put a paw on her knee. Beatrix reached down and smoothed a hand over the wiry coat. *The dog is small, we have a fenced back garden, and Birdy would be in love. I can see the dog on a leash trotting right next to Thomas and the baby as they take their morning walks. But a dog? No, not if we might have to flee the country.*

"I taught her to do that," Kay said. "They are great with kids when trained. This is Peanut. She came to me through a rescue organization, and I am planning to rehome her. Just think about it. She could be yours."

"You've been most helpful, and Peanut is adorable. When I find out anything about your husband's death, if it's okay with the police, I will let you know. Thank you, and good evening."

Beatrix arrived home safely, but her mind was so convinced that the young woman selling tickets was somehow involved that she didn't remember the drive at all. She told Thomas about her day and the interviews.

Thomas listened intently. "The lady with the snappy poodle is the sister of big game hunter Frank Buck? Why, she must have a dart gun that shoots tranquilizers. I hope you told the police."

"Thomas, she might be outspoken and less than cordial with neighbors. However, I simply can't imagine her shooting Grayson Welsh and then trotting across the street to finish the job in that quiet neighborhood."

"Maybe one of the numerous pillows you mentioned was the murder weapon? Now, what about Mrs. Number Five?"

Beatrix relayed their conversation, minus anything about terriers, as Thomas would have driven to Kay Welsh's house at once, she feared, to see the potential animal companion. "I like her. I just don't see her as killing her husband, even though she made him out as a rat of the first order."

"The leading suspect, then, is the young woman who sells tickets at the depot?" Thomas asked.

They were tucking Birdy into her crib when Beatrix responded, "I'm on the morning shift tomorrow. If I can, I'll slip a note to Detective Davies, who is there too, asking to gossip about Grayson and to watch the girl's reaction. Wish I could, so I could read her face, but that would be weird since I'm Chuck when I'm there."

After dinner, they both knew that she'd need time alone to recall the conversations with Kay Welsh, Mrs. Du Bois, and

Gordon Blackfoot before she'd be able to sleep. Thomas understood and seemed happy listening to Dick Tracy and Superman radio shows while she processed.

Beatrix's shift as a conductor started at six that morning, so an hour later, when Thomas came downstairs, the tea in the pot was barely warm, and Birdy was hungry. He'd managed to shower and dress before the baby woke and just as Lillian arrived, bringing in the day's mail.

Lillian, as always, walked right into the house. "Morning, Thomas." She gave him a strong, one-armed hug. "Where is my baby Birdy?" She pretended to look around, and while the joke went over Birdy's head, the girl giggled. She reached up to be hugged.

"What in the Good Lord's name are you dressed up like that for? Have you lost your senses, mister? Maybe you need to go back to the university if you're going to dress like a vagrant. Wait, no. Tell me you're not going to try to build anything without Sam being here."

He looked down at the tattered trousers and ripped shirt, the ragged baseball cap in his hands, and the scuffed, cement-covered boots. "Beatrix asked me to do some research on the free-spirited community up on Mountain Drive. I'm going there to ask some questions. Thought they'd talk more easily if I didn't look too posh."

"Nothing posh about you in that getup, Thomas. Now get out of here with those muddy boots."

"I'll be back well before five, and Beatrix is on the four o'clock train from Los Angeles, so she'll return around six. Ah, Lillian, could you kindly keep my research idea of infiltrating the commune hush-hush? I want to surprise Beatrix with my brilliance on this if I find anything out. You see, recently, a member was shot with a stun gun, like the one used on that executive from Union Pacific, and maybe I can find out more. Have I shocked you?"

"Just seeing you dressed like a hobo would surprise anyone. Okay, mum's the word. That letter on the top looks important, Thomas," she said, nodding toward the mail.

Thomas glanced at the stack of letters and flipped through them, noting the return addresses. There was one from his parents in London, another from a colleague at Cambridge, and the third was postmarked from Princeton, New Jersey, and the sender was an A. Einstein. He slipped it in his back pocket. *The great man probably wants to tell me he made a slipup, a terrible blunder, and I am not qualified to work with him. I'll read it later. Now, off to Mountain Drive.* He couldn't think about Albert Einstein when he had to pretend to be a down-and-out, disgruntled former soldier.

It took just under a half hour for Thomas to drive the back roads toward the commune. He'd traveled it the previous day, constantly reminding himself that he was in the States. He'd already discerned where he'd hide the Ford Woody in order to cover that he'd driven to Mountain Drive. He parked under a sprawling California oak, looked around to make sure he was alone, and got out. He bent down, picked up a handful of dirt, noted his fingers were quivering, and scrubbed it into his hands, unsuccessfully trying to get dirt under his well-trimmed finger-nails. Then he wiped his right cheek, spreading the dust on his face. The morning was cool, and he hoped the dirt would cling to the nervous sweat on his face.

A car came toward him, and he put out a thumb. The driver sped away without a glance. *I must look shabby,* he was pleased to imagine. When yet another vehicle increased speed as Thomas put out his hand, he was certain of it.

There was a wooden welcome sign as big as a refrigerator indicating the entrance to the community, and he hiked down the graveled road. He walked on, guessing at least a mile, and thought, *They certainly want to be alone.* He stopped when he heard someone shout a greeting.

"Friend? Are you in need of food or drink?" the stranger called out.

Thomas saw him then, with scruffy long hair, dressed in a T-shirt of some faded brown color, boots, and short dress pants cut off just below the knees.

Thomas had previously decided it would be useless to try to conceal his British accent. He could speak a multitude of languages, but American was not one.

"Both would be appreciated." He waved and attempted to look thirsty and in need of a meal.

"You English? I was stationed outside Dover, Royal Air Force Swingfield. Would have been nice if the Nazis weren't bombing the hell out of your country. You're a long way from home, brother." The man was far cleaner than Thomas appeared. His hair, which reached his shoulders, had a healthy shine in the sunlight, and his smile seemed genuine. His face, arms, and hands were browned from working outdoors. "Come on, pal, let's get you some grub." He patted Thomas's back.

This is far from what I expected. Where are the nude orgies? Where's the debauchery? He smiled at his notion of what would be discovered among the commune's residents and followed the man to an outdoor eating area set with rough-cut picnic tables and benches. There were no walls to the open enclosure, but the roof seemed adequate should there be rain. Thomas could see two more men chopping wood, and there were women clipping wet clothing to a line. Some children, who should have been attending school, were chasing each other around and playing a game that only they seemed to know the rules. The little ones were half dressed and a few not at all, which made Thomas shiver, whether it was from his protective nature as a dad or the chilly breeze or both. He didn't have time to consider that conundrum.

"Here you go, pal."

A pretty young woman brought a tray of refreshments to the table and winked at Thomas. The commune member patted the girl's bottom, and she slapped his hand away, giggling back to the circle of others who were watching.

"Thank you." Thomas accepted a steaming cup of something the deep shade of an avocado peel, which he hoped was tea, and a bowl of lumpy porridge. "I've been walking a long time."

"You got a name? I'm Gus." Gus stuck out his hand, and Thomas accepted it.

"Tom."

"Been in California long?" Gus pulled back his shoulder-length, saggy blond hair and tucked it behind his ears.

"Here and around. Seeing America, I suppose," he replied, sipping the tea and then spooning in a helping of gruel.

Gus yanked his hair into a ponytail and pulled a string of leather from his pocket to secure it. "I did that for a while, lost myself a bit after the war. I'm originally from the South. A few people I've had the unfortunate experience to be related to prefer the bad old days, wanting to turn back the clock regarding hot ticket social issues and commentary."

This was not the grubby, drunken Mountain Drive resident Thomas had expected. He actually liked the man.

Gus looked out toward the mountains, now in the morning sun nearly a pale purple. "My old man is about as closed-minded as they come. Mom goes along like a faithful retriever. Don't know if she's ever had an original thought, although she and her siblings are close."

A breeze whipped around some fallen leaves. Thomas tried to "read" the man's features as he'd seen Beatrix do hundreds of times, but nothing came.

"What kind of work did you do before war, Tom?" Gus asked.

"Ah, laboratory stuff."

"I was a teacher. English, can you believe? Just got my first teaching job the day my draft notice arrived. Now, I make pottery, which we sell during events and fairs. We sell our wine, and the women take the wool from the sheep we have, and, like magic, knit shawls, hats, and scarves to be sold. We don't really need much here."

"How do you all make ends meet? You must need money for some things."

"I do odd jobs around town, sometimes drive delivery trucks, help out for a small company. That kind of stuff. That guy over there stacking firewood? He's a local dentist who comes up here to get away from it all. The one chopping wood? Was a barber. He had a rough patch in the war. North Africa and a POW for a while. Now, his hands tremble like crazy. All he can do for money is manual labor, which doesn't pay enough for him to rent a room. He stays in the community most of the time. He's offered to trim this," Gus tossed his hair side to side, "but, man, I don't want him near my head with a sharp pair of scissors."

Thomas eventually recognized Gus's accent, or what he thought it might be. "Prefer life in the hills? Do you like California? You, see my wife . . "

"You gotta' wife? Yeah, me, too. Three, actually." He chuckled. "Sisters. We're a close family. More's the better, I always say."

Thomas was momentarily stunned. "One is all I need, but right now, we're apart. I reckon you're from Louisiana? My wife and I spent some time there during the war. Before . . . before everything happened to me." He wanted Gus to believe that an unfortunate event had occurred. Not true, of course. When he met Beatrix, she flipped his pedestrian world upside down, and he never looked back. *Best thing that ever happened to me when I collided with Beatrix Patterson*, he thought.

"Heard the twang, huh? Spent time in New Orleans. Good music, good food, good drink, good people." Gus patted his knees as if he were playing the drums.

"Right you are. Someone once told me that it's a criminal offense to serve a bad meal in that city. Would not be Monday without red beans and rice, would it?"

Gus patted Thomas's back. "Darn straight. Hey, now, Tom, I hope you know you're safe here with us. We don't put up with any trouble, no fights, no swearing, or spitting either. Well, spitting is okay, and swearing happens. Some of the men get a bit rough and resort to their fists at times. It's all settled quickly."

"When you mean that you don't put up with trouble, it's all relative?" Thomas asked.

"Especially with our relatives," Gus bent over with laughter. "I gotta remember that, Tom. You heard about us? Heard of Mountain Drive, I'm guessing."

"I hopped on an empty freight train yesterday in San Francisco and ended up here. A fellow traveler I was riding with told me that there were some veterans up on the hillside trying to make peace with what happened to them in the war and themselves. You're not a group of Communists, are you? Reds?" Thomas widened his eyes and tried to look concerned. Which he was.

"If we are anything, it's that we want to be free. Some think we're bohemians, but it's more than that. Some say we're Socialists. Others say we're crazy."

"What is Socialism?" Thomas asked, knowing full well what the answer should be. He scrapped the last of the porridge from the bowl. Although not appetizing looking, it was flavored with banana, honey, and walnuts. The tea, however, tasted a whole lot like the smell of freshly mowed lawn. *Not unpleasant, although it has a bitter aftertaste,* Thomas thought as he finished the cup. It was quickly refilled by one of the women, and he smiled at her.

The women were dressed respectably, not a naked one in the bunch, Thomas noted. They seemed to all wear long flowing skirts, some with embroidered flowers or like a patchwork quilt. Their shirts were of plain fabric and they wore scarves around their heads. Some were adorned with strings of beads, some had on sandals and others wore boots. A couple were barefoot.

Thomas stifled a yawn, not even realizing that he was tired, which he shouldn't be as it was still not even ten. He was relaxed and happy. The sky was intensely blue. A flock of blackbirds skittered in the trees, and then they chirped in unison. It was as if they were singing just for him. The breeze through the tall trees seemed to be whispering to each other, looking down on Thomas, and one attempted to smile. A fat squirrel stopped across the meeting area and lifted a paw. *Did that animal just wave at me?* He laced his fingers together, overriding the desire to wave back.

Gus sipped tea. He smiled, and his eyes seemed to be focused on something in the distance.

Thomas turned to look but just saw the swaying of the huge trees. Yes, they *were* happy, and Thomas had the urge to paint them, although he'd never painted anything in his life—except the outdoor furniture in the garden.

Gus poured more tea. "Socialism is a populist economic and political system based on collective, common, or public owner-ship of the means of production. Those means of production include the machinery, tools, and factories used to produce goods that aim to directly satisfy human needs."

Thomas blinked, finished the tea, and had a third, realizing his mind was keenly aware of what his new friend was saying. The idea of becoming a Socialist seemed sensible, and Thomas always considered himself an open-minded, levelheaded man.

Thomas found he was nodding in agreement.

"All we have, we share. We have enough. Enough is all any of us need, right, Tom?" He nodded toward another man who was raking leaves. "He's a tuna fisherman. Well, he was. Something happened with his boss and possibly the boss's wife. Never knew the details, and he's settled in here now. It's calm and quiet except for our grape festivals when we invite the county to come up for wine, dances, and crafts. None of us want to toil in a factory or work in an office with some old fat cat bureaucrat." The man rubbed his scruffy beard and swung his legs out from under the worn picnic table.

Thomas understood at once what the American meant. In the British newspapers, a fat cat is often depicted as a cat-faced, corpulent, middle-aged man clad in a pin-striped suit and holding or smoking a thick cigar, representing a venal banker, a greedy executive, or "captain of industry."

"Come on, Tom, walk around the compound with me. Steady there, man. The tea is sometimes too strong for newcomers like you." He grabbed Thomas's shoulder.

"I am not looking to stay here, Gus. Just passing through and heard about how disenchanted citizens were forming a community. Wanted to see it for myself, you understand." Thomas internally cheered as he was wondering if he could make a complete sentence because his tongue felt disjointed from his brain. He had to concentrate doubly hard, checking in his mind that the comments included verbs and nouns.

He'd been drunk one or two times, if he was honest, during university, and the wobbly feeling of his knees and the cooked spaghetti sense of his body shouted that there was more in that "tea" than tea. "Just visiting, Gus." Thomas followed the man along a path that led to what he assumed were sleeping tents and outbuildings, taking deep breaths of the clean mountain air, which seemed to clear his mind.

"A lot of us, after being discharged, floundered. I did and got in trouble once or twice. Now I've got a prison record, so it'd be tough to get a teaching job even if I wanted to, which I don't. The community is just building here, Tom. I predict when more vets learn about us, more free spirits, clusters like ours, will grow. We might even start another over in the Solvang area. Been talk already.

"We don't have a name yet, but outsiders call us The Mountain Drivers, and some call us names, think we're up to no good. You see, we just don't fit the mold. Like I said, we just want to live, to be free. This isn't utopia, not some Shangri-la in the hills. Think of it much like the neighborhood where you grew up. It's got problems, but we choose to work for the good of the whole. We celebrate diversity. Think that's the magic of the place."

Thomas breathed in the pine and eucalyptus scent carried on the breeze, felt the sunshine on the back of his shirt, and realized, quite suddenly, that he was happy and at peace. "It is nice in the mountains," he said, surprised that he'd verbalized the thought. He vowed to think before speaking again, or possibly he'd give away his disguise.

"Quiet, too," said Gus. "During the war, I swore if I made it back home alive, I'd never get angry with anyone of any color or persuasion again. When I was discharged, I was broken and broke. It was in a police cell in LA, arrested for being drunk and disorderly, when I heard about Mountain Drive. I thumbed my way here and haven't left."

"Was that when the group started?"

"Close after. Mountain Drive's founder and culture shaper, Bobby Hyde, acquired fifty acres of fire-scorched land for a relative pittance in 1940 and then sold parcels to like-minded free spirits and bohemians-in-training. The first group was building houses when I arrived, mostly from adobe. We have a lot of dirt around here. No building codes required. No interference from city authorities. We have about twenty loose-knit families, some monogamous, and some people like me have connections but prefer to be less encumbered. What is marriage anyway? Do we need yet another contract, another restriction?"

Thomas looked west and saw the Pacific. He took a deep breath, and this time, the scent of sage mingled with the sunshine. "You've created a communal enclave of societal outliers."

"You look like you could fit in here, unless you're itching to travel. We could use strong men like you to help build structures and work in the fields. We've got a vineyard that's producing wine grapes and plan to bottle more next season to sell. Sorry you missed the fall grape stomping and festival. Although it was a cool day, and with clothes being optional, we didn't get as many visitors participating as we anticipated. As word spreads, the festival will grow. We even crowned a Miss Grape." He pointed to a young woman chopping vegetables and then waved to her.

"Clothes optional?"

CHAPTER EIGHTEEN

"Yeah, man, but only if a person wants. There are no rules, including the fact that if you want to drink your day away, like that guy against the tree, it's your call. Our mandate is we do no harm to others, and we have no set laws like in the city, state of California, or America. We have leaders known as 'the cluster' and these are the men who make the decisions about what's best for the collective. We discuss any issues that arise, vote, and then tell the rest of the group."

"This is a lot to absorb, Gus, especially for a Brit like me brought up with too many regulations and mandates of etiquette. Seems to me that this is a male-dominated domain," Thomas said, knowing that he and Beatrix were partners and he could hear her opinion of the workings of the community in his head.

"You noticed that, huh? Some are old fashioned and think drinking and having sex with nubile teenage girls is their right in life. A lot of the men have the idea that we need to keep 'em barefoot, in the kitchen, and pregnant. We're not all that way. I'm certainly not, even if I do have more than one wife. How about lunch and meet the cluster?"

They walked more and talked about the worries of the world, the Cold War, the problems in education, and the strength of the country against the power of the Soviet Union. Time slipped away, and Thomas was shocked, if he were to admit it, but he shared many values with Gus and the folks on Mountain Drive.

The communal lunch was served from great steel pots, and it was some kind of thick soup or stew. Thomas didn't want to know what the protein was. He feared for the worst and thought it might be rat, since he'd seen one earlier in the day that had been about the size of a small cat. It scurried between the buildings and if there was one rat, there were more rats. He pushed the brown gloppy meal around in the handmade ceramic bowl. He could identify potatoes and carrots, and something slimy that could possibly be onion. He nodded politely, accepting another hunk of brown bread which tasted like molasses. Then had a few more mugs of grass-flavored tea.

Lunchtime conversations were heated about President Truman calling for workers not to strike, the weather, and the birth of two babies, with one of the men taking great pride that he was the father of both. The mothers were sisters, and somehow that made the delivery and the commune members even happier.

This is crazy, he thought. *Has to be the tea.*

Thomas started to look at this watch, then realized he'd left the shiny Rolex on a bedroom dresser. He glanced at the sky and the shadows. They were starting to lengthen and he needed to get back to his real life. A part of him, not connected with his scientific brain, wondered if he could survive in the commune. What would happen if he slipped out of his shirt and dashed straight away into the bubbling creek he'd been mesmerized by? Then he thought of Beatrix, undercover on the railroad line, dealing with racists and thugs. Then of tiny Birdy, so sweet and perfect. He would never let his child run naked in front of strangers. He would not expose her to loud drunks, rough language, and then there were wandering eyes and possibly the hands of older men. What kind of caring parent could do that to an innocent child?

"Mind if I walk around alone and maybe come back, Gus? You've thrown a lot at me, and I don't know if I'm ready to settle down."

"Sure, man. You can help make bricks tomorrow. We're going to enclose the eating area so we can share meals and have meetings even in bad weather. With the rain like we had last month, we've got to get the gathering hall done."

Thomas turned and waved, heading back up the steep climb to the paved street and eventually to his car. He longed for a hot shower only after a cup of builder's tea and a long, strong hug from his wife. Once again, he marveled at her resolve to right wrongs, her bravery, and how, too often, she'd dealt with criminals. Now she was undercover asking perilous questions of dangerous people in order to flesh out the KKK. *Beatrix is so brave, and I can't stay six hours in the strangeness of Mountain Drive.*

Muddled in the memories of the morning and whatever had been in the tea, Thomas recalled laughing, a lot, with Gus as he boasted about an "over the banks" club for residents, where members egged each other on to drive their cars over the side of the road after perhaps imbibing too much Pagan wine. Too much "tea."

"Never again . . . if there is an again," Thomas said, then felt the pain of remembering the children. The adults would have hangovers, which would be their own fault. Yet, the kids? These boys and girls would likely have a lifetime of emotional aftereffects experienced as children of alcoholics and the free-spirited lifestyle. Those would be more lasting than the consequences of their parents' alcohol consumption and moral decisions. His heart felt heavy as he drove through the city and finally pulled the Ford into the carport. His head felt as if someone were playing a steel drum inside his brain.

He sat there for the longest time after he took out the letter from Dr. Einstein that had been stuffed in the back pocket of his shabby pants. He looked at the typewritten address and the return address. He'd been rejected from scientific institutes before. *The great scientist came to his senses and doesn't want me or my work to be done at Princeton. I still have my position here at the university. Nothing will change, and we're happy here. Why am I even considering working with him? Because, you dolt,* he thought, *it's Albert Einstein.*

Finally, he slid an index finger under the seal and pulled out the letter. He closed his eyes knowing that whatever it said would be the right thing for him and his family.

The message was just a few typewritten lines:

Dear Dr. Ling.

I am enroute to California on another matter. If you are available, I would like to meet to encourage you on your vital energy work, possibly here in my lab. My secretary, who is already in your city, will telephone you when I arrive at my lodging. Then we must confirm a time and place to meet.

A. Einstein.

As he walked into the kitchen, smelling a savory meal on the stove and fresh baked bread cooling on the counter, he knew returning to the commune was imperative if he was going to discover a link between the man who died there of a tranquilizing dart to the foot and the Union Pacific executive. If, in fact, there was one. He'd been too drunk of "tea" to even remember the stun gun question. He wanted to help Beatrix complete the investigation quickly, so he could focus on stopping the blackmailer and contemplate uprooting his family and his work to New Jersey. He had to return and get answers.

He longed to wrap his arms around Beatrix, hold their baby, and praise God that he was normal, or normal-ish. *Other than getting blotto on that crazy, alcoholic tea and having a tour of the compound, I accomplished nothing today,* he thought and looked at the clock over the stove. Beatrix would return in an hour, and he'd tell her everything.

"She'll know what to do," he said. "Including my meeting with the world's leading scientist. Oh, I'm staggered. I will probably not even be able to speak a coherent sentence when I meet him, the greatest living scientist in the world."

At this same time, Beatrix was monitoring the passengers on the afternoon train from Los Angeles to Santa Barbra. After she ended her shift in Santa Barbara, the train would continue on to Lompoc, San Luis Obispo, and eventually to San Francisco. There it would switch engines and crew again, heading to Seattle.

Lunch in the crew room was far more uneventful than the first day. She read, others chatted, one man listened to horse races on the radio. Ken Purdue didn't stop to talk with anyone. She saw him rush from one place to another, and when the train was heading north, he disappeared altogether.

Back on board, Marcus, the kindly porter, gave her coffee from the serving tray and refused when she tried to pay. "You look like you can use a cup, Chuck."

"Been a porter long?" Beatrix leaned against the door that led to the next car.

"Daddy was a porter, big brother was, and looks like my oldest boy's going to join us. I do my job and take home my paycheck. Been a good life."

"Planning to retire soon? You used a past tense for that verb, so I assume you're nearing the end of your career. I've got years ahead of me," she said, keeping her voice as baritone as possible.

"Six months more. I seen stuff in my day that might shock a young man like you. In the old days, long before the war, there were times when it wasn't safe for a Black man to walk through the railroad yard at night alone. Especially when I started in Mississippi. Wife and I came west in 1939. Safer out here."

"I am sorry. What of the ghastly prejudices these days, Marcus? Still around?" She liked Marcus, his open smile, and his easy manner.

"Sure thing, there is. Scrape the surface and ugly is just under it. You can put lipstick on a pig, Chuck, but you're still going to have a pig. Because I'm just a porter and about ready to live a quiet life, I got no troubles. Everybody knows I'm not one to make no fusses, so some of the conductors let things slip."

"Like what?" she whispered and inched closer, keeping her head cocked.

"Like the Union. A few of the men are against it privately, how the dues go to things that aren't needed. Then there are the ones who are in cahoots with secret clubs, and I heard even one wanted to disrupt the schedule."

"Think these are the Communists we keep hearing about?"

He looked at his well-polished shoes, straightened his black hat, and said the next thing so quietly Beatrix had to lean further in. "Not the Commies, my friend. I'm talking about homegrown factions, been around since the Civil War. You might want to steer clear—" He stopped, his chin went up, and he saluted as Ken Purdue stepped through the sliding door at the back end of the train car. "Afternoon, sir."

"Yeah, Marcus," Purdue barked. "What's with you? Knock of lounging about, man. You think it's your break time or something? Chuck has more important stuff to do than to listen to your whining and gossiping. Besides, you're needed in the next train car. A kid just peed all over the aisle. Go clean it up," he snapped.

"Yes, sir, right away." Marcus grabbed some towels, and

without making eye contact with Beatrix, he dashed to the next train car.

"Mr. Purdue," Beatrix started, noting they were about to pull into the tiny Santa Barbara depot. "Friendly of you to ask me to the bar. I thank you."

"We'll do it again, but I've got a big meeting tonight. Thought of inviting you there, too, but someone said I'd better get to know you more. You a traditional thinking man or one of the gawd-awful liberals?"

"I don't have an opinion, sir. Been in the service and seen battle and just want to have everything good and right just like America should be," she said, wondering if that made sense at all.

Apparently, it did, as Purdue gave her a thumbs up and slapped her on the back. "Yes, we need to keep things as they were, in the old days when everybody knew their place, and we were safe. Where'd you grow up, young man?"

Where had Chuck George grown up? Her mind raced to the only other city in America she knew well during her time as the Robin Hood of fake psychics. "Way outside New Orleans, sir. Family been there awhile. After being discharged, and with this game leg, I wanted to see America, the country I fought for. The railroad suits me."

"Louisiana? Hmm, good folks there. My wife's got a relative in public service, a highfaluting brother. You don't happen to know anyone in the government there?"

"My family farms, sir. Been to the city. Too busy for my taste. I'm from one of those Cajun parishes. Tiny town, sir."

Purdue puffed out his chest. "This relative is an important man. You might have heard of him? His name is Ben Long."

Beatrix blinked. "No? Yes? Your wife is related to the governor of Louisiana? Bennington Long? That is a big deal."

"Known Ben all my life. We spent a lot of time together before the misses and I came here. Want to know a secret?"

Beatrix nodded enthusiastically.

"Now don't tell a soul, however, he's going to make an announcement next month. Ben's going to throw his hat in the ring against that nut job Harry Truman. Somebody's got to get our country on solid ground again, especially since we won the war. I think he's got a good chance to win. Plenty of money backing old Ben. Not everybody," he aimed a thumb to his chest, "agrees on Truman's foreign policies, like how he's giving money right and left to the Greek government to keep the Commies out."

"The Soviet Union does seem to be threatening Europe," she said.

He looked like he wanted to spit. "I say let the Reds have Greece. We got enough problems with our own people, keeping them under control, especially some folks who should know better, but then Truman goes giving money away like it grows on trees." Ken Purdue's face slowly splotched with quarter-sized spots of red, and his breathing shallowed. He rubbed his left arm and then shrugged, as if trying to shake off his dislike for the president.

"Times are changing," Beatrix offered.

"You're right, Chuck, and some of us like-minded citizens need to stick together to bring back what's right. Now, you go check on that lay-about Marcus, and make sure our cars are spick and span. I heard we're having an important guest tomorrow. They're putting on the VIP car, all plush cushions and even a small kitchen, with a private restroom. You on that shift from LA?"

"Yes, sir, I am, and I'll check to make sure the cars are ship-shape. You can count on me," she said and headed toward where Marcus was cleaning in the next car.

"Chuck?"

Beatrix turned. He walked closer and looked at her intently. Had he found her out? Was he searching her face for stubble and failed to find it? She yanked out a handkerchief, and pretended to sneeze so she could move away from his curious appraisal.

CHAPTER NINETEEN

"BEEN THINKING, SON," PURDUE BEGAN, "I WANT YOU conducting in the executive train car tomorrow unless it might be too much responsibility for you? Being new and all."

"I'll make you proud of the Union Pacific Railroad, sir."

The train pulled into Santa Barbara, and Beatrix walked through the empty cars, gathering the debris that humans leave behind, picking up trash, and discarding afternoon newspapers.

"That's kind of you, Chuck," Marcus said, wheeling a trash container down the aisle and taking a moist cloth to the leather seats. "Some conductors think it's beneath them to pick up even a chewing gum wrapper. You're good people, son."

"Mighty glad to help, sir." Beatrix put her chin down and smiled, exiting the train. She stopped in the depot, and Maria, undercover, was still at the ticket counter. She waved and called Beatrix over. "Easy shift, Chuck?"

"Just like I like them."

"I know you're alone in town, and I thought you might like this book if you have time in the evenings. It's called *The Big Fisherman*." She slipped the book across the counter and smiled, nodding toward it.

Beatrix walked to the ticket counter, knowing there would be a note inside. "I've heard of the novel, ma'am. Isn't it about teaching in the time of Jesus?"

"Didn't know if you were a religious man, but there's a lot of adventure in it. I thought you'd like it."

"Kind of you. Good evening." Beatrix slipped the hefty novel under her arm and limped out of the station. She would not allow herself to open the book until she was safely back at home. As she did previously, she traveled a convoluted route home, making sure she wasn't followed or attracting any attention.

Beatrix's mind poured over and over how Purdue's eyes zeroed in on her face. His facial muscles and eyes revealed no hint of surprise. *Can he be that good of an actor?* she thought.

Finally in the carport, she stopped, shrugged out of the uniform's jacket, put it on the hood of the Ford, and opened the book. There was a note folded in three, and it said:

The young ticket agent Dora and Grayson Welsh were lovers. He dumped her last week. He had the audacity to come into the station and demand she return all the jewelry he'd given her, or so the rumor mill says. She refused, and a couple of the porters had to pull her off of Welsh. Then she meekly followed Welsh out. Sorry I missed that spectacle. Could it be part of the inquiry? I'll tell the detective when I finish my shift.

Beatrix opened the kitchen door and stopped. Someone who looked exactly like her always-immaculately dressed husband was reading a story to their child. The man was scruffy and dirty. "Thomas, are you going to a costume party as a vagrant?"

"You will not believe the day I have had, Bea. I'm busting with news although I don't know that I have helped with the research at all. This is my undercover costume. Good for the gander and so on . . ."

"Mister Goose, you never stop amazing me with how clever and resourceful you are. You invaded the commune, didn't you? Should our baby hear about the wantonness, nude orgies, debauchery, and drunken parties that you have been exposed to?"

He laughed, and little Birdy reached out for Beatrix, squealing, "Mummeee."

She kissed the plump infant and breathed in the intoxicating smell of cookies and baby lotion. "I missed you, too, Birdy. Mummy's been on her feet all day." She sat at the kitchen table and slipped off the black sturdy work boots. She rubbed her feet with one hand while drinking the water that Thomas offered with the other. "I have news, too, Thomas. But you first. I am still in shock about how rough and ruggedly handsome you look. I love your debonair persona, yet there's something extremely appealing to this new side of you that we can talk about later, if you like." She winked and smiled.

"Oh, Bea, I certainly do like that a lot. I definitely do. Now, about my day?" He explained how he created his clothing to look like a vagabond and how Gus, who seemed in a position of leadership up on Mountain Drive, accepted him without too many questions. "The tea, which smelled just like when our lawn is being mowed, was odd. I've never tasted anything like it, not unpleasant, mind you, just odd. With a lingering fresh, almost apple taste. I think it was dodgy—good but peculiar. It did not taste alcoholic. However, possibly it could have been a hallucinogenic tea. The other community members were often laughing and smiling, even when standing in the sun and chopping wood."

"Did it feel like when you were drugged by that crazy neighbor? Did you experience any psychedelic effects? Did it change the way you saw, heard, tasted or felt, or your mood?"

He massaged his forehead with the heel of his hand. "I did feel a bit wobbly. Nonetheless, it could have been because I skipped breakfast, although they shared their food with me. Truthfully, I was starving when I left. I also enjoyed the outdoors more than I remember, hearing the birds chirping their hearts out. Truth be told, darling, I briefly pondered running into the shallow creek that goes through the property. I've never been an outdoorsman, yet I think I could like it. Have you ever been camping, dear? Slept in a tent and eaten meals by a campfire?"

Her forehead knitted. "How are you feeling now, darling?" She looked closely at his face to read it as well as listen to his words while checking his pulse and feeling his forehead for a fever. "You look absolutely intact, except for those grubby clothes. Have you discussed this outdoors he-man transformation with Birdy yet? I think it's a marvelous idea, actually. Truly, are you okay?"

"Fit as a fiddle, whatever that means. As soon as I got back to the car, the tea's effects disappeared, and the cheese and pickle sandwich I packed helped immensely. The members there were a fascinating example of societal nonconformists."

"Tell me about the people you met?"

"Gus? Kind and a good listener. He explained their free-spirited group, and intellectually, it sounded like a utopia. In reality, I did not like it. The residents looked happy, well-nourished, and seemed to be working together if they wanted to."

"Except?"

"It was the macho dominance and lower status of the women in the community that troubled me. Then there are the children, Bea." He kissed Birdy's pudgy hand and ran a finger down her cheek.

"Were they neglected or seemed to be abused in any way?" Beatrix asked.

"I am not a prig or a stuffed shirt. Am I?"

"You're British, so being a bit of a stuffed shirt comes with your accent or how others perceive you, Thomas. I've never ever found you to be a prude at all. As you know, I'm quite fond of your posh ways."

"Well, that is a massive relief. You see, I found it disquieting that quite a number of the children ran around unclothed or only partially dressed. The ones just learning to walk," he nodded at Birdy, "just had T-shirts on, nothing on the bottom. I had heard of the clothing optional part of the commune, but these little tikes were everywhere, some of the older ones, well, how do I put this . . ."

"Were starting to develop? Is that what you mean?"

He swallowed. "I am a prig about this. The majority of the group, as I perceived it, were men. A few uncomfortable times during the hours I was there, I could see the children getting sly, interested looks from the blokes. I was appalled and, yes, shocked. Gus, who gave me the tour, didn't lift an eyebrow, so apparently, this was a common sight. I longed to speak out yet said nothing. I am extremely uncomfortable about that situation, Bea. I'm ashamed that I tried to ignore it."

"For that alone, I am not at peace with this community," Beatrix stated.

"Should we consult with the authorities about this issue?"

"Instead, let's return there for more information. I'll go with you, and we'll not tell them we're married. I'll pose some questions pretending that I'm considering setting up a free-spirited community near San Diego, near the beach. I'm sure they don't have a business model, but they will want to talk. Suppose there is even appropriate sanitation? That could be a legal issue if the Santa Barbara county government wants to bother with the free spirits. Are the children sent to school, even? I can check for neglect in that area. Then, by observing their microfacial expressions, I should be able to tell if the children and women are feeling threatened or in danger."

"One more thing. They practice polygamy. Gus was quite boastful about his 'collection' of wives."

"Unless they're all legally married to him and others, that's not against the law," Beatrix said.

"Are you sure?"

"Thomas, we should visit. I've been in treacherous situations before. I doubt that visiting a chauvinistic group of partially clad and drunken people is going to muddle with my psyche, do you?"

"As for tomorrow, I have an appointment in the late afternoon. Are you also conducting on the train tomorrow?"

"Yes, so it'll have to be Friday. Ken, the senior conductor, told me that a VIP is going to be on the train from LA tomorrow. That's why I'm late tonight. After we pulled into the depot, Ken barked out orders that every surface needed to be immaculate. No one was to leave until he inspected the nooks, crannies, and toilets. We had to polish the brass fittings until they sparkled and wipe down the seats with a special leather cleaner. Whomever the guest is, they've commissioned a special luxury car, and Ken wants me on it. Has to be a superstar."

"Why you, darling? Not that you aren't the best conductor I've ever kissed, but why? Wait, I take that back as I've never kissed another train conductor. You do know what I'm rambling on about, right?"

"A marvelous question, dear husband of mine. Maybe the others don't want the extra responsibility or to be at someone's beck and call for four hours when they can lounge in the other cars. I imagine the person will be a famous movie star like Ingrid Bergman, Rita Hayworth, or, wait, Humphrey Bogart or Ronald Coleman? Should I try to get their autograph for you, or would that be too gauche?"

Thomas laughed when Beatrix giggled like a teenager. "Maybe it'll be a movie mogul, and you'll be discovered as a dapper leading man. Oh, wait, you're my lovely, most feminine wife. I concede that wouldn't work for the long term. Could it?" he teased.

Beatrix's face clouded. "Seriously, I'm glad you went to the commune. I never thought of the dark side of Mountain Drive and the children involved. It's unfortunate, and honestly, I believe there are other cults and subgroups around the country also functioning this way. Thomas, might we, if John goes through with asking me to be the executor of his fortune, somehow create a group that will put the welfare of children first?"

Thomas picked up Birdy from where she was now sitting on the floor, chewing on her teddy bear's ear. "We could work to get laws passed to protect little ones and make abuse a criminal offense. Blimey, one more thing. I never got around to asking my new friend Gus about pumas and why their compatriot was using a stun gun when he shot himself in the foot."

"We'll find the answer. The women, I think, are more likely to tell me when we visit. As a male-dominated group, they'd be hesitant to say anything to you, especially a stranger, about how they're treated. Or if they can simply walk away from the life-style or not."

Thomas held Birdy, and Beatrix took a moist kitchen towel and wiped her hands. "I never thought when I joked about the orgies that I would come away so disillusioned with these free-spirited nature lovers."

"What is that delicious smell? You haven't magically created a meal for a hungry conductor, have you?" She lifted the pot lid and sighed. "Did Lillian make us dinner?"

Thomas leaned into Beatrix as she peeked into the large pot that was bubbling on the stove. "She's amazing, you know. Can we adopt her away from Jo and Sam? Yes, it's chicken stew with loads of veggies. She instructed me to let it cool and then chop it into tiny cubes for Birdy, which I'll do right now."

Thomas popped the little girl into her highchair and placed a

handful of oat cereal, known as Cherioats, on the tray. "That'll
keep you busy while Daddy gets your food."

"I need to change before dinner, Thomas, and then you must
give me a full report on whatever else it is you need to tell me.
Yes, I did read your face, and even with the weight of visiting
the compound, you're excited. I can tell. I'll be back in a jiffy."

By the time Beatrix washed off the day's dirt and grime,
changed into a loose gray pullover and jeans, and returned to
the kitchen, the table was set, candles had been lighted, and the
red wine had been poured. Birdy was again carrying on an unin-
telligible conversation with her stuffed toy and crawling around
the kitchen floor, dragging the bear behind her.

"Sit down, my lady." Thomas folded a cloth napkin over his
forearm, bowed elegantly, and pulled out her chair. "I tried to
slice the bread, but it is so fresh that I made a mess."

She took a chunk the size of an orange from the breadbasket
and said, "Let's not leave a crumb. Then it won't matter."

Between mouthfuls of the savory stew, Thomas shared Dr.
Einstein's latest note. "He wants to meet with me on Thursday
or Friday. The man is making a special trip. Actually, apparently,
he has other business in Santa Barbara, but I'm gobsmacked. I'm
terrified that he will learn I'm noddy and nervous."

Beatrix grabbed his hand. "You are being silly, you know.
Thomas, I'm so proud of you. The work you're doing is being
noticed, dearest, and you really are going to make the world a
better place. Have you thought of inviting him here, to the
house, for dinner? I won't cook, I promise, but we can hire our
Lillian to create a feast. I'd be over the moon to meet him, but I
completely understand if you want to keep the meeting at their
hotel."

"I have not mentioned any of this to the staff or provost at
the university. But the timing might be off, especially if Long
goes through with blackmailing John and us."

"That governor must be stopped, but how?" Beatrix asked.

"In my mind, I pour over every detail and cannot fathom what we can do so that John is free of the crook and we can continue our lives. It's so blooming frustrating."

"I don't see a simple solution or even a complex one, Bea. By the way, although he didn't ask, I have not told anyone of Dr. Einstein's visit. Otherwise, there would be fans of the doctor lining State Street, or maybe protesters, too. He can be quite controversial." Thomas poured more wine and sat back in the kitchen chair. "I would never have imagined when I discovered you in New Orleans that fateful day in 1942, our lives would have brought us here, doing what we do, whatever that is. And our beautiful little daughter chewing on the leg of this kitchen table."

Beatrix looked under the table and gasped. "Thomas, oh my goodness, stop her."

Birdy and Thomas were asleep when Beatrix slipped into the wool conductor's uniform, grabbed the messenger bag with a sack lunch tucked inside, and left the house the next morning. If there was time, on her way to the train depot, she wanted to call in at the police station and talk with Detective Rodriguez to see if there was anything to the liaison and subsequent argument between Grayson Welsh and Dora Smith. *I just can't see Dora, tiny thing that she is, firing a tranquilizing gun. She has money. She could hire someone. However, I can see her doing it if she wanted to retaliate against Grayson for breaking her heart. Smothering the man, even if he was paralyzed, would take muscle. She doesn't look that strong. Maybe I don't either, but I could fire a gun.*

Beatrix reached the courthouse, and no matter how often she visited, the shockingly expansive emerald-green lawns and wide, white marble steps always delighted her senses. As soon as

Birdy could walk, they'd picnic on those lawns, like the locals did.

As she moved toward police headquarters, passing the coroner's office, the door was ajar, and young Rudy was, per usual, sitting there, feet up at his desk with a Superman comic in his hand. A spark connected. She felt, more than knew, that somehow, she had a solution to John's dilemma and their tragic decision, but like the fog that came into the city at dusk, it suddenly slipped away, opaque.

As much as her mind tried to grab that vague idea and turn it into reality, it flitted away like a butterfly gliding on the breeze. She put her frustration aside, hoping that the brilliant notion that would solve the blackmail issue might come around again.

Just outside the bullpen were Maria Davies and Stella Rodriguez huddled in the corner. "Good morning," Beatrix said, knowing that whatever they were whispering about would either be shared or not.

"Hey, there, young man. Chuck, long time no see, as your precious mama always says to me." Stella shook Beatrix's hand, then introduced Maria as a friend.

That was her cover; the young conductor's mother was a friend of Stella's. No one in the bullpen, filled with police, even gave Chuck a second glance after that.

If there was corruption in the department, news of Beatrix being undercover with the Union Pacific could get back to whomever was instigating the violence and put Beatrix's life in danger.

Stella slid her arm under Beatrix's elbow and said in a louder-than-necessary voice, "Now, Chuck, you tell your mama to call me. Thank her for the letters and all the news from my hometown." Then, in a whisper, she said, "We're investigating Kay Welsh's connection with Mountain Drive. I'll call you tonight." Again, for whoever was listening, "Tell your mom that I'll be visiting in June."

"Yes, ma'am." Beatrix tipped her conductor's hat. *Kay Welsh and Mountain Drive. Kay Welsh and her swim partner. Kay Welsh and the pool maintenance staff. Kay Welsh and Mrs. Antoinette Du Bois. Then there was the frisky, to be polite, Grayson Welsh and most probably countless women who had motives to hurt or kill him for what he had done or tried to do to them.* As Beatrix headed down State Street to the depot, she reviewed all the pieces of information on his death, and there was no headway. It was like a complex jigsaw puzzle, and half the pieces were missing.

She walked past a military surplus store. Army green uniforms, leftover or sold by veterans after the war, were stacked in the window. There was a great pile of surplus knives and shovels. She stopped. Turned. Walked into the shop.

She lowered her voice in an attempt to sound like a man. "Excuse me, this is an odd question, but do you get any surplus from Africa?"

"What ya lookin' fer, kid?" came the response from the grizzly clerk, scratching his beard as he looked Beatrix up and down.

"I have a friend who needs a gun that can shoot tranquilizers. He's an avid hiker, and he's afraid of the wild pumas."

"Had two, ways back, and nobody touched them for five years or more, then bang, sold 'em in one day. Never know when I'll get more."

"Are these considered dangerous guns? Does a man need a permit for them?"

"Not in California, not yet anyhow. Lots of vets kept their weapons when they were discharged. I sure as shootin' did. You in the war, young fellow?"

"Yes, Guam and places I'd rather forget."

"You say a friend wants a gun? I might know who bought one of the guns. Since the two guys here in town got shot with them, I'm not surprised, especially after the stories in the news-paper. Come back, say, on Saturday. The folks who bought it don't have a telephone, so I'll drive out there after I shut the shop and ask."

Beatrix reached into her pocket and pulled out a five-dollar bill—enough money to buy groceries for a family for the week. "To make it worth your while. If your contact wants to sell the gun, can you make sure it works?"

A smile formed on his beaded face, revealing several missing teeth. "Always do. No use carrying a gun if you aren't prepared to use it."

CHAPTER TWENTY

Could this army surplus shop be where the murder weapon was purchased? Beatrix stuck out her hand. "I'm Chuck. I'll stop in next week, okay?"

They nodded to each other. *The people who bought a dart gun don't have a telephone, he'd said. Not everyone does, but I wonder if the clerk could be referring to Mountain Drive. What happened to the gun that the member used to shoot himself in the foot? I need to ask that when Thomas and I go to the camp.*

She limped on toward the depot; trying to stay in the character of young Chuck George was not easy. *Hopefully, there'll be a lead in the killing of Grayson Welsh, and I can return to being a psychologist, wife, and mom. And wearing my own clothes.*

When she got to the Santa Fe Depot, an old-fashioned wood and metal railroad car was being hooked to the end of the train and the caboose was being realigned second to the end. Sam Conrad was watching as well. "I always walk the entire train before we leave in the morning and again when we reach the destination. Not my job, but the safety of the cargo and these folks is my responsibility." Beatrix nodded as she walked next to him.

"Sir, will that be for the VIP who's going to board when we get to Los Angeles?" she asked her friend.

"Yep, just waiting to have the final connection, and then I'm going to look inside. Been with the railroad my whole working life, except during the war, and I never been in one of these babies. Might never again. Got to see how the other half lives. Really fancy. Don't you think, Chuck?"

"Ken assigned me to work alone on the car. There won't be anyone in there on our trip south to LA except one, but the person or persons coming back are still a mystery. Do you think Ken even knows who our passenger is? The president? A movie star?"

"My money's on a movie star getting the full Hollywood treatment. I didn't read anything in the newspaper about Truman coming to California, but it could be the governor. Nah, he loves publicity. He wouldn't travel without the press corps and all his entourage." One of the workers signaled to Sam that it was safe to board the train car. He climbed the polished steel steps, and Beatrix was right behind him.

"It's like an extravagant living room, not a train," she said. Overstuffed sofas and chairs in azure-blue velvet lined the walls. The tables, a small writing desk, and the side chairs were mahogany so polished they glowed. Velvet drapes patterned with Art Deco geometrical designs covered the windows. Plush blood-red carpet lined the floor. A small kitchen was partially concealed with a pale-blue velvet curtain. It was gaudy and glitzy, over the top, as if it were last used to transport silent film stars in the Roaring Twenties, before the Great Depression, before the war. Seemed to be deemed appropriate for the VIP who'd use it that day.

"This is where I'll be serving the passengers." She looked in the cupboard and found green tea, black tea, and Earl Grey. The coffee was already ground and in a smart-looking glass jar. The cabinet next to the sink held a bowl of apples, oranges, and bananas, and in another, there was a selection of cookies that looked like they came from a high-end bakery. Packets of individually wrapped sugar cubes were in a crystal bowl on the counter. "Our guests certainly won't starve during the two hours from LA to Santa Barbara."

Sam tested the cushion. "I need one of these puffy pillows for my engineer's seat in the front of the train." He laughed and fluffed a sofa cushion.

Beatrix checked the ice box. Champagne, beer, wine, and a pitcher of water were neatly arranged. "Oops. There's no milk or cream for the hot drinks," she said.

"Maybe that's why Purdue asked you to operate on this car. I have a feeling most of the conductors wouldn't think to give the place a look-see, and we cannot have our VIP drinking coffee without cream." Sam laughed. "Takes a woman's touch after all, and I, for one, know the rails would be better if more women were hired."

Beatrix checked her railroad pocket watch, which was connected with a chain looped to her uniform's vest. "I'll dash to the market the next block over and get some. We're not leaving for fifteen minutes."

"I won't let 'em leave without you," Sam assured her.

She was just exiting the train when the older ticket lady waved and yelled, "Wait up, Chuck. Stop right there. You're not to leave." She awkwardly jogged to Beatrix. The woman's face was deeply lined as if she were a cigarette smoker, and her gravelly voice confirmed it. "Don't you move. Ken said you had to be in the executive car. Told me to keep an eye on you. Wants to make sure you are in that car and ready to help the important people coming from Los Angeles." She swung her hand out to grab Beatrix's arm, but missed as Beatrix took a step back. The woman's breath came in puffs as if that was the first exercise she had gotten in a decade. "You are forbidden to leave the depot." There was authority in her words, but her face was filled with fear.

"Excuse me, ma'am. I am working on the executive car, and you can tell Ken not to worry."

"Don't you lie to me, mister." Her face was blotchy and red. "I can see with my own eyes what's going on. You were running away." She swiped again. Beatrix jumped back, but the woman snagged the fabric on the uniform, clutching it in a death grip, her knuckles white with pressure.

Beatrix put her palm toward the angry woman's face. Lowering her voice, she said in a calm, singsong way, as one might speak to a traumatized child, "You need to let go of my arm, madam. Relax. I don't know what you think I've done to be pounced on like this, and if I've neglected my duties, I will rectify it. Why are you holding me back?"

"You were escaping, and the train will leave the station in fifteen minutes. You must be on the train." The words squeaked back.

Beatrix peeled the woman's fingers off the fabric of the jacket. "You are greatly mistaken. I am an employee, and I know my duties. Explain why you're stopping me."

"Ken told me you were a slick one. Now you're lying." Her lips puckered as if she'd just eaten a lemon. "Ken knows what everybody is thinking."

Beatrix read the fear in her features. She took a breath and, in Chuck's voice, said, "I suppose you might think I was leaving, but that's far from the case. You see, madam, there is no cream or milk for our important passengers' tea and coffee. Someone neglected to check the provisions." Beatrix stepped away and then added, "You can tell Ken that unless he wants to send someone else, I must dash to the corner market to get what is needed."

"Oh. Well, I just didn't want you, being that you're new and you were injured in the war, to get fired. Thought you'd get in trouble," she said, sighed the lie, and studied her bulky shoes. She blinked and clasped her hands tightly, still unable to make eye contact when she said, "I must find Ken. He's got to know this."

Beatrix read the falsehoods on her face and the dilation of her eyes' pupils. *Why is she so upset? It's Ken behind this. He's threatened her. The bully.* She knew the feeling yet preferred not to acknowledge it. She was walking straight into an ambush. There was no alternative but to be caught in order to learn the truth. *What will happen then?*

Returning with the small glass bottles of milk and cream, she placed them in the icebox. Out the car window, she saw Ken and two of the other conductors in a tight circle. *I can't leave to call Thomas or the police. If I tried, I know they'd stop me. Why? Ken specifically wanted me on this route, on this car, on this day, with their celebrity, and now I'm about to be a player in this subterfuge. It's the only way to stop what Ken and the others are trying to orchestrate.*

She paced the stylish car, looked under the sofas to make sure everything was tidy, and took a soft cloth from the supply cabinet and removed smudged fingerprints from the brass handrail and doorknob leading to the private restroom. Then, she looked again.

This time for explosive devices. It was a peculiar notion, but one that made sense.

Right then, there was nothing to fear, yet the ticket lady's reaction to seeing Beatrix about to leave was bizarre. She tried to shrug off the notion of danger, but it lingered like an unwanted guest.

Making a cup of tea, she sat away from the window so that the other conductors couldn't monitor her movement. *No, wait, they know. Somehow, they know I'm not Chuck George. They're keeping me contained so . . .? What? So I don't tell the VIP that I think they've adopted the horrible agenda of the Ku Klux Klan? That makes even less sense.*

There was a rumble, and she heard the whistle just as a conductor hollered, "All aboard."

She crouched down below the window and went to the side door. It was locked. She'd been locked inside.

"I'm safe as long as I'm here. At Los Angeles, I'll make a commotion and escape. Whatever they're trying to do, I'll have to be faster," she said.

Her senses were on high alert. The sun seemed brighter, and the beach sands whiter as the train moved south through the cozy coastal towns. There was also no place to hide in the upscale car. She'd looked. *I'm a sitting duck. Now, I wait. Wait and hope that I'm prepared for whatever is about to play out.*

Reaching LA, Beatrix believed someone would come for her, whisk her away, possibly by gunpoint, and then what? *Shoot me for accusing them of being part of the Klan? Okay, that's a horrible and honest assessment.*

Still, no one came. She sat alone for two hours, trapped in the rail car as the business of unloading passengers and cargo continued around Union Station. She reviewed every possible evil scenario and threw each out.

The return train to Santa Barbara was scheduled to leave at one o'clock. At ten minutes to the hour, the door opened, and adrenaline shot through Beatrix. *This is it.* She held the edge of the writing desk.

A conductor Beatrix didn't recognize unlocked the door, yelled, "Hello," and stepped aside, still holding the door.

Escaping at that second was her only hope, and just as she was about to push past the burly conductor, a small, bespectacled man with a mass of frizzy gray hair climbed the steps. His eyebrows were inky black, and his eyes seemed to be everywhere, calculating, comparing, and making decisions.

Everyone had seen his photo in countless magazines and newspapers. His untidy appearance was unmistakable.

In person, he looked older, slighter, stooped at the shoulders, and even more fragile. When he smiled, however, it was as if he knew all the answers in the world and wanted to share them. Perhaps he did.

"Good afternoon," he said to Beatrix and held out his hand. "I'm Albert Einstein." His German accent was as soft as his fingers.

Beatrix was close friends, still, with Eleanor Roosevelt, the former first lady of the United States. She knew her share of celebrities, politicians, and the wealthy, especially as she was part of Santa Barbara's circle of philanthropists, including her friend John Brockman.

This was different. This man was one of the greatest scientists to ever live.

Just as Beatrix shook the scientist's offered hand, she heard a click and knew they were both now locked inside. "Good day, sir. Please sit down. What I am about to share with you is of grave importance."

"I am confused, but that happens often. I'm on my way to Santa Barbara to meet a fellow researcher. What can be so urgent?"

Beatrix handed him a glass of water. "Please sit." She joined him on the opposite sofa. "Everything is not what it is supposed to be, Doctor. We've been locked together inside the rail car. I have a hunch as to why, and it's a convoluted, frightening reason."

"I like complicated problems, young man. You must explain it all to me. Unless the train stops, we have hours for you to do so. Do not leave out any details. It's the truth in the smallest element that often brings sense to chaos."

"First off, I am not a conductor."

His bushy eyebrows dashed up. "No? Why are you in a

uniform and on a train? Isn't the most obvious often the correct answer?" His eyes twinkled, clearly fascinated with their situation.

"I am a consultant with the Santa Barbara Police Department, and I am currently working undercover as there has been some trouble. My name is Beatrix Patterson."

"What has happened that the police are involved, Miss Patterson?"

She read his microfacial expressions as he'd spoken, and while there was no shock or concern that she was a woman, there was a worry about their vulnerability. "There's been violence all along the Union Pacific route from Seattle to San Diego. The police believe it to be an anti-union push, but I've ascertained proof that the dreaded KKK is trying to stop African American workers from further joining the union. Their methods, as usual, are ripe with intimidation and bullying. I'm a trained psychologist, and during the war, I worked with the army and our federal government to expose Nazi terrorist cells in New Orleans that were planning to disrupt and cripple commerce along the Mississippi and in the factories there." She removed her hat and felt relieved not to have to talk like Chuck.

The eminent man rubbed at his head, and the hair sprang back in all directions as if a mini tornado had control of it. "You are widely known, Miss Patterson, and I am pleased to make your acquaintance, though perhaps not in these circumstances. You are well spoken of among my circle of colleagues and friends here in California, in Washington, DC, as well as the American South. Perhaps you are not aware that I am visiting Santa Barbara on business, yes, and further to consult with a noted scientist who lives in the city. I am looking forward to staying with my long-time friend, John Brockman."

"I didn't realize you knew John." Beatrix shook her head. "I must explain, then, sir, that Dr. Thomas Ling is my husband,

and while I have longed to meet you, I didn't expect you to be a fellow prisoner in this train car. How small the world is."

He smiled. "John and I have known each other for some time, before the war, and support the same causes. He has written to me about his friend and colleague, the intelligent and clever Beatrix. Furthermore, I have much regard, madam, for the work of your husband. He's insightful and creative with his research, while most in the field prefer to rehash theories. Dr. Ling is willing to risk failure for the advancement of science. That is a quality I highly regard.

"Do you know why our abductors have chosen me? I am no threat to the Klan or any other global movements, except perhaps some of the American lawmakers, if they chose to listen to me. Which I doubt."

"I know we'll have that answer shortly, sir. We're in grave danger. You especially."

"What must we do?" Dr. Einstein asked.

The train bumped along the track, then in the tiny beach hamlet of Oxnard, it slowed, steel wheels squealing as it came to a full stop at the platform. The view from the car stole Dr. Einstein's full attention.

Beatrix peered out the windows and watched a handful of passengers exit the train, greeted by loved ones and striding away. The conductor yelled, "All aboard," and the reverse happened, with a half dozen people boarding the train. On the west side of the train was a row of slightly shabby yet quaint cottages selling local art and ceramics, antiques, coffee, and nooks that sold beachy trinkets. At any other time, she would have made plans to drive to the town and shop for collectibles. Now, however, they were prisoners.

Five minutes later, as Beatrix checked her railroad watch, she heard the screech of the steel wheels again. With a bounce, they were on the move, and her heart beat in the rhythm of the train, chugging along the track. She'd always enjoyed taking the train;

it was rhythmic and comforting. Now the danger could not be denied.

The next stop would be Ventura as they headed north. Then, with a jolt, a resounding thunk, and a clunk, the car slowed. Beatrix assumed there was something on the tracks as had happened in the past when rocks, mud, and debris tumbled from the unstable cliffs above the track. This part of the rail line was precariously close to the ocean on the west and a sheer dirt wall on the east. The bluff of sandy soil was pock-marked with crevasses eaten away by rain and earthquakes. When there had been mudslides the previous winter, the track had been closed for a week from just a small mudslide. As she'd previously read in the paper, for the smaller disruptions, the train crew would drag out shovels to clear the rubble before the train could continue the journey.

She knew that when the biggest boulders slipped down the hillside, the Union Pacific workers brought in tractors to clear away the rocks, some the size of an automobile, and she spotted a skip loader sitting on a small mound as if guarding the mushy soil, in wait for the next avalanche of earth.

She peered out the window, seeing the roof of Casa Verdugo, and on any other day, when she was not imprisoned and heading for whatever horrible end the KKK was planning, she'd dream of owning a home like that. The lavish villa with full ocean views had been the venue of a recent wedding she and Thomas attended, and she had marveled at the architecture, learning that the founder of Oxnard, Miguel Verdugo, built the Spanish Colonial Revival home for a large family as his representation of the California dream in 1927. The story was told that Mr. Verdugo patterned the development of the rest of the city after this property. She and Thomas had visited the hacienda again during the summer for a fundraiser to benefit the arts community in Santa Barbara.

She sat back down, and Dr. Einstein's eyes were closed,

seemingly unbothered by their isolation. She scanned for any activity. *There was none. There are no crews working. Maybe there is a failure with one of the cars.* It was a relief to know that her friend Sam Conrad was steering the massive train engine. *When we get to Santa Barbara, I'll make a huge fuss. Someone will notice.* She tried to relax and sipped water. It did not help. There seemed to be no concern for the workers' safety or an impending landslide above their heads. Everything was far too quiet.

Then, far in the distance, she heard a train whistle. The northbound and southbound trains had to be staggered. There was only a single track in this region. The sound was vibrating from far north. It was the law that the engineer blew the whistle at each road intersection, and Sam blasted the horn twice. He did this as it crossed the main thoroughfare to the beach, and she knew it well. The car that was their current prison did not move. She looked outside; she ran to the door. They were deserted as the main train barreled north.

She swallowed hard and ran through every scenario for escape because there had to be plans for whatever was about to happen. The doors were locked, and the windows had been fitted, at one time, with elaborate-looking bars that bolted shut to protect the prestigious passengers who had traveled previously in this car. She saw the scientist's eyes flicker, and he sat up, scrubbing his fingers again through his outrageous hair. "Have we arrived, Miss Patterson, at our destination?"

"Dr. Einstein, you and I are about to discover just why we've been kidnapped." She folded her hands in her lap. Waiting.

If this had been a movie rather than real life, the next sound would have made a Hollywood director smile. At that instant, the door to the car door swung back. Whatever the scientist was about to say was cut short as he and Beatrix waited.

Beatrix could not help fear that this was how it all would end. Her life did not, as rumored, flash in front of her. Rather time seemed to slow as her mind raced through what would happen. She was hemmed in on all sides, and the sheer audacity of whoever was behind this, abducting the leading scientist in the world, was formidable. She'd heard, from Eleanor Roosevelt and others in the state government of California, that many were against Einstein's radical politics, but to go this far to take him hostage made icy droplets of sweat dash down her back.

Beatrix had studied the life of the scientist, and while he was reportedly an agnostic, he'd been raised as a secular Ashkenazi Jew. He had fled the brutality of Naziism early on, but she knew in her heart that Einstein's family and friends would have been destroyed in the gas chambers and death camps of Germany when war shattered everything.

Yes, he knows fear, has seen it, and yet he is outwardly calm.

She tried to match the older man's appearance and composed demeanor. She'd been in crisis situations and held at gunpoint before, yet this time, she'd made the choice to put her life on the line. She always wondered, because of the death of her beloved parents when she was twelve, how she'd die. It was not a negative idea but rather yet another instance of the rational thinking and problem-solving she was so good at. It never seemed possible that it would be in a fancy railroad car with an internationally known scientist or at the hands of KKK-inspired killers. Instinctively, she knew who was behind this, and that made it even more frightening.

The odds of ever again loving Thomas and baby Birdy vanished. She let her back fall against the cushioned sofa and saw Dr. Einstein breathe in deeply and slowly exhale. He was alarmed, as was she, but his face was stiff. There was no way out of the train car, and the man who approached them was pointing a pistol first at Dr. Einstein and then at Beatrix, waving it with demonic pleasure written on his face.

Ken Purdue stepped inside the rail car. In his right hand was a handgun pointed at Dr. Einstein, and in his left was a writing tablet. Quickly, two other men, both of whom Beatrix recognized, climbed the steps. They had been in the scuffle with Sam the day that Grayson Welsh was murdered. Their likeness had appeared on the front page of the newspaper.

Now they were dressed in cheap black suits, white shirts so starched the collars were making red welts on their necks, and wide, silky black ties. One skinny and the other overly muscled, they looked like actors in a low-budget Hollywood gangster movie.

"Sit still, and nobody's going to get hurt," Ken barked what had to be a lie, although Beatrix and the doctor had not moved or shown any sign of wanting to. "I'm calling the shots now, Dr. Einstein and *Miss* Patterson." A cold, smug grin twisted his lips.

"You know me, Ken?" she asked, in the most quiet and calm voice she could muster considering they were about to be murdered.

"I didn't know you at first. Just thought you were a different kind of guy. You pulled the wool over my eyes. Ya see, one of the gals in the ticket office and my wife play bridge. She told my wife she thought you looked familiar; that was on the first day you came into the depot, but I thought she was being ridiculous. She's a foolish old biddy. Can't keep her crazy conspiracy theories and gossip straight. I ignore her, mostly. Turns out she was right. You two were at some kind of charity bazaar. She remembered you because you're so rich. My wife confirmed it when she stopped at the depot to bring me lunch.

"Crazy, I know. You'd met once at a Mardi Gras party. You were telling fortunes for some stupid animal cause in New Orleans. My wife telephoned her brother, who's going to humiliate Truman in the upcoming election. He asked around. Rest is history."

"What is your agenda in taking us prisoner?" Einstein asked; his voice was smooth, and the question was not threatening. Nonetheless, Beatrix saw his pupils were dilated. He was well aware of their vulnerability and was no stranger to the voice of a madman, having warned Germans since the 1930s about the danger of Adolf Hitler. She saw it on his face: the scientist would not back down if the bully pushed too hard.

Einstein's jaw tightened. "I fled my home country because of people like you who think that laws do not matter." He nearly spit out the words, and anger rose to his eyes with the cold, dark resentment born from experiences of the worst the world has to offer.

Ken raised the pistol and took a deep, steadying breath. "I've got no beef with you, Doctor. You help me, and I'll get you safely on your way." The promise came from his mouth, but to Beatrix, the senior conductor's face shouted the lie.

Beatrix pleaded, "Wait, Ken. This is insane. What do you want of us?"

"You're just collateral damage, honey. We could ask for ransom as you're both plenty rich, and the money would help our members, our group, and our future. Which is the right future for America. However, your inferior female brain just can't grasp what's going on under your pointy little nose, can it? This is bigger than you and the geezer here." He indicated to Dr. Einstein with the weapon. "It's bigger than even me. This is big. Big-big. We won't be stopped now."

Eighty-five miles north of where Beatrix and Dr. Einstein were being held at gun point, Thomas was cheerfully on his way to Jo and Sam Conrad's tidy bungalow on Garden Street. He had said he'd wait until Friday to go with Beatrix. But she was so involved in the dispute at the depot that he felt the only husbandly thing to do was help her out.

Before dressing in his undercover tramp outfit and returning to Mountain Drive, he decided he needed to unburden himself of the worry for his wife that was stiffening his shoulders, and Jo was a wise and kind listener.

The March day was clear, and the earth was shouting that spring had arrived, so he had bundled Birdy in the pram and set off to Garden Street. "Nana Lillian will pick you up from Auntie Jo's along with your cousins Jackson and Jefferson. It'll be a play date while Daddy is away."

Reaching the tidy Conrad house, Thomas saw Jo bent over the kitchen table, closely reviewing the papers that were spread out there. He knocked on the back door.

"I'm wearing my chapter's hat for the WCTA," she said after a quick hug.

"I don't have to leave Birdy with you. Lillian had an appointment, and I'd like to dash off. But you're busy. Please don't feel obligated," he responded, seeing the stack of notes and papers spread out in front of his friend.

"I'm nearly finished writing a petition to Governor Warren about the effects of domestic violence. There had been a recent court case where a young mother shot her children's father when he threw one of their toddlers against the kitchen wall. The woman was sent to prison, and her three children were placed in foster care," Jo told Thomas as she took Birdy from his arms and kissed her pudgy cheeks as he parked the elegant baby carriage in the living room. "It's criminal. If a stranger did that, *he'd* have been arrested and charged." She shook her head.

"Will your letters make a difference, Jo?" Thomas asked, seeing the fury on his friend's face.

"Maybe not today. Maybe not even tomorrow. However, if we as citizens recognize that domestic violence is a crime, someday, this will change. Hold Birdy, will you?" She returned the tot to her father's arms. "I need to grab the telephone." She dashed to the front room.

Thomas sat in the cheery kitchen that smelled of dish soap, sugar cookies, and a hit of sea breeze. Jackson and Jefferson were now running in circles around them, and their antics made Birdy giggle. The twins, whom Thomas still could not tell apart, never crawled. They went from being stationary to full-blown running at top speed overnight. The two families felt closer than any friendship Thomas had ever experienced from his upscale background and formal education. While his biological family was close, California families seemed to be even chummier, much more apt to share emotions than his British clan.

He was just explaining all this to Birdy, being bounced on his knees, when he heard a scream. Then, Jo shouted, "Oh, God in Heaven, no."

Thomas put Birdy down on the linoleum and rushed to the front room. Jo stood there in shock.

"Something horrible has happened, Thomas. Something I cannot even think how to tell you. That was Sam. He was calling from the depot in Ventura. It's the train." She steadied herself against the back of the sofa and then started to sway, looking about to faint.

"Jo, tell me. What is it? Is Sam hurt again? Are there riots at the station?" Thomas put an arm around his friend and guided her trembling body to sit on the sofa.

She covered her face with quaking hands. "Sam said the train was going from Oxnard north at about fifty miles an hour along that stretch. Just a normal day. However, when they pulled into the Ventura depot, he got down from the engine to stretch his legs. Then he saw it. Or rather," she gulped, "didn't see it. The car with Dr. Einstein and Beatrix wasn't connected. It had disappeared."

"What? Ridiculous. A thirty-ton railway car cannot disappear. He must be wrong." Thomas felt torment in every fiber of his body constricting, and he could hardly breathe. But Sam was, Thomas knew, telling the terrible truth. "My Bea is on that train. My Bea . . ."

Jo was crying. "Thomas, Sam is there. He's just over ten

miles from the last stop. Sam," she fought tears, sitting up straighter, "has to continue to drive the engine to Santa Barbara. They have to, according to the regulations, but they are sending investigators out right now."

"How long until Sam's here in the city?" Thomas didn't know how his voice could sound so calm to his ears while terror gripped his heart.

Jo grabbed Thomas's hand. "About thirty minutes. Something is horribly wrong, Thomas. I can tell. I've hiked the cliffs north of Oxnard, and they're sheer. There was a landslide in that area two years ago, and some folks who were camping on the beach below were hit with an avalanche of mud and debris. They were never found. That storm washed them and the landslide out to sea. Wait. Thomas, where are you going?"

"Care for Birdy, please, Jo. I don't know how long I'll be," he raced out and sprinted back to his house. He grabbed the station wagon keys from the hook near the back door and stopped in the garage for the work boots and two shovels. He kept blinking away the image of Beatrix and the illustrious scientist trapped inside the railway car beneath a behemoth mudslide. Or suspended and dangling from a cliff, tossed about like leaves ripped from trees in a violent storm.

Tires squealed. Gravel on the driveway kicked the undercarriage as he pulled the Woody out of the carport, onto Anapamu Street, and careened down State Street. Traffic inched along, and Thomas considered taking to the sidewalk with the automobile, just as he had when Beatrix's life was in jeopardy at the beginning of the war.

Sanity kicked in as afternoon shoppers and children returning from school paraded down the thoroughfare. By the time he'd reached the Santa Fe Train Depot, the big engine and what was left of the afternoon train from Los Angeles was in the distance. He parked the car, not caring where or how, and jumped out, dashing to where Sam would maneuver the enormous engine to a screeching stop.

Thomas paced, fists tight against his trousers as he glared at the train, moving at a snail's pace in order to cross Highway 101 and get into town. With each blast of the horn, warning drivers and pedestrians of the oncoming train, Thomas gasped. He knew if he stopped walking, he'd bawl, so he slammed his feet to the pavement, casting menacing stares at anyone in his way. He smashed his right fist into his left palm, and in what seemed like a month later, the train finally stopped.

Sam Conrad threw open the engine door and jumped down, not taking time for the stairs. "Tom. Get in the car. Let's go. Want me to drive?"

Thomas tossed the keys to Sam. "You know the way better than I do. I've brought shovels, Sam. Are the authorities on their way? Any police coming?"

"Don't know. Don't care. Hold on, man. I'm about to break all the speeding laws in this county."

Thomas's hands shook while in a death grip on the dashboard as the car skidded out of the station and south at a breakneck speed, stopping, but just barely, to let a school bus pass as Sam twisted the steering wheel, making a left turn from State Street to Highway 101. He didn't bother with the brakes as he swung the bulky station wagon in a sliding left turn to head south. Thomas clutched the door handle, gulping in air from fear of the speed they were moving but more so of the fear of never seeing his beloved again. He shouted, "Drive this thing faster, Sam. If the hillside collapsed, they may be suffocating right this second." He cried out in pain, like a wounded animal, imagining the crumbled railcar under a mudslide. His heart pounded in his ears. He began beating the dashboard with his fists and screaming.

Sam slammed on the brakes and pulled to the side of the highway. "Listen up, and listen good, Tom. We'll be there, where

I think the slide most likely occurred, in five more minutes. You cannot fall apart on me. If we have to use our hands to dig them out, we will. We'll find them. You're suffering, I get that, but pull yourself together, man. You are not doing Beatrix or that scientist any good in this state."

Thomas took an unsteady breath and turned to his friend. "Let's go." He wiped his dripping nose on the sleeve of his suit jacket and pulled his shirttail from his trousers to wipe his eyes. "But faster, Sam. I beg you. Go faster, man. Beatrix could be hurt or dead."

CHAPTER TWENTY-ONE

THE HEAT IN THE ENCLOSED RAILWAY CAR NOW FELT like summertime in Florida. When the car was disconnected from the rest of the train, the electric fan in the ceiling had stopped.

"Uncle" Ken looked from Beatrix to Einstein. His face was stiff. Evil was written in his eyes as sweat dotted his cheeks. His eyes darted around the railway car. The paper tablet he'd previously been holding was on a writing desk along with a folded newspaper, and both jumped when Ken slapped his palm on it.

"Girly, you just behave, because if you don't, I will slowly, one-by-one remove your pretty little fingers. You see, I want him," Ken nodded in Einstein's direction, "to write something, and then, we'll get you out of here."

"What is it, sir, you wish me to write?" Einstein looked from Beatrix's fingers to the anger boiling on Ken's face. "Leave this lady out of whatever you want of me. She is innocent."

Ken laughed, but the corners of his mouth were pulled nearly to his chin. "I thought you were supposed to be smart, Mister Important Foreign Doctor. She's got you fooled. That woman is famous in Santa Barbara for stopping a serial killer and exposing Nazi war criminals. All with no assistance from the authorities. She might look like a damn damsel in distress, but I know better than to turn my back on her."

Beatrix sat with her hands folded on her lap. Whatever Ken and his ilk wanted Einstein to write could change history, she sensed as bile twisted in her stomach.

"Okay, old man. Here's the deal. I want you to write in bold letters: Nobody is safe from the KKK. Not even me, Albert Einstein." He handed the doctor the tablet and a fountain pen. "Write, or off go her fingers. Think I'll start with the pinkie. Less blood but enough to get your attention." Out of his back pocket, the conductor pulled a pair of huge wire cutters. "Snap. Snap. Snap," he said, clicking the tool.

He smiled as the steel blades reflected the sunshine coming through the window, nodding at Beatrix. Then he walked closer to her, twisting and turning the steel cutters under her nose. Then drew the blades gently across her hands. Touching each finger with their points.

The worst she could do right then was make a scene. *Why Dr. Einstein needs to write this for the KKK makes little sense—unless,* she thought, *they're planning to kidnap other high-ranking Americans. Yes, that's it.*

The scientist repeated what Ken wanted. "Nobody is safe from the KKK. Not even me, Albert Einstein."

Einstein complied, never sharing his emotions or meeting Beatrix's eyes.

Ken snatched the tablet away the second the doctor finished, and from a cabinet, he produced a Brownie camera. "Hold the newspaper up in front of you and the note too. I am going to take your picture, and it'll show the day we snatched you." The flash went off, and then he nodded to his henchmen as Dr. Einstein replaced the lid on the fountain pen and put it in the inside pocket of his tweed jacket. It was such a common reaction the kidnappers didn't even notice.

Beatrix did.

Beatrix knew what he'd just done.

It was their only hope.

She realized that Einstein might appear old and fragile, but he wouldn't go down without a fight. She felt her resolve strengthen.

"Gentlemen," Ken spoke to the goons. "Handcuff these two and take them to the car. I'll be there shortly. Got a loose end to tie up."

Beatrix went down the steps and turned to let Dr. Einstein use her body to steady himself as he nearly teetered to the ground. Getting off the train, he looked back to her and, in a smooth, innocent motion, slipped the fountain pen into her hand. The abductors didn't notice. Otherwise they would have, Beatrix knew, broken fingers or her arm to get the pen. She palmed it, slipping it into the cuff of her shirt, and followed the trail to a waiting black sedan.

This cannot be the same car that Mrs. Du Bois saw driving in her neighborhood when Grayson Welsh was shot, could it? What in the world is the connection between a Union Pacific executive and the KKK?

The men and their captives looked up toward the cliff and the residence of Casa Verdugo. Ken Purdue sat atop a huge, yellow skip loader as the machine roared to life, spewing inky exhaust smoke. They froze as they watched the tractor push soil and a few huge boulders over the cliff. The first two rocks missed their mark. The biggest and third boulder directly hit the railway car, twisting the car on its side and crumbling the steel and wood frame as if one would crunch a piece of paper. Then Ken ran the tractor back and forth, scooping up sticky soil and dropping it onto the tracks.

At the moment when the tractor inched forward with another load of rocks and dirt, the cliff began to slide toward the tracks, the loose earth creating a slide that covered the car completely, leaving a mountain of soft mud, sage brush, and large rocks. Ken must have seen the slipping movement as he'd quickly thrown the tractor in reverse, or he would have tumbled, too.

If they had been in the train car, they'd have died, smothered by the slide.

Beatrix felt the ache of fear spread through her body. Terror seared her thoughts. "Where are you taking us? You're going to kill us anyway, so tell me," Beatrix demanded, her voice squeakier than she'd anticipated. She looked into the younger man's eyes and was shocked. He was fearless. *The trim man shows no regret, fear, or empathy on his face. The muscular one is laughing, and he's finding pleasure in scaring us, planning to hurt us. Could I talk any sense into these two, who seem to have no heart?*

The brawny thug turned to the skinny one, who seemed to be second in command of their snatch-and-grab operation. He shrugged and said, "Guess it won't hurt. You're going someplace safe for a few days. Just until Uncle Ken can get the photograph developed and take that and your statement to the local newspaper. He's going to get the story out to all the major papers. The KKK isn't sticking to the South—no way, no more, no ma'am. Get in the car. Nobody's going to rescue you, and if they come looking for that fancy railway car, they'll find it. If they dig long enough," he sniggered a high-pitched, nearly hysterical sound, clearly of someone mentally unwell. "I said get in the car, lady. You, too, Mr. Geezer with the big brain. Yeah, we've heard of you. Now who's smart? Let's go. We gotta get out of here."

The burly one spoke, as if he hadn't heard anything that his partner just said. "The Klan's going global. Uncle Ken told us all about it. We're going to be leaders. We're going to rid the world of the wrong sort of people. Folks like you—you're a Jew, right?" he poked a finger toward the scientist. "Yep, we're going global."

"Not global, young man. It is correct to say national if you are going to expand in America," Einstein remarked. His posture was as tall as he could make it, and his voice was steady, even knowing his life could end in a second by one of the unhinged kidnappers.

"Shut up, fella, or I'll shut your mouth for you. You don't know nuffin'," the skinny one snapped. He gave his pal a thumbs up and slammed the backseat door after shoving Einstein inside. Then, barely waiting until Beatrix got her feet into the waiting car, the other goon heaved the door. The anger and intensity made Beatrix flinch as it banged shut.

The KKK had been scheming this for a while. The backseat door handles had been removed. The locks gone. They were hemmed in. The muscled thug continued to point a pistol at the passengers from the front seat, hefting the weight of the weapon with a look of perverse pleasure. He sat sideways, sneering, laughing, and squinting at them as the car drove along the gravel, kicking up dust and rocks at a nerve-racking speed. The driver turned onto a side road that led to Highway 101. They headed north to the destination that Beatrix felt, in the pit of your stomach, would be their end.

She peered out the window, seeing the landscape speeding by, drivers whizzing along on the two-lane busy highway, off for a family gathering or maybe a business appointment.

Then a car she immediately recognized whooshed by. She stifled a gasp. Thomas and Sam were in the bulky Ford in the next lane over, driving south as their kidnappers zoomed north. *Oh, Lord,* she thought, *they're going to think we are under the mudslide. Oh, Thomas, be courageous. I am not there.*

Sam knew the graveled roadway on each side of the track. He saw it from the engineer's seat on the twice-daily trek along the rail corridor. The Ford careened down the loose rock, a racket of pebbles hitting the undercarriage. "There," Sam said in a breath above a whisper. "The cliff has collapsed, just as I feared."

Thomas stared, unbelieving, unable to speak. His body teetered. *It's not a time to crumble, old man,* he reprimanded himself. Yet, he folded over and had to put his head between his knees, fearing he was about to crumple. His ragged breath suddenly stuck in his throat.

"Hold it together, Tom. I'm going to need you to dig with me." Sam was out of the car and grabbing the shovels, dashing to the catastrophe ahead. "Keep an eye out above. The rest of the soft dirt could slip at any second. I don't want to be digging three people out."

Somehow by instinct, Thomas took off his dress shoes and put on the work boots. He followed his friend, unable to do anything but mirror what Sam was attempting to do, pushing rocks out of the way with his bare hands.

"Help me with this one," Sam called out, and Thomas put his shoulder into it, feeling the jagged boulder move slightly, and then, with one more effort, they pushed. It rolled like a toy, tumbling to the sea below.

"Is that the green paint from the top of the car?" Thomas cried out in joy and abject terror.

Sirens blared closer and closer, and a fire engine clanked out a thunderous sound as workers, police, and firefighters neared the scene of the disaster. In his chaotic digging and without warning, Thomas was back in London during one of the mass shellings of the war. Then, too, he had been on his hands and knees digging through the rubble.

It happened too quickly: The air raid sirens sounded. He'd been at the greengrocery picking out potatoes, and in a split-second, people were running in every direction. Some, he imagined, to the shelters; others, home to gather their loved ones.

Then the unmissable sound came from the distance: dreaded, vile, and frequent in the night and now in the day. It vibrated everything. It was as if the Devil himself was laughing at their vulnerability.

The reverberation came from heavy airplane engines flown by the German Luftwaffe. They were practically overhead. The sky was black with them, like a murder of crows flying over a cornfield. Thomas tried to remember the closest air raid shelter, praying that the building could withstand another assault from the bombs. He huddled in the darkness with crying babies, frightened fellow Londoners, and old people praying as if their lives depended on it—perhaps it did. The group seemed to be breathing in unison, taking ragged breaths of stale air, the smell of sweat and unwashed bodies stuffed into a small cement room. Not knowing if they'd live through this attack. When would Death come for them?

An hour or more passed, or perhaps just minutes. Time could not be quantified in the bomb shelters. Finally, when the all-clear siren sounded, the traumatized filed out into the mid-day sun to find smoke billowing from buildings, destroyed streets, and rubble where there had been flats and shops.

Thomas helped an older man find a place to sit. There was no way to tell him everything would be fine.

The greengrocery was now a heap of broken bricks and shards of glass. He heard what seemed to be a muffled voice. "Oh, bloody hell," he cried. It was his worst nightmare. "Help me. Someone's trapped inside," he yelled to the shell-shocked crowd.

A few stunned men came to his call, and tossing back the bricks, they dug for what seemed ages. They did it with their bare, bleeding hands, with one ear attuned to the return of the fighter planes and more bombs. Then they saw the man crumpled beneath a roof joist.

"He'll die unless we get him out," a stranger said. "You, man," he pointed to Thomas, now covered in soot and bits of dust from the crumbled bricks, "grab that end of the timber. He's alive. We must rescue him."

Two teenagers rushed to the chaos, and the six lifted the massive wooden board from the groceryman. "He's alive." was the shout, and in the distance, an ambulance siren grew stronger. The crowd cheered, most wiping tears from their eyes.

As the ambulance crew gingerly placed the grocer on a stretcher to transport him to a makeshift hospital, Thomas sat on the curb, stunned at the inhumanity of humanity. It was the fourth time in two weeks he'd had to dig into the bombed-out shells of a business or home. This time, the grocer was alive. Gazing at the rubble, others were not as fortunate, and the screams continued into the night.

CHAPTER TWENTY-TWO

THE SAME TERROR WAS WITH HIM AS HE DUG WITH HIS hands, ripping the skin and tearing his fingernails, trying to get to Beatrix. Every fiber of his body was back in the Blitz, and he was frantic, terrorized, and disoriented.

Suddenly, dozens of men were pushing away rocks, shoveling the grainy mud. "Better move back, sir," one of the officers commanded, but Thomas ignored him, unable to comprehend that they were going to help. By that time, he was pushing sandy dirt off the side of the car, off the window caked with slimy grit. He whipped out his handkerchief, pushed away the debris, and tried to look inside.

A broad-shouldered firefighter put a hand on Thomas's back and pulled him to his feet. "Stand back, sir." He waved a long-handled ax in front of Thomas at the same instant that Sam pulled his friend away.

Thomas couldn't catch his breath. Intellectually, he knew he was digging to free his wife and the scientist, but in his crazed nightmare, he was back in the middle of a bombed-out neighborhood, surrounded by death and devastation.

"They know what they're doing, Tom. Give 'em some room to work."

With that, the firefighter slammed the ax blade into the window of the train car. With gloved hands, he pulled shards of glass away, bent down, and peered in.

Behind him were ambulance drivers with stretchers at the ready, and police calling to others that the car had been found. People who had been driving on the highway stopped when they saw the emergency crews or came to the accident site after hearing news reports on the radio. They lined the edge of the highway above like greedy, squealing seagulls waiting for a scrap of bread.

"Get in there and see how the victims are doing," shouted an officer who seemed to be in charge. "Hand him the medical kit. Give the stretchers a clear path."

Thomas fell to his knees. There in the distance was the coroner from Ventura County, and on the man's heels was Detective Stella Rodriguez. Stella swayed as she took in the horror of it all, the crumpled railcar, and Sam and Thomas mute with fear. She stopped ten feet from the damaged car, stunned. She'd been on the scene of grotesque accidents before; she'd seen how horrible humans could be to one another more times than she wanted to recall. Beatrix was her friend, and she'd forever carry the guilt of asking her to go undercover with such a dangerous gang. She was certain what they'd find inside: broken, torn, bloody bodies whom she'd have to report dead. She muffled a cry.

Thomas couldn't move. His legs no longer seemed to be able to function. He made guttural sounds, unable to connect words. All he could think of was, "Gone." *That's what I'm going to hear next,* he thought, sobbing uncontrollably. *Gone. My darling Beatrix is dead.* He crumbled to the ground.

Sam knelt beside him and put his massive arms around Thomas, and they cried together.

Both men snapped up when they heard yelling, jumping to their feet as they watched an emergency worker pull himself out of the window. As his shoulders appeared, he called out, "Captain? You might want to come over here."

This time the two held each other up, shaking, teetering, and knowing the next words, the next few minutes, would change both their lives forever.

"What is it?" the captain called.

Now halfway out of the car lying on its side, the worker shielded his eyes and finally identified the captain. He yelled, "There's nobody inside."

"What?"

"No?"

"Can't be."

"It's empty."

"You sure?"

"What?"

"Yes. Empty"

"No, not possible."

"It's empty."

"What?"

"Nobody's inside, sir. No bodies."

The words echoed through the crowd of firefighters, police, and emergency responders. Sam and Thomas fell backward on the soft, mucky earth, and they repeated the words, "Nobody is inside."

The emergency crew member shouted to the crowd, "There's nobody in the car. It's empty. There's a briefcase with the initials of A.E. in gold on the handle and a blue conductor's jacket. I didn't even see any blood, sir."

A flood of emotion enveloped Thomas, and he bent forward and sobbed, arms around his folded knees. "She's not there. She's not there. She must be alive, must have been taken someplace. Along with Einstein? Yes, both of them. Alive. For now?"

Sam gave Thomas what he hoped was a reassuring one-armed hug. "We'll find her. I don't know what in God's green earth is going on, but you can be sure, Tom, we won't rest until we find your wife and your friend."

"Should we wait here?"

"There's nothing more for us to do here."

Thomas scrubbed his muddy hands together, the fragments of shale reopening the wounds. "Do you have the addresses of the conductors in the office at the depot?"

"You bet. Let's get Ken Purdue's and pay the man a visit. He was on this train, and he didn't get off when we arrived in Santa Barbara. Is he mixed up in this, Tom?"

"Bea told me," he was sucking air, attempting to still his frayed nerves, "that Ken was suspected of being involved with the KKK."

"Cripes and cripes again. That makes nasty sense. Knew Purdue was selective in hiring only Whites for conductors and treating some of the crew like they were halfwits. Never did it to me, but I'm twice his size."

"Any idea where the Klan meets or heard any rumors?" Thomas asked as they climbed the trail to where they left the Ford.

"I wouldn't touch that miserable group with a ten-foot pole and pray none of the younger men on the rails would either."

At least for now, he steadied himself to find his wife. Alive.

Ken Purdue had left his minions in charge of Beatrix and Dr. Einstein and got into a waiting car. He screamed some orders at the two, and they waved him off. These misfits didn't seem in any urgency to reach their destination and sedately drove at a moderate speed along the highway. They were perverse in how they relished being kidnappers. The power of the bullies was making them giddy with dominance over an old man and a trim woman.

"You two are awful quiet back there," the driver called over his shoulder. "Cooking up how you'll escape, are you?" he cackled.

The nauseating sound of his laughter twisted in Beatrix's stomach and threatened her throat. "Can't you take these handcuffs off? A woman and an old man are no match for you," she said, feeling the fountain pen in the sleeve of her shirt and thinking, *What an abysmal excuse for a weapon. I'll use it if I can. Even if it stops these thugs for a moment. Maybe a moment will make a difference.*

Beatrix had been in tight situations before and each time she had assumed it would be the end of thrills in her life. Yet, her heart to help others, to be their protector, continued to entangle her into investigations where her life dangled on a thread.

"I cannot run, young man," Einstein shouted over the engine noise. "Please, won't you do one kindness? My wrists are aching."

The car slowed to a stop just before the Santa Barbara city limits, and the driver pulled to the side of the road. The skinny one bellowed for them to get out of the car as he wrenched the backseat door open. "No funny stuff, you two, or you'll wish you hadn't messed with me."

The muscular one concealed the gun in his jacket pocket but kept his hand on it. The barrel was evident and pointed at them.

His partner grabbed Beatrix by the shoulders and twisted her around, throwing her against the car. He unlocked her restraints and then the doctor's. "We're going to your new digs, pretty Miss Buttercup. Maybe, when we're settled, you and I can get to know each other better?" He winked at Beatrix, and a lecherous sneer appeared on his lips.

The driver growled as evil replaced lechery, "If you've got any ideas about jumping out of the moving car, I swear, I'll back up this car to drive right over the top of you."

As the car returned to the highway, Beatrix pulled the fountain pen out of her sleeve, and the temptation to plunge the tip straight into the scrawny neck of the driver was almost too powerful. *Wait*, she told herself. *Not yet. I should wait until the car stops.*

She turned to Dr. Einstein. He stared for a second, blinked, and, with a tiny dip of his chin, nodded.

He knows. He's ready. Am I? There was no choice.

They exited Highway 101 and headed north on State Street, taking a side road to pass the famous Santa Barbara Mission, called the Queen of the Missions, and then up a curving country road. Every single traffic signal was green on their journey, every intersection empty, and nothing was stopping the path to their murders. The beefy thug turned sideways in the front seat. "You two, no funny business." He shoved Dr. Einstein toward the middle of the seat just to punctuate his statement.

"Stop it," Beatrix protested. "He's an old man. He has nothing to do with your cause or what you're doing."

The kidnappers cackled a laugh and steered the car to a country road, driving on the wrong side and pulling over before they would have collided with an oncoming car. The road twisted and was filled with blind curves, throwing Beatrix and Einstein into the doors as they ascended the mountain. The thugs shoved each other rowdily, and at one time, the driver took his hands off the wheel, pulled up his knees, and drove with them.

The husky one barked, "You're wrong about the doctor, little lady. If we can kidnap him, then, like the statement you signed said, pal, nobody and his mama is safe from us."

Beatrix felt her bottled fury explode. She looked briefly at Einstein. He crouched down, folding himself nearly in half. She knew he realized what she was about to do.

When the driver twisted the steering wheel as they reached a hairpin curve, she swung her right arm back and, with all the power she could generate on pure adrenaline, plunged the sharp tip of the fountain pen into his neck.

He screamed.

She yanked it out and again dug the pen's pointy steel nib into his neck.

The other thug whipped around, trying to see what was happening. Panicked, he tried to grab Beatrix, but she slid across the bench seat, just out of his reach.

The driver swerved, managing to keep the car on the road, only to collapse and hit the massive trunk of a eucalyptus the size of an elephant.

Beatrix gripped the seat and watched in horror as the men's heads crashed into the front window, shattering the glass with a horrifying thud.

Beatrix and Dr. Einstein tumbled to the floor. No sounds came from either. Or the men. Everything was still. Smoke began emerging from the car's engine in just a trickle. The trickle turned into a cloud and then billows of stinky smoke poured out from under the hood.

She touched Einstein's shoulder, and he moved. "Are you able to get out of the car, Doctor?" she whispered, all breath knocked out of her. "Take my hand, steady yourself, but we must get out."

"You are brave, my dear. I do not feel any pain. And you? Are you able to walk?" he moved gingerly and sat back on the seat.

"I don't know if they're dead, but we must get out of the car." Smoke was starting to seep into the interior of the car. She used all of her weight and the power of her shoulder to try to open the door. Jammed in the crash. "We've no time." She rolled down the oversized window and climbed out. "Give me your arms, sir. We have to get you out now."

"You'd better call me Albert, Beatrix, after all this," he said, and he stuck his torso through the window, pushing off the seat with his legs. "Oh, that hurt, but no broken bones that I can detect."

She grabbed him by the shoulders, forgetting the ache in her left arm, and they limped off to the far side of the road. The smoke increased, and when the explosion Beatrix expected came, she jerked with a shock. They could feel the heat from the burning car fifty feet away. Whether the men inside were alive after the crash was a moot point. "There was no saving them," she whispered, more to herself than her companion.

The doctor coughed from the inky smoke, thick and smelling like gasoline and motor oil. "Beatrix, I have lived a life that has been marked with fear, unimaginable horror, panic enough to turn my hair white, and yet this nightmare and your bravery? I will never forget."

She managed a slight smile. "It all happened so fast."

"You are courageous, my new friend."

"I don't think we should leave the site. Someone will see the smoke and call the fire department. God willing, it will not spread. Wildfires are a huge threat here in California. We had a good soaking storm last week, and that just might keep everything from going up in a fireball."

"Another miracle, then, madam, as the tree is not ablaze." He pointed a shaky finger to the now flaming car.

"Someone will pass by, I'm certain." She wasn't, but what else could she say? On the weekends, there were day trippers and tourists. On a weekday, in the early evening, traffic was sparse. "Let's sit someplace to wait. Your face is bleeding. Are you going to faint, Albert?" She took the handkerchief from his suit's pocket and applied pressure to the scrape on his cheek.

"It is nothing. This old body has seen much worse. You and I are alike. We are fighters."

Beatrix quickly scanned the landscape, and there was a tumbled tree away from the smoldering remains of the car. They leaned against it. Waiting. She lifted the railroad watch from the uniform's vest; it was almost six, and her left arm was throbbing. *My pain will have to wait.* She looked around for the first time, seeing and knowing where they were. It was the road leading to the compound. They were on Mountain Drive.

We need to get there before twilight—before the coyotes and pumas come looking for supper. He need not know we're in danger from the wild things that are watching us right now. Overhead, as if hearing Beatrix's thoughts, a massive turkey vulture swooped low and glided on the wind's currents, circling back as if keeping an eye on his next meal.

"It will be dark shortly. Can you walk, Albert?" She knew from traveling this road before, on all the Sunday road trips her parents had taken when she was young, that the entrance to the commune had to be about a mile away as Thomas had explained after his visit. *Can he make it? There's nothing to do but walk,* she thought. *Or plan to fight off a mountain lion with my good arm.*

She scanned the rugged hillside, and a memory immediately flashed in her mind. "If it's still there," she said to herself and the trailhead hidden behind a boulder. Beatrix was about ten, hiking the hills with her father. They'd left her mother in their car—not far from where she and Dr. Einstein now stood—crossed the road, and meandered along a footpath, eventually coming out where Mountain Drive ended. It had been spring, she recalled the memory, and bright orange California poppies and deep, purple-colored lupine made the meadow a riot of wildflowers. When they arrived at the end of the short hike, her mother was spread out on a plaid blanket, a book propped in front of her, looking like a fairy princess with her long hair loose being tickled by the breeze. She hadn't thought of the moment in time in years and now she would have to remember to pull it out again later, to relish the peace-filled day when there was more time to delight in it.

"This way, Doctor. There's a short path just in back of this massive stone," she called out. The trail, she knew, was under a half mile and with just a slight incline. Again, she thought, *Can he make it? He has to. No help is coming. No one even knows where we are, especially Thomas.*

The commune would not have telephones, so even if one of the members had seen the smoke from the crash, she realized they wouldn't have called the fire department. Most likely, they wouldn't even have sought out the reason for the smoke, possibly chalking it up to someone on the hillside having a bonfire.

"If you are willing to walk slowly until I test my strength, yes, I will be fine." He leaned heavily against Beatrix, allowing her to put her right arm around his middle. "Look, I am not even limping, as I had expected."

They gradually took to the trail, well-trod by deer and possibly members of the commune, or Beatrix supposed. While the afternoon shadows grew longer, they headed to Mountain Drive's free-spirited community. "We'll have shelter soon, Albert. Maybe even a cup of tea or coffee."

Thomas and Sam stood next to the Ford. So much adrenaline had coursed through Thomas's body, coupled with the terror of his wife's disappearance, that his emotional state was frazzled. He unexpectedly felt giddy. Crazy, uncontrolled laughter erupted from his throat, and Sam flipped his attention to his friend, shocked at the sound. Then, without warning, he joined in the inappropriate reaction, knowing that trauma causes emotions that collide with reality to often surface.

Thomas pointed an index finger, and the laughter froze in his chest. He wiped more unexpected tears off his face, leaving streaks of mud and dots of dried blood.

Detective Rodriguez turned at the laughter, knowing shock when she heard it, and came over to where the men were standing. "I've got to get back to my car and call this in. You guys need any medical help?" She nodded to the ambulance.

"What do we do, Stella?" Thomas begged.

"Go home. Get cleaned up. Come to the station. I'll meet you there in an hour or so. I've got to talk with some of those folks gawking on the hillside above us. Maybe somebody was walking a dog and looked down. Could we even hope there were folks with binoculars waiting to see if the whales were migrating out there?" She pointed to the Pacific. "Maybe somebody saw something or someone? It'd take more than one kidnapper to snatch both your wife and the scientist."

"A train car doesn't just come unhitched, ma'am," Sam said, turning to the police officer. "Someone did this on purpose."

"You're right, Sam. An avalanche of mud and boulders could happen, but what are the odds this was a coincidence? Zero," she replied. "I'm going to hike around to see if there are any footprints or tire tracks."

They all stared at the rubble, thoughts of what might have been and the whereabouts of Beatrix and the doctor were unspoken and heavy on them.

Sam was one of the least violent men Thomas had ever met, but glancing down to see his friend's fists clenched and the knuckles bulging alarmed him.

"Okay, Tom," Sam began, "let's do what Stella says. We'll get cleaned up and meet at police headquarters. Want me to drive?"

As they got into the Woody, glancing up at the lingering crowd, spying the detective walking along the tracks where the railcar should have been. They saw her stop, remove a camera from her army surplus backpack, and aim it toward the tracks.

"Look, Tom, she's found something."

"We should help?" Thomas asked, one foot in the car, the other hesitating to follow.

"Best if we let her do her job." Sam lowered himself into the driver's seat.

Thomas got into the passenger's seat and covered his face with his palms, trying to slow his brain from spiraling out of control. "We have no idea who's done this or where they are."

"My bet," Sam said, turning left onto Highways 101 heading north to Santa Barbara, "is that Purdue, whom some of the younger workers affectionately call Uncle Ken, is involved. Before we get you home, mind if we make a stop at the depot? I've got a few questions to ask some of the crew."

Thomas beat his fists on his knees; his knuckles were white. "Beatrix said he was dodgy. I'm going with you. You may need me to knock him around if he gets violent with you." The men drove in silence, far too fast for Thomas's liking, yet knowing if he were behind the wheel, they'd be passing cars at ninety or more. He remembered years back, after he first met Beatrix and she'd been kidnapped by Nazi sympathizers when they were in New Orleans, he had driven like a maniac in irresponsible circles around the city trying to find her. "Thank you, Sam."

"Nothing you wouldn't do for me or my family, Tom."

At the depot, Sam skidded to a stop, and both men jumped out. Sam dashed toward the outbuilding where the workmen gathered to smoke, drink coffee, and swap stories. "Anybody seen Marcus?" he yelled, then saw the spry, old porter lifting wooden cargo crates onto a dolly to take into the station. "Never mind, I see him." Thomas and Sam ran toward the man.

"Where's the fire?" Marcus started to laugh and then saw Sam and Thomas covered in mud, blood smeared on their faces, and their hands bloodied and bruised. "What the—"

"Long, ugly story. Where's Purdue, Marcus? Seen him?" Sam asked.

"Not here, I'm thinking." He rubbed his wrinkled, chocolate-brown forehead. "Matter of fact, I don't think he even got off the train when we arrived. Didn't see him, anyhow. A lady, in the family way," he looked down, somehow embarrassed about the woman's pregnancy, "needed me to help her down the stairs. I hesitated and looked both ways before I took her hands. The conductor doesn't like us porters touching the passengers, or maybe it's because they're White. On any normal day, Purdue'd be standing on the side, whistle at the ready, to hustle passengers along before the northbound customers are allowed on. And to hold a pretty lady's hands or even put his arms around her to help her down the stairs."

"He was not on the train? Are you sure?" Thomas asked.

"I could have missed him. We were short staffed. I always walk through all the cars, from engine to caboose, at this station before it leaves north for Lompoc. It was empty before the Santa Barbara passengers were allowed to get on. There are no stops between Ventura and Santa Barbara. Don't know where he could have got to."

Thomas paced, the muscles from his martial arts training in fight mode. "Marcus, I'm Thomas Ling. The young conductor you know as Chuck is actually my wife, Beatrix, working undercover with the police."

Marcus nodded. "Sam let me in on it, sir, first day out. Asked me could I keep an extra eye out for your spouse. Nice lady. I'm so sorry. Heard how their fancy car came disconnected from the rest of the train." He looked at the men more closely. "Did you have to dig them out? Mudslide hit 'em?

"No, they were not in the car when we dug through the rubble," Thomas said. "Beatrix thought that Purdue might be affiliated with the Ku Klux Klan from something she saw."

"Lordy, bad news." Marcus cast his eyes toward the pavement. "Think you fellas need to know something I saw a while ago. I saw Purdue walk by another conductor and give what I thought was a Nazi salute. This was after the war, and I knew Purdue had a son who saw action in North Africa and then in Europe. I was shocked. He got lathered up about Hitler, so I decided I'd been mistaken."

Thomas cocked his head. "What did you actually see, Marcus?"

"I was raised in the South, seen it there. In the open. In my face a few times. Horrible. Terrified me, and rightly so. They salute with the left arm. Seen Klan members separate the fingers of their hand when making the salute."

Sam interrupted, "Supposed to represent four Ks for the official name, which is the Knights of the Ku Klux Klan." Sam's face got hard. The men didn't have to say that people were fearful of the despicable organization; everyone knew it.

"I believe you saw what you saw, my friend," Thomas said and reached out to shake the porter's callused hand, pulling it back regretfully, seeing the dirt and dried blood on his knuckles and under his fingernails. "One more question? Did you ever hear Purdue mention a secret meeting place or some location where he frequented other than home or Garcia's Bar and Grill?"

"People talk a lot of secrets in front of you, Marcus, because they imagine you won't test their power," Sam said.

"Yeah, we porters are invisible." He rubbed his forehead, his eyes flickered. "A few months back, a long-haired hobo came to the depot before the train arrived. I figured he was looking for a handout, so I was going to the lockers to get my lunch tin for him. When I walked back out, right over there," he pointed to the depot office, "Purdue was talking with the man."

"Like they knew each other?" Thomas asked.

"Definitely. The hobo tried to hug Purdue, and the conductor jumped back as if the kid had leprosy or something."

"There's more?" Thomas leaned in.

"I picked up a dolly and walked closer, pretending to move

some cargo. I heard the younger man call Purdue 'Pa,' I think, which knocked me sideways. Didn't look a thing like Purdue. The guy was grubby, and his blond hair hung past his shoulders. Then he said something about needing supplies for a building, a dining hall, and asked Purdue to get it up to him on the mountain. That he needed him to drive to the mountain or something like that."

"The mountain?" Sam asked.

"Marcus, was it Mountain Drive? Is that what you heard?" Thomas's head flipped from the porter to Sam. "Mountain Drive, is that it?"

"Sure, could be, mister. That's what they were talking about. That back-to-nature foolishness Nat King Cole sang about? Remember hearing that song everywhere for a while. Excuse me. Sorry I can't help more. The next train will be here in an hour, and I've got crates to move."

Thomas had walked a few steps away, stopped, and then turned. "Marcus, any chance that Purdue called this man by name?"

"Don't know. I did hear 'August,' but it was December, I believe, when this happened."

Thomas did a double take. "Mountain Drive. August. Gus." The words tumbled out in spurts, his brain swirling. "Could Purdue have kidnapped Beatrix and Dr. Einstein and taken them to Mountain Drive? But why? Why snatch them? If he wanted them dead, no reason to take them from the car. No reason."

Sam said, "A reason is a hefty ransom. You're rich. Einstein might not be, but he knows rich folks."

"Not possible, mate." He looked shocked. "Gus? Can't be Purdue's son, can he? Nothing makes sense. Now, they're holding them for a ransom? We've got to get there," Thomas ran toward the Ford.

"No, we've got to get Stella Rodriguez in on this. If I know Purdue's kind, bullets are going to fly, and people could get hurt. Let's figure this out, real smart, Tom—or Beatrix and the doctor could get shot. Or worse."

Thomas scowled. "Right." He sighed. "Right. We'll wait for the cavalry." But in his heart of hearts, he knew waiting was impossible. *As soon as Sam goes to get cleaned up, I'm driving straight away to that blasted commune. Beatrix needs me.*

CHAPTER TWENTY-THREE

BEATRIX HAD LEFT HER CONDUCTOR JACKET IN THE railway car, and now the late afternoon chilled her skin through the flimsy white dress shirt and the uniform's vest. "We must trudge on, but if you need to rest, Albert, we can do that." There had been a storm that had blown in from Alaska just earlier that week, and a sprinkle of snow still clung in the shady spots on the craggy Santa Ynez mountains.

His breath came in puffs. "*Nein*. No, I am all right. In my years of living, I have survived much worse than an arctic walk in the woods, Beatrix. We move on. How far?"

"As I remember, if my husband's description of the location is correct, the community is just beyond that meadow. If we keep moving, we should be there by five, and the mountain lions and bears will have to find something else for dinner." She laughed. It sounded authentic, but it was not.

They crossed the valley and ascended a small hill. The trauma to her left arm throbbed to the rhythm of their footsteps, and she was certain it would require medical attention once she got the scientist to safety.

Beatrix stopped, as Einstein's breath seemed more ragged.

"Just behind that grove of eucalyptus trees. See the flicking of a campfire? Do you want to stay here, sir, and I'll ask some men to help you?"

"No, Beatrix. I am old, but I am not feeble. I will walk with you and then rest once we've arrived." He smiled and nodded. "In my youth, a million years ago, I was quite the wanderer. Hiking through the hills in Munich, I felt alive. I was a quiet child, always curious." He seemed to be talking to himself, perhaps to keep his mind off the accident and the fatigue and the cold air. "I must take more wanders. I spend far too much time in the laboratory. Wandering helps me think."

"What advice would you give to a younger person just going out in the world, Albert?" It seemed that if his mind was occupied that he walked faster.

"Learn from yesterday, live for today, hope for tomorrow. The important thing is not to stop questioning."

"My husband Thomas would say that."

"Ah, Dr. Ling. I have only known him through correspondence and the research articles and monographs he's written. His work is stellar. Oh, how peculiar our world can be. Here I am, my coconspirator in escaping a kidnapping, and you are the spouse of the man I plan to lure away from the University of California."

"He's honored to be meeting with you," Beatrix replied, thinking even as they climbed the hill what a change it would be to live in New Jersey: to bring up Birdy in an environment less accepting of mixed races, with more traditional roles expected of a wife. *Would there be a conflict for Thomas, whose wife works?* "Yes, he's honored." *Should we make the move? Leave this city, our home, and our close friends? But Thomas's work is valuable. He could save our world or slow the process of destruction, at least,* she thought. *Or will we find ourselves fleeing America after being accused of association with the Reds?* Her thoughts wrestled for dominance with no clear solution any closer.

"There it is. The commune," she pointed and then called out as they walked toward the little group of buildings. "Hello? We need help."

A young child raced up to her but stopped when he saw the dried blood on the strange woman's face. He wore just a pair of jeans—no shoes, no shirt. He looked at the strangers with deep distrust yet hollered, "Daddy, come quick. People are here, and they're all dirty."

A man appeared from one of the makeshift homes that looked as if a good wind would knock it down. "Friends, welcome. Are you in trouble? You are safe here."

"Thank you. I'm Beatrix, and this is Albert. There was a car accident." She wasn't about to share the fact that she'd caused it by repeatedly jabbing the point of a fountain pen into the neck of one of their kidnappers. The crash caused the fire and ended the lives of the ruffians yet saved Beatrix's and Albert's lives.

"Come inside. Sit, please. I'm Gus, and this is my child. Son, find one of your mothers to bring tea, bread, hot water, and towels." The boy scampered away, and Gus motioned that they should come into his rustic house.

One of your mothers, Beatrix repeated in her head. *This was the man who was gracious to Thomas when he pretended to be a lost soul looking for community.*

"You are kind, sir," the doctor said, looking around the one room hovel for where to sit, settling on an overturned wooden crate, not knowing if it was a chair or Gus's dinner table.

Beatrix perched on the end of the bed. "We've hiked in from the crash. You wouldn't possibly have a telephone so I can call for help?"

Gus shook his head. "It's getting dark, and it's not safe to roam the hillsides until morning. Tomorrow I'll go to a neighbor just south and use their phone. Or if you're well enough, Beatrix, you can come with me."

Two young women who looked like twins, barely teenagers,

Beatrix guessed, came in with a bowl of steaming water, a bar of tan-colored homemade soap, and towels that were surprisingly white. "Food will be here soon," said one as she wrapped a roughly woven, sky-blue knitted shawl around Einstein's shoulders and offered another to Beatrix. "There will be bean soup and bread and tea."

"You are compassionate to strangers, thank you," Beatrix responded and pulled the rust-colored shawl closer to her body. She suspected that the deep chill was from the shock of the afternoon and the accident, and she avoided dwelling on the constant throbbing in her left forearm. There was nothing for it. If she was fatigued and in shock, Dr. Einstein must certainly be suffering as well.

Until Beatrix washed her hands and face, she didn't know how crusted with dirt and blood she'd been. Dr. Einstein apparently felt the same because as he cleaned himself up, he started talking to Gus, asking questions about the little society, how it got its name, when it started, what their goals were, and who was in charge.

He truly is curious about everything, Beatrix said, seeing the man's face become more animated with the conversation and looking ten years younger.

In a lull, as they finished their mugs of spicy, thick soup, Beatrix asked, "Gus, you said that there were wild animals in the hills. That's normal, but does the commune have any way of protecting itself if someone had to leave the compound in the night?"

"Not right now, and that's why I would prefer you stay put. It's spring, and the wild creatures out there have babies that they're mighty protective of. As for protection? We did have a dart gun to tranquilize animals. I lent it to a friend, and it's not been returned."

Beatrix nodded. *A friend? Kay Welsh? Mrs. Du Bois? One of the louts who kidnapped us?* "I read in the newspaper, my goodness, possibly a week or two ago, that someone here in Mountain Drive had been shot in the foot by a gun like that."

"It was an inane mistake. The man had been drinking our homemade wine—much too much. He decided to take a walk and took the gun with him. I found him the next morning, alive and angry at his stupidity. He seemed to be getting better, then he got a fever . . ."

"He died?" she asked.

"Yes. So distressing, so useless to have happened. I hope it taught the children that guns are dangerous. I really see no reason, if this friend gives it back, why we even need it. We love peace. We want tranquil lives and to live in harmony with nature and our neighbors. I saw too much misery caused by guns. I finished my duty near Dover, England, at the end of the war." He reached up and took down a photo from the wall. Young service members smiled for the camera. "I was among the American paratroopers, the 509th Parachute Infantry Battalion made up the US Army's first airborne combat jump near Oran, Algeria, on November 8, 1942."

"I have read about the distinguished service you provided. Thank you," she said.

"All these pals, guys I would have given my life for, died in one operation. I still have nightmares and waves—tsunamis—of survivor's guilt."

Dr. Einstein stifled a yawn and attempted to blink away heavy eyelids. Beatrix and Albert were safe, even if the members of the community were non-conformists.

Gus stared at the photo and then put it back on the shelf. "We have an empty house with two twin beds, and my wives are getting it ready for you. Here's a candle. I'd recommend sleeping in your clothes as it is going to be about thirty tonight. It's still cold from that freak snowstorm. We have blankets for you."

Moments later, the twin teenage girls escorted Beatrix and Einstein to a cabin at the end of the row of tiny houses. "There's another candle on the shelf if you need it. You should shut the door, too, to keep the critters out," one advised.

Dr. Einstein looked around. "I've been in worse, Beatrix. Your arm, I've seen you favor it. Is it broken?" He sat on the bed and slipped off his shoes.

"I'm afraid so, or perhaps very badly bruised. In this cold, however, the pain isn't terrible, and when we're rescued tomorrow, I'll get medical help. Let's try to sleep."

Thomas dropped Sam at his home on Garden Street and then stopped at the house on Anapamu for a flashlight, a baseball bat, and a warm jacket. He filled the car with gas, reviewed the map, and determined the fastest route to Mountain Drive.

The road was quiet in the late afternoon, and as he drove by a burnt-out automobile, he slammed on the brakes, pulling the car to the side of the road. He jumped out and touched the ash-encrusted fender. It was still quite warm. He peered inside and then jumped back. There were the charred remains of two humans, one slumped over the steering wheel and the other thrown against the door. He tried to get the scream that was in his throat out, but it was stuck. He bent over and gagged.

"Bloody hell. What has happened?" He looked around, and there were no houses or signs of life. At his feet was a white handkerchief, the same kind that he'd seen Beatrix stuff into the pocket of her conductor's uniform, and he froze. "She was here." He picked it up and breathed in the faintest smell of the rose perfume that Beatrix wore. "Blasted and bloody bullocks. At least I need not worry that the skeletons are those of Beatrix and Albert." His head swiveled. He wanted to race to Mountain Drive's commune but felt the moral duty to report the accident first.

"Help, I need to get help," he said and grudgingly made the

choice. He'd passed a tiny country store a few miles back, leapt into the car, made a U-turn, and headed to the shop.

He tried the front door. "Locked." He hammered a fist on it and then walked around to the little shack behind.

The front door cracked open, and Thomas was met with the barrels of a shotgun. "Stand back, stranger. I know how to use this," growled the voice of a man.

Thomas backed up, yet even from five feet away, the smell of whisky was unmistakable. "I mean no harm. I need to call the police. Is there a telephone I may use?"

"What's your problem? Those maniacs on Mountain Drive up to some mischief? Stole your lady friend or something?" Inside the shack, it was dark, and it felt as if the shotgun was doing the talking.

"An accident. Up the road. Two people died inside it appears."

"You talk fancy. Need a drink?" The door flung wide, revealing a hefty old man, not much taller than the length of the gun. Deciding that Thomas was not a threat, he pulled a bottle half full with amber liquid from his back pocket and shoved it at him.

"Thanks, but not right now. I'm driving up the hill and must use your telephone. The authorities need to be called. There's no time to lose as I'm in pursuit of some extremely dangerous criminals."

"Criminals? Oh, come on, mister. My daddy told me that moonshiners used to hang out here in the hills, especially during Prohibition, but that's all over. Here's the key to the store. Telephone's on the table behind the cash register. My old legs feel a bit wobbly, so I'll wait here. Just lock the door when you're done and leave the key under the doormat. You understand?"

Thomas snatched the key and thought, *I can't waste more time. The police must be called, and every second matters. Where is my*

Beatrix? Adrenaline kept him moving, kept him focused on finding her.

❧

Inside the bungalow on Garden Street, Sam Conrad paced around the compact living room. "Where is Tom?"

Jo held the twins, one under each arm, rocking them and watching the anguish on her husband's battered face. "Honey, you know Thomas. He could be anywhere. Maybe he's at Brockman's house getting advice? Have you telephoned John?"

Sam dialed the Brockman estate. "Henry? Good, it's you. I've lost Thomas."

Henry and Sam had hit it off like brothers, especially since Henry was now pen pals with Jo's sister, a doctor in Chicago. "You lost him? Where?" Henry asked.

Sam told Henry about Beatrix working undercover for the police, the possibility of the KKK involvement, the accident with the railcar, and the disappearance of Beatrix and the illustrious Dr. Einstein.

"Dagummit," came the loud acknowledgment. "Don't leave. I'll be there in twenty minutes. I've seen what happens when Thomas goes rogue. No telling what he'll do when he's panic-stricken." Henry replaced the receiver with a slam, and the big, black Bakelite telephone trembled.

"Beatrix and Thomas are in a jam. She's been kidnapped, and Thomas has probably gone alone to find her," he calmly explained to his employer.

John got up, and the book he was reading slammed to the floor. "I'm going with you. I think all this might be solved by a visit to that commune in the hills. There's trouble in that place. Bank on it. Hurry, man."

"Mr. B., wait." Henry rarely stopped his boss from anything —he actually never had, but if there was going to be trekking in the rough terrain, he wouldn't be any help at all. "I'll telephone you as soon as we find something. You're better off here. You can coordinate the effort."

"You're right, my friend. Take my gun." John opened the wall safe and handed Henry a Colt pistol.

Henry nodded, accepting the responsibility as he dashed from the house.

CHAPTER TWENTY-FOUR

THOMAS WAS CONNECTED TO THE POLICE STATION and learned that Detective Rodriguez was not in. "May I take a message?" came the inquiry.

He hurriedly explained about the burnt-out car.

"Wait there, sir, and police will arrive within an hour."

"No. Absolutely not. My wife has disappeared, and I fear she's been kidnapped." He replaced the receiver, rubbed his hands together, and looked out the grubby window of the grocery store. It was twilight. Thomas was athletic and power-ful, but he'd spent most of his life in the bustling metropolis of London. The wildness of the outdoors was foreign to him.

"Spiders come out at night. Snakes, too." He muttered and felt his body sway at the concept of coming face to face with these and other critters. "Coyotes and bobcats." He dashed back to the Woody and slammed the door as if a spider could crawl in and grab him. Locked it, too. He turned the key, and the engine purred. Speeding on the two-lane road, he hit a rock and then a pothole that nearly made his head collide with the car's ceiling. Moments later, he smelled gasoline and, in horror, watched the gas indicator slip from half to E. "Empty? Impossible." He glided the car to a wide place on the side of the road.

He depressed the clutch and pumped the gas pedal. He twisted the key. The engine was silent. He did it again, knowing that the faithful old car sometimes took a moment to decide if it felt like starting. Why he tried, he didn't know, except that he felt completely helpless. He didn't know a spark plug from a carburetor, but he got out, walked to the back of the Woody, and there, like a line down the highway, was a stream of gasoline, glittering like a silver thread in the last ray of sunshine. He might not be a car guy, but he certainly understood the law of cause and effect.

He slammed his right hand against the back of the car. "Bloody hell, I've nicked a hole in the gas tank." He looked back toward the market and knew it was a good two miles. Just up the road, he remembered, was where he'd left the car the first time he came to Mountain Drive. Then it was just a quick walk. Yet, in the fading light, he couldn't judge distance as all of the chaparral looked the same, gray and dangerous in the evening.

There was no other choice, and time was slipping away. He grabbed the khaki jacket, flashlight, and baseball bat from the car.

The sun winked out of sight over the ocean, and the breeze had picked up, rustling the leaves in a frightening, moody dirge that could have been used as background music for a horror film. Clouds covered the moon that looked like a sliver of cantaloupe. He flicked on the flashlight, and the trees and bushes became crouching monstrosities ready to pounce on him, the dreadfulness of childhood nightmares coming true.

In the distance he heard a guttural sound. "Just the eucalyptus branches scraping against other limbs," he said in a loud voice, edged as false bravado that echoed against the hillside. He still didn't believe himself. He flipped around, focused the flashlight in the direction he'd just come from, and swore again, but this time in a quivering whisper. The light reflected a glimmer of something shiny. "Eyes, oh, Lord, no. I am going to be eaten while Beatrix is held at the hands of those devils."

He ran, knowing it was the wrong thing to do but feeling helpless against the primal urge. "Stick to the road, man," he shouted to himself. "Move, move, move." In his mind, he could feel the collective breath of a pack of coyotes on his neck. At that second, there was a crack from overhead. He swung the bat. It collided with a tumbling, massive branch of a splintering eucalyptus that had snapped like a twig in the fierce gusts of wind. The bat ricocheted, hitting him in the face, and the limb twisted over him.

The bat was lost in the inundation of foliage, and the limb tossed him as if he were a feather. The force of the thick branch flipped him over the road's guard railing and then down the cliff, plummeting Thomas to the bottom of a ravine. The dark of the night circled in waves around his eyes. The hefty branch landed on top of him as utter blackness closed in.

Not five miles away, Beatrix woke with a start, momentarily confused by the snoring elderly man in the twin bed just feet from her. She sat up, gathered her thoughts, and gently rubbed her damaged arm. She'd need to find something to secure it before she hiked to the store with the telephone. She slipped into her sturdy boots and pulled the woolen shawl around her. The air was crisp and clean as she exited the cabin, quiet not to wake Einstein. She checked her watch. It was a few minutes to six, and across the clearing, smoke was coming out of a makeshift chimney. The commune was up and running.

She walked into the kitchen structure. The women nodded but didn't say anything, and Beatrix wondered if this was more of a cult than a society of free thinkers. Gus was setting a long wooden table.

"Good morning, Beatrix. Coffee's on the stove over there if you need a cup. Your friend, Albert?"

She waved. "Still asleep. He doesn't, I believe, get much outdoor exercise." *Or any,* she thought. *Would Thomas look like Albert in twenty years and to all the world like a mad scientist? If we move to Princeton, will he ever get out in the fresh air? Get to go on adventures with Birdy and me? I don't want to move,* she finally admitted. She filled a thick, hand-thrown earthenware mug with inky coffee. It was surprisingly good. "What direction is the house where there is a telephone, Gus? I must call in that accident and tell our family that we are safe."

"Down the road a piece. There is a little market, not much, but we get flour, sugar, and coffee there. It's a good five-mile hike. Get to the highway and head back toward Santa Barbara. But if you take the trail through the hills, same one you used when you came here, it'll knock off three miles."

"Would it be an imposition if my friend stayed with you until I can get a car to pick him up?" she asked.

"We'll take good care of the old man, Beatrix. I like him. He's clever and sharp. There's paper and a pencil on the dresser over there if you want to leave him a note."

She wrote: "Albert, we are going to be safe soon. I've gone to get help, and then I'll return with an automobile. Please stay with Gus and his family. I do not know how long it will be, but please don't worry, I promise to be back as soon as I can. Beatrix."

After quickly creating a makeshift sling from a measure of cloth offered by the women at the commune, she was off, recalling with precision the same trail they'd traveled the evening before. *After I call the police and Thomas, I'll see if I can find the accident site,* she thought, scurrying over fallen branches from the previous night's windstorm, protecting her injured arm.

The terrain was rough, and she gave credit to the scientist for not complaining, although she knew his breath had been labored. Eventually, and far longer than she thought it would take, she reached the highway. "Gus said to walk south, away from the camp." She looked at the sun in the east and followed his directions.

No cars passed, and the sun was warming on her back as she reached a tiny shop. The weather-beaten sign said, "Santa Ynez Grocery Store." She twisted the handle. Locked. Her railroad watch said 7:30 a.m., but stores in the country opened when they wanted and closed without notice. Everything seemed still except crows squawking about her intrusion. She followed a path between knee-high weeds to the structure beyond, a ruggedly built wooden shack. As she approached, she called out, "Hello?" The door inched open, and a double-barrel shotgun faced her.

"If yous want to see tomorrow, you'd best stay right there," growled whoever was pointing the gun.

"I won't harm you, sir," she said, slowly moving closer. "There's been an accident. I must use your telephone. Gus, on Mountain Drive at the commune, told me you have one." She put her hands above her head.

A stocky, grizzled-faced man opened the door and lowered the gun. "You're the second person to barge in on me to use the phone. Crips, it's like Grand Central Station here." His breath reeked of whisky, and his hands trembled. He fiddled in his filthy red flannel shirt pocket, extracted a key, and tossed it at Beatrix.

"Just leave the money on the counter, lady. It'll cost you two bits," he barked, remembering that the stranger with the funny accent had scammed him out of his rightful money for that phone call. He mumbled, "Foreigners. Can't trust them." He closed the door and then opened it again, yelling, "Leave the key under the doormat. Don't need you to bother me again. I'm too busy."

Beatrix unlocked the door. It smelled of mold and overripe fruit. She went straight to the phone. "Operator, this is an emergency. Please put me through to the Santa Barbara Police Department."

The sergeant who answered reported that Detective Rodriguez was out of the office on the scene of an accident. Could he take a message?

"Please tell her I'm at the Mountain Drive commune, and Dr. Einstein is safe with me."

Then she dialed her home telephone number. It rang a dozen times. Thomas wasn't there. *But where are you?* She let it ring a dozen more, then called John Brockman's number.

The housekeeper told her that Henry had been gone since late yesterday afternoon, and John was in a meeting with his attorney. "May I leave a message for him, Miss Beatrix?"

"Yes, Yuri. Please tell Mr. Brockman that Dr. Einstein and I are at the Mountain Drive commune. And when Henry is available, please send a car to pick us up."

"Wait, please. I must tell you. Henry and your friend Mr. Conrad believe that your husband went to find you at the commune. They have not called or contacted us since they left. Mr. Brockman is beside himself with worry."

"Thomas was not at the camp, Yuri. I just left there an hour ago. Oh, no," she breathed back the fear. *What's happened to Thomas?*

Beatrix sat on the wooden stool by the cash register. It wobbled, and she felt the same. *I need to walk back to the accident site. Could this be the same accident Stella's working? Hardly. Too much of a coincidence.*

There would be no need to send aid to the thugs who died in the car fire, but she felt the need to tell what happened, to be respectful to the men who'd died, even though they probably would have killed her and the doctor. *Perhaps someone reported the smoke, and the police are there already.*

Her arm throbbed in the makeshift sling. The now stabbing pain was making her nauseous. She held the arm tightly against her body. She'd placed a quarter on the counter, locked the rickety door, left the key under the threadbare mat, and headed south once more.

Going down the grade was much easier than the other way, and when she reached the blind curve in the road, she knew the crash was just beyond. She wished she'd brought water, wished she was home with Birdy and Thomas, wished she was anywhere but a lonely highway in the middle of rural Santa Barbara county with a broken arm. The pain, she realized, had started to cloud her mind.

She walked around the curve, and there, like a miracle and answered prayers mixed together, were two patrol cars, an unmarked police vehicle, and an ambulance. She swayed, found her balance, and waved. "I've never been happier to see all of you in my life," she hollered.

Stella Rodriguez looked up from the tiny notepad in which she was scribbling. "Oh my goodness, Beatrix." Heads turned, and Beatrix moved as quickly as she could to the detective. They hugged. "You look like you've been in a catfight, honey."

"You will hear the whole story soon." Beatrix glanced over at the burnt-out car. "The men?"

"Nothing left. An explosion gutted it. Melted some of the metal, and there's no way to identify them."

"They were the two who grabbed us from the disconnected rail car and kidnapped us. The same goons who hurt Sam in that ambush at the station. I saw their faces in a newspaper article the next day. Where is Ken Purdue?"

She chuckled, but it was not from joy. "Bullies. They're a mystery to me. We arrested Purdue about two hours ago. Went to his house, wasn't there. Wife refused to cooperate. She swung a punch at a patrol officer and got the cop straight on the nose. She's been arrested, silly woman. Had a hunch, so I called in the scent dogs. Found him cowering in a back room of the depot.

"There was a group of naturalists on a hike right above where the train had been derailed. By a quirk, a member of the group lives next door to Purdue—not a big fan of the guy. He watched the railway car tumble over the cliff and then saw Ken climb onto a skip loader and push boulders and dirt over the cliff. At the same time, he saw a woman and an old man, I assumed was you and Dr. Einstein, being manhandled into a car.

"Lucky break for us. His neighbor then followed Purdue back to the rail station and called us. My guess is that Purdue heard the sirens and thought he could hideout in a cupboard." She shook her head. "I'm often astounded at how stupid supposedly smart men can be. He blurted out a confession on the spot. Quivering. Mind you, Grace, a bloodhound the size of a pony, was standing on top of him. Drooling. What a pretty sight.

"Purdue admitted to trying to disrupt rail service in order to prove to the world that the Klan was mighty. Thus, the roughing up of your friend Sam, who would not let the hoods stop him from doing his job. Then, when that didn't grab national head-lines, Purdue learned that Dr. Einstein was traveling for a special visit to Santa Barbara."

"Oh, Stella, what a mess."

"Purdue got the idea to abduct Dr. Einstein. He sang like a bird about his daft allegiance to the KKK. He said his aim was to get the higher-up members of the Klan to notice how effective he was as a leader of the California arm of the hideous organiza-tion. Those thugs were blindly following a maniac."

"Stella, I need to tell you something."

"It can wait. You need to sit down. Get the lady some water, guys," she instructed one of the emergency crew.

Beatrix ignored the opportunity to rest and walked over to

the shell of the car. She'd feared that the fountain pen would still be sticking in the driver's neck. She'd have to tell the police that she caused the accident and the deaths of the two kidnappers. Charges would be brought against her for attempted murder, which was only right. She peered through the burnt-out window. The skeletal remains were charred beyond recognition. She looked at where the driver's head connected to the body.

The pen was gone. She took a full breath. *Could it have been burned in the fire?* She held the side of the car, felt the grit of burnt paint, and then pulled back. *If I hadn't defended me and Dr. Einstein, we'd probably be dead right now. Would that be enough testimony to make it self-defense? Dr. Einstein is a viable witness.*

A fireman brought her a tin cup of water. "You need to sit in the ambulance, ma'am, and have one of the guys look at that arm. Broken?"

"I think so or badly twisted."

"Get them to give you something for the pain, then. Detective Rodriguez wanted me to find out where the man who was kidnapped with you ended up? Let me know, and I'll tell her. You're going to feel better soon," he said and, in a fatherly way, patted her good shoulder, smiling down on her.

She believed him. However, she refused the pain meds. *If we're going to find Thomas, I can't have a head full of cotton.* "He's at the commune, Mountain Drive."

The fireman nodded and walked over to a patrol car, chatting for a moment with the older patrol officer.

Beatrix approached the plump officer standing by the second police car, explained that Dr. Einstein was safe at the Mountain Drive commune, and asked, "Will you drive me there?"

"Hop in," the officer said, opening the passenger door. "Been there before? That commune? Messy place. Who knows what really goes on there. They think they're above the law because its outside of our city police jurisdiction. Heard about the festivities and all, but gossip probably is better than the real thing. Least, that's been my experience."

They drove the narrow, zigzagging road, her right hand tightly grasping the door handle. Then, without warning, she saw it. "Stop. Please. Wait. I know that car." She pointed to a long, black Cadillac. "Why is John Brockman's car parked on the side of the road? Where is he? Where is Henry?" She turned to the officer, "Stop the car."

The officer was out of the squad car and on Beatrix's heels as she dashed across the road. There was a steep hillside below and jagged rocks poking through the sage and stubby, red-barked manzanita trees. The wooden guardrail was shattered, and splinters told the story. A massive eucalyptus limb, the length and width of a telephone pole, had crushed it.

She cupped her uninjured hand around her mouth and called out, "Henry? Where are you? Henry? Sam?"

"Maybe your friend just stopped the car to, um, well, relieve himself?"

"Henry?" She called again and then peering down over the ravine, searching for Henry and Sam. Then she saw something glitter. The sun was reflecting light onto metal caught halfway down the rugged hillside. Her hand covered the scream that was in her throat, and she knew at once what it was.

"Look," she shouted and pointed down the cliff, just three or four yards away. "That's my flashlight. But why?" She leaned against another massive eucalyptus branch that had been ripped off one of the trees during the previous night's windstorm, trying to get a better look.

The two scaled down the terrain. The officer struggled to gain a foothold as he retrieved the flashlight. He handed it to her. "Maybe your friends have one that looks like yours?"

She turned the flashlight in her hand. On the side, there was a deep dent in the aluminum casing—a result of dropping it down from the attic when they were renovating the house. "It's mine. Ohhh, no." Words stuck in her throat. "My husband would have taken it. He's here somewhere. We have to find him." She started screaming Thomas's name as she gingerly struggled, on the seat of her pants, down the hill.

The officer tried to tell her to wait, to say they'd get a rescue crew, but she was deaf to his orders.

Slowly and with only one good hand to grab onto the red bark of the spindly manzanita trunks so she wouldn't end up in the gorge below, she scooted her way down the slope. Then she saw what looked like a piece of cloth—khaki cloth. "It's Thomas," she called back. The officer was edging closer, his eyes wide, watching the injured woman move through the brush.

"Thomas? Thomas? It's me, Bea." There he was, in the sand on the edge of the creek at the bottom of the gully. She gasped at how close he was to the bubbling stream. Another few inches, and he would have drowned. A large, bare eucalyptus branch had pinned Thomas to the ground. As she reached him, she tumbled over an outcrop of river rock, falling on her injured arm. She gasped but shoved back the pain and went to her husband. She knelt down, touched him, spoke to him, but there was no response. He was cold, and his face was badly scratched, his body bent in an awkward position.

Holding her breath and fearing the worst, she felt for a pulse.

CHAPTER TWENTY-FIVE

"OH, THOMAS. OH, MY DARLING," SHE HUGGED HIM with her right arm and laid her body over his. The pulse was there, and she kissed and kissed his blood-splattered face just as his fingers started to move.

It was then that the officer finally reached the creek bed.

"He's alive," she gasped, wiping tears off her face.

"Can you help me get this limb off him, lady?" he asked, breathless from the descent and his age.

"I've been hurt. I don't think I can help . . ." She began to unravel, angry at her throbbing arm, angry at a world where bad things happened. Angry that there was no way to free her husband.

"Beatrix?"

She pulled her attention away from Thomas's crumbled body and listened again. Her imagination?

No.

The voice came from the distance, beyond a grove of trees on the other side of the ravine. Then she saw them. Henry and Sam were bolting through the chaparral.

Minutes felt like hours.

Eventually, the men reached them. "Oh, Lord, is he?" Henry couldn't get the word "dead" out of his mouth.

"Stand back," Sam told the officer, and the two men pulled the limb off Thomas while Beatrix held Thomas's hand, whispering to him. In the distance came the sound of sirens.

"Help's coming. I called for backup when you scurried down the cliff. When you saw the flashlight," the officer said.

Thomas moved his other hand. "Bea, oh, I thought you were dead." His voice was scratchy.

"Don't move, Thomas," Sam instructed. "Keep him still, Beatrix."

Thomas spoke in ragged puffs, "The wind was wild, I heard a tree crack. I must have blacked out. I didn't see or hear you come to me."

Two emergency workers scaled down the cliff, a stretcher over their heads. "Mister, we're going to have to get you out of here. Don't know what's broken, but the only way to find that answer is to drag you up the hillside. You going to be okay with that?"

Thomas lifted his head. "I feel quite right now that that blinking log is off my back," he tried to laugh, to make a joke. "See, darling, everything is going to be aces."

"We're going to roll you over, sir," one of the firefighters said. "Don't like doing it, but there's no alternative. If there's too much pain, stop us."

"I must live under a lucky star," Thomas said. "I'm not dead. Or is this heaven?"

She squeezed his hand. "If it's heaven, we're here together, Thomas. See you at the top."

Sam and Henry assisted the workers in carrying the stretcher up the hill to where the ambulance was waiting, Beatrix hot on their heels.

A medic, with worry lines deep on his face, said, "We'll meet you at Cottage Hospital, ma'am. Looks like your husband here was damn fortunate."

"Beatrix?"

She'd pushed through the scratchy chaparral and grabbed Thomas's hand before he was loaded into the ambulance.

"All the time I was down there, I thought I'd failed you once again. Geez, Bea. I reckoned if I could get to Mountain Drive after our car conked out, I could rescue you. Then the wind came up, and the branch and I landed in the gorge. I knew the KKK had kidnapped you and Dr. Einstein, and when I heard that Purdue's son was named Gus, it all came together."

"Shhh, we can talk later." She smoothed her right hand over his tattered shirt and onto his cheek. Kissed it tenderly.

"No, I've been rehearsing this for hours. I was going to break into the compound at night, when I finally reached it, and I was planning to beat those kidnappers silly with the baseball bat. I was going to save your life, but instead, you found me. Saved me. I am most grateful, shocked, happy, and in love. After spending the night under that tree truck, Bea, I have reconsidered whether I'm an outdoorsy camping bloke."

"You are a valiant and heroic man. You're hired again. You are officially and forever my bodyguard."

The police officer, catching his breath, barked, "Let's get you two lovebirds on the way to the hospital."

Beatrix quickly explained to Thomas, Sam, and Henry that Ken Purdue had been arrested for attempted murder and kidnapping. "Gus is there at the camp. In case he's like his evil father, I'll take Sam and Henry with me. Nobody will trouble me with those two by my side. I have to go, Thomas. I need to collect Dr. Einstein, and then I'll see you at the hospital."

"Go. I am balmy from the bump on the head, but go get him before the good doctor rips off his suit, does a primal scream, and joins the mischief-makers on Mountain Drive. We must save him from himself." He closed his eyes and grimaced.

Henry and Sam were more than happy to drive Beatrix back to the compound. As they walked down the long gravel drive, they saw a group of men sitting on overturned wooden crates. Dr. Einstein was standing in the middle, and a black chalkboard was scribbled with equations. He looked up mid-sentence and gave them a jaunty wave.

"Beatrix, good you are here. Hello, gentlemen," the doctor said. "I have just completed explaining to these fine people my theory of relativity."

"Dr. Einstein, may I have a word with Gus?" Beatrix asked.

Gus nodded and crossed the meeting area, hands wide in a welcome.

"Bea, glad you got back safely. Let's talk in the dining hall."

Away from the group, Beatrix lowered her voice. "It's about your father, Gus. He and two of his henchmen had Dr. Einstein and me kidnapped so he could brag to the world about how strong the Klan was, and how no one was safe from them."

Gus's mouth tightened; his hands clutched into fists. "That's one of the reasons I'm here, Beatrix, turning my back on the brutality in the world, the cruelty my own father perpetuated. It was that way when we lived in the South, and he dragged his tainted philosophy and heartlessness along when he and Mom moved to California."

"He's in jail, Gus, for the crimes he committed, including kidnapping and attempted murder. He can't bully anyone anymore."

"Thank God. Best news I've had in a lifetime."

"I have a question, not concerning your father or the KKK. That tranquilizer gun that was inadvertently fired and ultimately caused the death of one of your members. Did you get it back?"

"Yeah, actually, my new wife Dora brought it with her when she joined us yesterday."

Beatrix tried not to show shock. *Weird coincidence*, she wondered. "Dora?"

He nodded toward the group of women who were intently pretending not to listen to every word.

Beatrix smiled and then realized who Gus was looking at. "Your wife is Dora, who worked at the railroad ticket counter?"

"Yes. You know her?"

"I must talk with her."

Gus turned around to the women quietly preparing a meal and called out, "Dora, come over here. This lady wants to meet you."

Dora, minus several layers of makeup and dressed comfortable in loose, beige cotton trousers and a brown linen shirt, smiled. All pretense seemed to have been cleaned away when she washed her face. "I know you. You look just like one of the conductors."

Beatrix chuckled. "You're quite right. So tell me. Why did you shoot Grayson Welsh with the tranquilizer gun?"

Her fist flew to her mouth. "I didn't kill him. I promise. I wanted to hurt him, okay, and stun him. I wanted more than anything on earth to embarrass him. Mortify him as he did with me when he came to the station demanding that I return all the jewelry and clothes and furniture he'd given me. Told me to get out of his apartment or the police would arrest me. He said all this in front of the passengers and the staff. He was the boss, barking and yelling at everyone to stay back. Then he dragged me with him to hand over all the stuff he gave me. All the presents.

"I wanted to humiliate him. I wanted to have him wake up lying on his driveway. Yes, of course, I knew he slept in the buff. I'd been stalking him for days. I just drove by and shot him while he was getting the morning newspaper. Before I could park the car to *really* expose his private parts, this fat old lady ran to him, dragging a tiny poodle behind her."

"Mrs. Du Bois."

"Don't know her name and don't care. I drove around the

block again, and when I came to Grayson's house, she was bent over him, the poodle on top of his face. I swear, ma'am, it looked like she was trying to smother Grayson with her dog."

"Oh." Beatrix rubbed her hurt arm. "Oh. I never saw that coming, Dora. Are you willing to testify in court about this?"

"Sure, it's the truth."

Weeks later, the fruit trees in the Patterson-Ling garden were bursting into bloom. Western bluebirds were nesting in the oak tree by the picnic table, singing as they established their avian-size homes. Birdy had started to hold onto furniture to steady herself as she moved around the house. Every time she bounced on her diapered backside, she scampered right up again. The girl had spunk.

The doctors reported that Thomas had truly been fortunate. His concussion was mild, and because he was fit and strong, even a large tree branch couldn't slow him permanently.

Beatrix's left arm was in a cast for six weeks. As life settled, however, she could not manage to come up with a solution to halt the ruthless Governor Long from keeping his vile promise to ruin John, Thomas, and Beatrix. Life smoothed out, but the intensity of their worry grew.

Beatrix and Thomas were sitting in their living room as Birdy gently snored in her downstairs cot, listening to the evening radio programs.

There was a commercial, and the announcer shouted, "Palmolive Soap is 100 percent mild to help you guard that schoolgirl complexion look." Then another for cornflakes: "We've found the secret to happy breakfasts. Switch to something they like. Kellogg's Corn Flakes."

Thomas turned up the volume slightly as the show he eagerly waited to come on started. The announcer yelled,

"Faster than a speeding bullet. More powerful than a locomotive. Able to leap tall buildings in a single bound. Look. Up in the sky. It's Superman."

Thomas cocked his head. He stood up so quickly that the book, previously balanced on his knees, flew halfway across the room.

"That's it, Bea. By Jove. That's the solution. I've got it." He shouted, and Thomas never shouted. He jumped up and down, clapping like an excited six-year-old, then kissed his wife and turned off the radio.

Beatrix squinted in surprise. "Isn't that your favorite program?"

"Chalk this up to fanciful scientific reasoning or my jammy cognitive ineptness. If Superman is that invincible, which we all know is true, what if Superman stopped the KKK?"

"Thomas, darling, I hate to break this to you. Superman isn't real, right?" She cocked her head and smiled.

"Don't be cheeky. Do you have any idea how vast the audience is? That program reaches into living rooms around the country. Superman can and must stop the Klan. I know how."

At once, she knew exactly what her husband was thinking. "Wait, are you saying that one of the show's writers could create a script about Superman taking down the Klan by revealing its secrets? If all of America knew the secrets, it would cripple the group."

"My dearest, you are wicked sharp. Yes. Didn't you say you recognized their secret handshake?"

"That's it, Thomas. You are brilliant. If we could just get the writers to do that. It could be dangerous, but the risk would not last once it was all exposed. I have to call John. I'm certain he has connections with someone who can make this happen." She kissed Thomas soundly. "You are brilliant." Then she went to the front room and dialed John's number. She heard the radio click back on as her friend's telephone rang.

"Listen to this idea, John, and please don't laugh. It's Thomas's concept, and it's crazy smart. It could work. We need to disarm the KKK by having Superman, on the radio, divulge the Klan's secrets and, with it, expose that silly and frightening handshake." She whisked away a happy tear that was trailing down her cheek. "Long won't be able to destroy you or us and, God willing, his career will be in ruins. We will have our lives back, John."

"I like it, Beatrix. I like that a lot. I do happen to know the owner of Action Comics that publishes the comic books. We grew up in the same tenement neighborhood in New York."

"And now that Ken Purdue is in jail, I bet he might make a plea bargain and identify that his wife's brother, Governor Long, is a part of the group. Superman can and will take down the Ku Klux Klan. And to quote him: 'I believe in truth, justice, and a better tomorrow.'"

They made plans for the following day to meet and call in some favors. Beatrix would have hugged John tightly—something he would have found embarrassing—if they'd been together.

John was quiet for a moment. "Would you be shocked, Beatrix, if I admitted I'm in love?"

She smiled at the phone and said, "Not at all, and I'm so happy for you and Mariam. I could see it in your faces when we were together."

"We'd like you, Thomas, Birdy, and the entire Conrad family to be at our wedding."

"I am over the moon, John. You and Mariam seem right for each other."

"Not to upset you, but what of the elephant in the room? Are you moving to New Jersey?"

"No. I'm relieved. Dr. Einstein liked Santa Barbara immensely, liked Thomas's heroism and even the folks up on Mountain Drive, and he's decided to open a branch of his research facility here in the city. I didn't want to, but I would have moved, of course. However, this is so much better. It would be hard to take Birdy from you and all our friends."

"The case concerning Grayson Welsh, Beatrix, is that concluded?"

"Yes, John. Grayson Welsh died of a heart attack after he was hit with the tranquilizing gun. Dora was fined for shooting off a weapon in the city limits. Mrs. Du Bois did try to smother Welsh and that's why there were hairs, black poodle hair, in his mouth. But it would have been impossible to do that without killing the dog. She was reprimanded and released. A complaint was filed against her for attempted murder by poodle. I kid you not."

"And what of Kay Welsh, the wife?"

"I met her yesterday, and she's returning to Hollywood and her first love, teaching dogs to be movie stars. By the way, John, you're going to be an honorary uncle again. Sam and Jo are in the family way." She smiled at the receiver. "More so, Thomas and I are expecting."

"Oh, congratulations. I'm so happ—"

"We've decided to adopt one of Kay's little Welsh terriers."

"Oh, um, well . . ."

"That was to make you laugh, John. Yes, we are going to get a dog, but we're on the list to adopt two infants who were relinquished, mixed-race babies. Two little boys. You're going to be an uncle again, three times over, and Birdy will have brothers."

"A dog? Are you sure of this, Beatrix? Might you want to postpone this until Birdy is older and her new brothers are settled in?"

"John, life is uncertain. Why would I want to wait and miss out on a second of the future?"

THANK YOU!

Thank you for reading! If you enjoyed this book, please leave a review on Amazon, Goodreads, BookBub, The Story Graph, or anywhere else you like to track your recent reads. Alternatively, you could post online or tell a friend about it. This helps our authors more than you may know.

- The Team at Torchflame Books

ABOUT THIS BOOK

Beatrix Patterson and Thomas Ling would not stop talking with me. I could hear them planning this book months before I put my fingers to the keyboard. And the other characters whom you have come to know, if you've been following the series, were just as chatty. I wanted to yell, "Give me a break." But then I would have missed their ideas and comments and snarky remarks as well.

I didn't set out to write about racism in our country in the late 1940s when the story takes place. It came about organically, perhaps, but with America and the world in conflict over skin color, country of origin, religious beliefs and disbeliefs, and conspiracies that boggle the mind, the topic of racism was there in me. Just like it's probably there in you.

Beatrix and I have no answers other than to love one another and be kind to our neighbors, but this book tackles the issue of racism when it was ugly and when elected officials pointed fingers and made accusations based on nothing but a witch hunt. There's a plot twist that I won't spoil for you, but it's all true, quirky, and weird. So, google it at the end of the book to learn more.

My grandparents, to whom this book is dedicated, were all targeted with racial contempt because of their country of origin, their religion, their language, and even the food they ate. During World War I, when my maternal grandparents took a day trip away from their Connecticut farm, racists burnt down their house because the Millers spoke broken English. (A clerk at Ellis Island, it's been said, couldn't understand my grandfather and decided Miller was the man's new last name). The ignorant, deadly neighbors mistook the language my grandparents were speaking. If they'd just asked, they would have discovered this quiet couple had fled from the horrors of European wars. But alas, anyone who didn't speak perfect English was assumed to be the enemy.

On my father's side were the Ashkenazi Jews, and throughout "modern" history, they were subjected to brutality, discrimination, and genocide.

Because of this personal history, I feel a kinship to immigrants. Hence, the theme of my book was established and shows, I hope, how racism destroys lives.

I have changed some facts to make the story flow, but the twist at the end of the book is real. I hope you enjoy reading this as much as I enjoyed writing it, especially since Beatrix and Thomas are evolving and growing with each book.

You can follow me on Instagram @evashawwriter or contact me via my website evashaw.com.

P.S. If you want to know more about how Superman actually worked against the KKK, check out: *Superman vs. the Ku Klux Klan* by Rick Bowers.*

---

* Bowers, Rick. 2012. *Superman versus the Ku Klux Klan: The True Story of How the Iconic Superhero Battled the Men of Hate*. Washington, DC. National Geographic Society.

ACKNOWLEDGMENTS

In 1652, French mathematician and philosopher Blaise Pascal wrote, "If I had more time, I would have written a shorter letter." I can relate. I can write an entire eighty-thousand-plus word book, and this is book four in the series, which means I've penned over three hundred thousand words for Beatrix Patterson and the gang. However, crafting a short and sweet acknowledgment is tough for me. It takes me forever to write a small greeting in a notecard.

"Do the hard thing" has never been my motto. I need treats every step of the way. So, as I write this acknowledgment, I'm going to pretend each person reading this is sitting across from me, having coffee, tea, or an adult beverage of their choice. I'm buying.

Big thanks to my good friend and now my publisher, Teri Rider. Teri and I met decades ago when we were both beginning our careers, never dreaming that in 2025, she'd be the CEO of the house that publishes my Beatrix Patterson mystery series. Truth be told, I liked Teri from the get-go, her laugh (which is contagious), her attention to detail, her creative energy, and finally, that there's never been an animal she wasn't willing to save, help, heal, and love.

Huge, heaping thanks to Chelsea Robinson, my editor. Her corrections, suggestions, and modifications in this manuscript made it shine. Thanks to Jori Hanna, PR person extraordinaire for Torchflame Books. Jori makes things easy, and that, as we all know, means she's knocked herself out when no one is looking.

Thanks to all the staff at Torchflame, consultants, editors, and freelancers. Thanks to my fellow authors at Torchflame, who are quick to praise and support others in the TF family.

Thanks to my bestie, Ellen, for being ready and happy to read a rough draft, to hear my laments over plot twists that were tangled, and there to celebrate when the book actually is "shareable" with the world. Appreciation goes to K. J. Bailey who was one of my beta readers and said all the right things with honesty; that's a friend. Another valued listener is my pal Nico Garafolo, a novelist and director, who understands that the voices we writers hear in our heads must be listened to and oftentimes shared. (Thank you, Nico, for letting me introduce you to these characters.)

Thanks, as well, to my chosen family, my bio family, and my friends. Love you all.

Enormous appreciation goes to my little dog, too, Welsh Terrier Coco Rose, who creates havoc whenever the mood strikes, multiple times a day when called for. This keeps life exciting, gets me out for miles of walks, and helps me make friends with everyone. You won't be surprised that there's a Welshie in this book, will you? How about three?

As with other books I've written and hope you've enjoyed, I'm donating 50 percent of my profit to charity. This time, the money goes to Welsh Terrier Rescue (welshterrierrescue.com). Coco is not a rescue, but my three previous senior Welshies were, and by buying copies of this book, you're helping these amazing, devoted, and wacky little dogs be placed in forever homes. Thank you.

Let me know if you'd like more adventures of Beatrix, Thomas, Birdy and the gang.

ABOUT THE AUTHOR

Eva Shaw, Ph.D. is the ghostwriter and author of more than 100 books, including *The Conductor* in the best-selling Beatrix Patterson mystery series. She's a dog mom to Welsh terrier Coco Rose, a sister, Aunt Eva, a godmother, a bonus grand-mother called Fifi to precious Dane and Gwen, a friend, a devoted Christian and volunteer with her church and causes concerning women and girls, a rabid reader, an ardent gardener, a seriously silly and passionate painter (canvases and not hous-es), an enthusiastic traveler who has visited more than 35 foreign countries, and an amateur banjolele player.

She is an online writing instructor with Education To Go and her five different courses are available through 4000 course providers worldwide.

When not hanging out with Coco Rose, family, and friends,

painting or playing music, you can find Eva enjoying her home-town of Carlsbad, California.

MORE FROM EVA SHAW

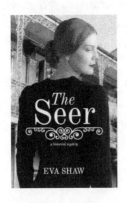

THE SEER

1942. War grips the world. Hired by the US Army to use her connections to expose Nazi saboteurs and sympathizers, Beatrix recruits the reluctant Thomas. Together, they pit their skills against a government conspiracy, terrorist cells, kidnappings, and murderous plots. As Beatrix grapples with the truth of her own past, she must come to terms with her ruse. Exposing the Nazi war machine about to invade the country could cost Beatrix everything she's worked so hard to build. But the information she and Thomas uncover could change the outcome of the war.

THE FINDER

Beatrix Patterson is good at finding things—people, the truth, missing evidence. As three Jane Does appear at the base of a nearby cliff, each with similar ceremonial markings, Beatrix grows more passionate. The deeper she digs, the less the pieces fit together. From a strange, disbanded cult to the drag queen desperate to claim an inheritance, Beatrix is soon stretched thin. Surrounded by new neighbors with shadowed pasts, she has to wonder: will anyone believe her?

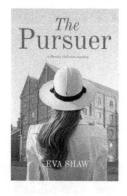

THE PURSUER

Set in 1947, Beatrix Patterson investigates suspected war criminals who may have killed thousands, a diabolical scheme to rob Indigenous Americans of their relics, and a person practicing voodoo as a means to murder a respected member of the Santa Barbara religious community. Who can she trust to speak the truth when everyone involved seems to be hiding something that could ruin their lives?